William Sharp, John Parker Anderson

Life of Robert Browning

William Sharp, John Parker Anderson

Life of Robert Browning

ISBN/EAN: 9783337416188

Printed in Europe, USA, Canada, Australia, Japan

Cover: Foto ©Raphael Reischuk / pixelio.de

More available books at **www.hansebooks.com**

LIFE

OF

ROBERT BROWNING

BY

WILLIAM SHARP.

———

LONDON:
WALTER SCOTT, 24 WARWICK LANE.
1890.

CONTENTS.

CHAPTER I.

CHAPTER II.

CHAPTER IV.

CHAPTER V.

CHAPTER VI.

CHAPTER VII.

CHAPTER VIII.

CHAPTER IX.

NOTE.

—

IN all important respects I leave this volume to speak for itself. For obvious reasons it does not pretend to be more than a *Mémoire pour servir:* in the nature of things, the definitive biography cannot appear for many years to come. None the less gratefully may I take the present opportunity to express my indebtedness to Mr. R. Barrett Browning, and to other relatives and intimate friends of Robert Browning, who have given me serviceable information, and otherwise rendered kindly aid. For some of the hitherto unpublished details my thanks are, in particular, due to Mrs. Fraser Corkran and Miss Alice Corkran, and to other old friends of the poet and his family, here, in Italy, and in America; though in one or two instances, I may add, I had them from Robert Browning himself. It is with pleasure that I further acknowledge my indebtedness to Dr. Furnivall, for the loan of the advance-proofs of his privately-printed pamphlet on "Browning's Ancestors"; and to the Browning Society's Publications—particularly to Mrs. Sutherland Orr's and Dr. Furnivall's biographical and bibliographical contributions thereto ; to Mr. Gosse's biographical article in the *Century Magazine*

for 1881 ; to Mr. Ingram's *Life of E. B. Browning;* and
to the *Memoirs of Anna Jameson,* the *Italian Note-Books*
of Nathaniel Hawthorne, Mr. G. S. Hillard's *Six Months
in Italy* (1853), and the Lives and Correspondence of
Macready, Miss Mitford, Leigh Hunt, and Walter Savage
Landor. I regret that the imperative need of concision has
prevented the insertion of many of the letters, anecdotes,
and reminiscences, so generously placed at my disposal;
but possibly I may have succeeded in educing from them
some essential part of that light which they undoubtedly
cast upon the personality and genius of the poet.

LIFE OF BROWNING.

CHAPTER I.

IT must, to admirers of Browning's writings, appear
singularly appropriate that so cosmopolitan a poet
was born in London. It would seem as though
something of that mighty complex life, so confusedly
petty to the narrow vision, so grandiose and even
majestic to the larger ken, had blent with his being
from the first. What fitter birthplace for the poet whom
a comrade has called the "Subtlest Assertor of the Soul
in Song," the poet whose writings are indeed a mirror
of the age?

A man may be in all things a Londoner and yet be a
provincial. The accident of birthplace does not neces-
sarily involve parochialism of the soul. It is not the
village which produces the Hampden, but the Hampden
who immortalises the village. It is a favourite jest of
Rusticus that his urban brother has the manner of
Omniscience and the knowledge of a parish beadle.
Nevertheless, though the strongest blood insurgent in
the metropolitan heart is not that which is native to it,

one might well be proud to have had one's atom-pulse atune from the first with the large rhythm of the national life at its turbulent, congested, but ever ebullient centre. Certainly Browning was not the man to be ashamed of his being a Londoner, much less to deny his natal place. He was proud of it: through good sense, no doubt, but possibly also through some instinctive apprehension of the fact that the great city was indeed the fit mother of such a son. "Ashamed of having been born in the greatest city of the world!" he exclaimed on one occasion; "what an extraordinary thing to say! It suggests a wavelet in a muddy shallow grimily contorting itself because it had its birth out in the great ocean."

On the day of the poet's funeral in Westminster Abbey, one of the most eminent of his peers remarked to me that Browning came to us as one coming into his own. This is profoundly true. There was in good sooth a mansion prepared against his advent. Long ago, we should have surrendered as to a conqueror: now, however, we know that princes of the mind, though they must be valorous and potent as of yore, can enter upon no heritance save that which naturally awaits them, and has been made theirs by long and intricate processes.

The lustrum which saw the birth of Robert Browning, that is the third in the nineteenth century, was a remarkable one indeed. Thackeray came into the world some months earlier than the great poet, Charles Dickens within the same twelvemonth, and Tennyson three years sooner, when also Elizabeth Barrett was born, and the foremost naturalist of modern times first saw the light.

It is a matter of significance that the great wave of
scientific thought which ultimately bore forward on its
crest so many famous men, from Brewster and Faraday
to Charles Darwin, had just begun to rise with irresist-
ible impulsion. Lepsius's birth was in 1813, and that
of the great Flemish novelist, Henri Conscience, in 1812:
about the same period were the births of Freiligrath,
Gutzkow, and Auerbach, respectively one of the most
lyrical poets, the most potent dramatist, the most charming
romancer of Germany: and, also, in France, of Théophile
Gautier and Alfred de Musset. Among representatives of
the other arts—with two of which Browning must ever
be closely associated—Mendelssohn and Chopin were
born in 1809, and Schumann, Liszt, and Wagner within
the four succeeding years : within which space also came
Diaz and Meissonier and the great Millet. Other high
names there are upon the front of the century. Macaulay,
Cardinal Newman, John Stuart Mill (one of the earliest,
by the way, to recognise the genius of Browning),
Alexandre Dumas, George Sand, Victor Hugo, Ampère,
Quinet, Prosper Merimée, Sainte-Beuve, Strauss, Monta-
lembert, are among the laurel-bearers who came into
existence betwixt 1800 and 1812.

When Robert Browning was born in London in 1812,
Sheridan had still four years to live ; Jeremy Bentham
was at the height of his contemporary reputation, and
Godwin was writing glibly of the virtues of humanity
and practising the opposite qualities, while Crabbe
was looked upon as one of the foremost of living
poets. Wordsworth was then forty, Sir Walter Scott
forty-one, Coleridge forty-two, Walter Savage Landor
and Charles Lamb each in his forty-fifth year. Byron

was four-and-twenty, Shelley not yet quite of age, two
radically different men, Keats and Carlyle, both youths
of seventeen. Abroad, Laplace was in his maturity, with
fifteen years more yet to live; Joubert with twelve;
Goethe, with twenty; Lamarck, the Schlegels, Cuvier,
Chateaubriand, Hegel, Niebühr (to specify some leading
names only), had many years of work before them.
Schopenhauer was only four-and-twenty, while Béranger
was thirty-two. The Polish poet Mickiewicz was a boy of
fourteen, and Poushkin was but a twelvemonth older;
Heine, a lad of twelve, was already enamoured of the
great Napoleonic legend. The foremost literary critic of
the century was running about the sands of Boulogne, or
perhaps wandering often along the ramparts of the old
town, introspective even then, with something of that rare
and insatiable curiosity which we all now recognise as
so distinctive of Sainte-Beuve. Again, the greatest
creative literary artist of the century, in prose at any
rate, was leading an apparently somewhat indolent
schoolboy life at Tours, undreamful yet of enormous
debts, colossal undertakings, gigantic failures, and the
Comédie Humaine.   In art, Sir Henry Raeburn, William
Blake, Flaxman, Canova, Thorwaldsen, Crome, Sir
Thomas Lawrence, Constable, Sir David Wilkie, and
Turner were in the exercise of their happiest faculties: as
were, in the usage of theirs, Beethoven, Weber, Schubert,
Spohr, Donizetti, and Bellini.

It is not inadvisedly that I make this specification of
great names, of men who were born coincidentally with,
or were in the broader sense contemporaries of Robert
Browning. There is no such thing as a fortuitous birth.
Creation does not occur spontaneously, as in that drawing

of David Scott's where from the footprint of the Omnipo-
tent spring human spirits and fiery stars. Literally indeed,
as a great French writer has indicated, a man is the
child of his time. It is a matter often commented
upon by students of literature, that great men do not
appear at the beginning, but rather at the acme of
a period. They are not the flying scud of the coming
wave, but the gleaming crown of that wave itself.
The epoch expends itself in preparation for these great
ones.

If Nature's first law were not a law of excess, the
economy of life would have meagre results. I think it
is Turgeniev who speaks somewhere of her as a
gigantic Titan, working in gloomy silence, with the
same savage intentness upon a subtler twist of a flea's
joints as upon the Destinies of Man.

If there be a more foolish cry than that poetry is
on the wane, it is that the great days had passed
away even before Robert Browning and Alfred Tennyson were born. The way was prepared for Browning,
as it was for Shakspere: as it is, beyond doubt, for
the next high peer of these.

There were 'Roberts' among the sons of the Browning family for at least four generations. It has been
affirmed, on disputable authority, that the surname is
the English equivalent for Bruning, and that the family
is of Teutonic origin. Possibly: but this origin is too
remote to be of any practical concern. Browning himself, it may be added, told Mr. Moncure Conway that the
original name was De Bruni. It is not a matter of much
importance: the poet was, personally and to a great
extent in his genius, Anglo-Saxon. Though there are

plausible grounds for the assumption, I can find nothing to substantiate the common assertion that, immediately, or remotely, his people were Jews.[1]

As to Browning's physiognomy and personal traits, this much may be granted : if those who knew him were told he was a Jew they would not be much surprised. In his exuberant vitality, in his sensuous love of music and the other arts, in his combined imaginativeness and shrewdness of common sense, in his superficial expansiveness and actual reticence, he would have been typical enough of the potent and artistic race for whom he has so often of late been claimed.

What, however, is most to the point is that neither to curious acquaintances nor to intimate friends, neither to Jews nor Gentiles, did he ever admit more than that he was a good Protestant, and sprung of a Puritan stock. He was tolerant of all religious forms, but with a natural bias towards Anglican Evangelicalism.

In appearance there was, perhaps, something of the Semite in Robert Browning : yet this is observable but slightly in the portraits of him during the last twenty years, and scarcely at all in those which represent him as a young man. It is most marked in the drawing by Rudolf Lehmann, representing Browning at the age of forty-seven, where he looks out upon us with a physiognomy which is, at least, as much distinctively Jewish as English.

---

[1] Fairly conclusive evidence to the contrary, on the paternal side, is afforded in the fact that, in 1757, the poet's great-grandfather gave one of his sons the baptismal name of Christian. Dr. Furnivall's latest researches prove that there is absolutely "no ground for supposing the presence of any Jewish blood in the poet's veins."

Possibly the large dark eyes (so unlike both in colour
and shape what they were in later life) and curved nose
and full lips, with the oval face, may have been, as it
were, seen judaically by the artist. These characteristics,
again, are greatly modified in Mr. Lehmann's subsequent
portrait in oils.

The poet's paternal great-grandfather, who was owner
of the Woodyates Inn, in the parish of Pentridge, in
Dorsetshire, claimed to come of good west-country
stock. Browning believed, but always conscientiously
maintained there was no proof in support of the
assumption, that he was a descendant of the Captain
Micaiah Browning who, as Macaulay relates in his
History of England, raised the siege of Derry in
1689 by springing the boom across Lough Foyle, and
perished in the act. The same ancestral line is said to
comprise the Captain Browning who commanded the
ship *The Holy Ghost*, which conveyed Henry V. to
France before he fought the Battle of Agincourt, and in
recognition of whose services two waves, said to represent
waves of the sea, were added to his coat of arms. It
is certainly a point of some importance in the evidence,
as has been indicated, that these arms were displayed
by the gallant Captain Micaiah, and are borne by the
present family. That the poet was a pure-bred Englishman in the strictest sense, however, as has commonly
been asserted, is not the case. His mother was
Scottish, through her mother and by birth, but her
father was the son of a German from Hamburg, named
Wiedemann, who, by the way, in connection with his
relationship as maternal grandfather to the poet, it is
interesting to note, was an accomplished draughtsman

and musician.[1] Browning's paternal grandmother, again,
was a Creole. As Mrs. Orr remarks, this pedigree
throws a valuable light on the vigour and variety of the
poet's genius. Possibly the main current of his ancestry
is as little strictly English as German. A friend sends
me the following paragraph from a Scottish paper :—
"What of the Scottish Brownings ? I had it long ago
from one of the name that the Brownings came originally
from Ayrshire, and that several families of them emi-
grated to the North of Ireland during the times of the
Covenanters. There is, moreover, a small town or village
in the North of Ireland called Browningstown. Might
not the poet be related to these Scottish Brownings ?"

Browning's great-grandfather, as indicated above, was
a small proprietor in Dorsetshire. His son, whether perforce or from choice, removed to London when he was a
youth, and speedily obtained a clerkship in the Bank of
England, where he remained for fifty years, till he was
pensioned off in 1821 with over £400 a year. He died
in 1833. His wife, to whom he was married in or about
1780, was one Margaret Morris Tittle, a Creole, born in
the West Indies. Her portrait, by Wright of Derby, used
to hang in the poet's dining-room. They resided, Mr.
R. Barrett Browning tells me, in Battersea, where his
grandfather was their first-born. The paternal grandfather of the poet decided that his three sons, Robert,
William Shergold, and Reuben, should go into business,

---

[1] It has frequently been stated that Browning's maternal grandfather, Mr. Wiedemann, was a Jew. Mr. Wiedemann, the son of a
Hamburg merchant, was a small shipowner in Dundee. Had he,
or his father, been Semitic, he would not have baptised one of his
daughters ' Christiana.'

the two younger in London, the elder abroad. All three became efficient financial clerks, and attained to good positions and fair means.[1] The eldest, Robert, was a man of exceptional powers. He was a poet, both in sentiment and expression; and he understood, as well as enjoyed, the excellent in art. He was a scholar, too, in a reputable fashion: not indifferent to what he had learnt in his youth, nor heedless of the high opinion generally entertained for the greatest writers of antiquity, but with a particular care himself for Horace and Anacreon. As his son once told a friend, "The old gentleman's brain was a storehouse of literary and philosophical antiquities. (He was completely versed in mediæval legend, and seemed to have known Paracelsus, Faustus, and even Talmudic personages, personally "—a significant detail, by the way.) He was fond of metrical composition, and his ease and grace in the use of the heroic couplet were the admiration, not only of his intellectual associates, but, in later days, of his son, who was wont to affirm, certainly in all seriousness, that expressionally his father was a finer poetic artist than himself. Some one has recorded of him that he was an authority on the Letters of Junius: fortunately he had more tangible claims than this to the esteem of his fellows. It was his boast that, notwithstanding the exigencies of his vocation, he knew as much of the history of art as any professional critic. His extreme modesty is deducible from this naïve remark. He was an amateur

---

[1] The three brothers were men of liberal education and literary tastes. Mr. W. S. Browning, who died in 1874, was an author of some repute. His *History of the Huguenots* is a standard book on the subject.

artist, moreover, as well as poet, critic, and student. I
have seen several of his drawings which are praise-
worthy: his studies in portraiture, particularly, are ably
touched: and, as is well known, he had an active faculty
of pictorial caricature. In the intervals of leisure which
beset the best regulated clerk he was addicted to making
drawings of the habitual visitors to the Bank of England,
in which he had obtained a post on his return, in 1803,
from the West Indies, and in the enjoyment of which he
remained till 1853, when he retired on a small pension.
His son had an independent income, but whether from a
bequest, or in the form of an allowance from his then
unmarried Uncle Reuben, is uncertain. In the first
year of his marriage Mr. Browning resided in an old
house in Southampton Street, Peckham, and there the
poet was born. The house was long ago pulled down,
and another built on its site. Mr. Browning afterwards
removed to another domicile in the same Peckham
district. Many years later, he and his family left Camberwell and resided at Hatcham, near New Cross, where his
brothers and sisters (by his father's second marriage)
lived. There was a stable attached to the Hatcham
house, and in it Mr. Reuben Browning kept his horse,
which he let his poet-nephew ride, while he himself was
at his desk in Rothschild's bank. No doubt this horse
was the 'York' alluded to by the poet in the letter
quoted, as a footnote, at page 189 of this book. Some
years after his wife's death, which occurred in 1849,
Mr. Browning left Hatcham and came to Paddington,
but finally went to reside in Paris, and lived there, in a
small street off the Champs Élysées, till his death in
1866. The Creole strain seems to have been distinctly

noticeable in Mr. Browning, so much so that it is possible it had something to do with his unwillingness to remain at St. Kitts, where he was certainly on one occasion treated cavalierly enough. The poet's complexion in youth, light and ivory-toned as it was in later life, has been described as olive, and it is said that one of his nephews, who met him in Paris in his early manhood, took him for an Italian. It has been affirmed that it was the emotional Creole strain in Browning which found expression in his passion for music.

By old friends of the family I have been told that Mr. Browning had a strong liking for children, with whom his really remarkable faculty of impromptu fiction made him a particular favourite. Sometimes he would supplement his tales by illustrations with pencil or brush. Miss Alice Corkran has shown me an illustrated coloured map, depictive of the main incidents and scenery of the *Pilgrim's Progress*, which he genially made for "the children."[1]

He had three children himself—Robert, born May 7th, 1812, a daughter named Sarianna, after her mother, and Clara. His wife was a woman of singular beauty of nature, with a depth of religious feeling saved from narrowness of scope only by a rare serenity and a fathomless charity. Her son's loving admiration of her was almost a passion : even late in life he rarely

---

[1] Mrs. Fraser Corkran, who saw much of the poet's father during his residence in Paris, has spoken to me of his extraordinary analytical faculty in the elucidation of complex criminal cases. It was once said of him that his detective faculty amounted to genius. This is a significant trait in the father of the author of "The Ring and the Book."

spoke of her without tears coming to his eyes. She was, moreover, of an intellectual bent of mind, and with an artistic bias having its readiest fulfilment in music, and, to some extent, in poetry. In the latter she inclined to the Romanticists: her husband always maintained the supremacy of Pope. He looked with much dubiety upon his son's early writings, "Pauline" and "Paracelsus"; "Sordello," though he found it beyond either his artistic or his mental apprehension, he forgave, because it was written in rhymed couplets; the maturer works he regarded with sympathy and pride, with a vague admiration which passed into a clearer understanding only when his long life was drawing near its close.

Of his children's company he never tired, even when they were scarce out of babyhood. He was fond of taking the little Robert in his arms, and walking to and fro with him in the dusk in "the library," soothing the child to sleep by singing to him snatches of Anacreon in the original, to a favourite old tune of his, "A Cottage in a Wood." Readers of "Asolando" will remember the allusions in that volume to "my father who was a scholar and knew Greek." A week or two before his death Browning told an American friend, Mrs. Corson, in reply to a statement of hers that no one could accuse him of letting his talents lie idle: "It would have been quite unpardonable in my case not to have done my best. My dear father put me in a condition most favourable for the best work I was capable of. When I think of the many authors who have had to fight their way through all sorts of difficulties, I have no reason to be proud of my achievements. My good father sacrificed a fortune to his convictions. He could not bear with slavery, and left India and accepted a humble bank-office in London. He secured for me all the ease and comfort that a literary man needs to do good work. It would have been shameful if I had not done my best to realise his expectations of me."[1]

The home of Mr. Browning was, as already stated, in Camberwell, a suburb then of less easy access than now, and where there were green trees, and groves, and enticing rural perspectives into "real" country, yet withal not without some suggestion of the metropolitan air.

> " The old trees
> Which grew by our youth's home—the waving mass
> Of climbing plants, heavy with bloom and dew—
> The morning swallows with their songs like words—
> All these seem clear. . . .
>   . . . most distinct amid
> The fever and the stir of after years."
>
> (*Pauline.*)

Another great writer of our time was born in the same parish : and those who would know Herne Hill and the neighbourhood as it was in Browning's youth will find an enthusiastic guide in the author of *Praeterita*.

Browning's childhood was a happy one. Indeed, if the poet had been able to teach in song only what he had learnt in suffering, the larger part of his verse would be singularly barren of interest. From first to last everything went well with him, with the exception of a single

---

[1] 'India' is a slip on the part either of Browning or of Mrs. Corson. The poet's father was never in India. He was quite a youth when he went to his mother's sugar-plantation at St. Kitts, in the West Indies.

profound grief. This must be borne in mind by those who would estimate aright the genius of Robert Browning. It would be affectation or folly to deny that his splendid physique—a paternal inheritance, for his father died at the age of eighty-four, without having ever endured a day's illness—and the exceptionally fortunate circumstances which were his throughout life, had something to do with that superb faith of his which finds concentrated expression in the lines in Pippa's song—"God's in His Heaven, All's right with the world ! "

It is difficult for a happy man with an imperturbable digestion to be a pessimist. He is always inclined to give Nature the benefit of the doubt. His favourite term for this mental complaisance is " catholicity of faith," or, it may be, "a divine hope." The less fortunate brethren bewail the laws of Nature, and doubt a future readjustment, because of stomachs chronically out of order. An eminent author with a weak digestion wrote to me recently animadverting on what he calls Browning's insanity of optimism : it required no personal acquaintanceship to discern the dyspeptic well-spring of this utterance. All this may be admitted lightly without carrying the physiological argument to extremes. A man may have a liberal hope for himself and for humanity, although his dinner be habitually a martyrdom. After all, we are only dictated to by our bodies : we have not perforce to obey them. A bitter wit once remarked that the soul, if it were ever discovered, would be found embodied in the gastric juice. He was not altogether a fool, this man who had learnt in suffering what he taught in epigram ; yet was he wide of the mark.

As a very young child Browning was keenly susceptible to music. One afternoon his mother was playing in
the twilight to herself. She was startled to hear a sound
behind her. Glancing round, she beheld a little white
figure distinct against an oak bookcase, and could
just discern two large wistful eyes looking earnestly at
her. The next moment the child had sprung into her
arms, sobbing passionately at he knew not what, but, as
his paroxysm of emotion subsided, whispering over and
over, with shy urgency, "Play! play!"

It is strange that among all his father's collection of
drawings and engravings nothing had such fascination
for him as an engraving of a picture of Andromeda and
Perseus by Caravaggio. The story of the innocent
victim and the divine deliverer was one of which in
his boyhood he never tired of hearing: and as he grew
older the charm of its pictorial presentment had for him
a deeper and more complex significance. We have it on
the authority of a friend that Browning had this engraving always before his eyes as he wrote his earlier poems.
He has given beautiful commemoration to his feeling
for it in " Pauline " :—

> "Andromeda!
> And she is with me—years roll, I shall change,
> But change can touch her not—so beautiful
> With her dark eyes, earnest and still, and hair
> Lifted and spread by the salt-sweeping breeze;
> And one red beam, all the storm leaves in heaven,
> Resting upon her eyes and face and hair,
> As she awaits the snake on the wet beach,
> By the dark rock, and the white wave just breaking
> At her feet; quite naked and alone,—a thing
> You doubt not, nor fear for, secure that God
> Will come in thunder from the stars to save her."

One of his own early recollections was that of sitting on his father's knees in the library, and listening with enthralled attention to the Tale of Troy, with marvellous illustrations among the glowing coals in the fireplace; with, below all, the vaguely heard accompaniment—from the neighbouring room where Mrs. Browning sat "in her chief happiness, her hour of darkness and solitude and music"—of a wild Gaelic lament, with its insistent falling cadences. A story concerning his poetic precocity has been circulated, but is not worth repeating. Most children love jingling rhymes, and one need not be a born genius to improvise a rhyming couplet on an occasion.

It is quite certain that in nothing in these early poemicules, in such at least as have been preserved without the poet's knowledge and against his will, is there anything of genuine promise. Hundreds of youngsters have written as good, or better, Odes to the Moon, Stanzas on a Favourite Canary, Lines on a Butterfly. What is much more to the point is, that at the age of eight he was able not only to read, but to take delight in Pope's translation of Homer. He used to go about declaiming certain couplets with an air of intense earnestness highly diverting to those who over-heard him.

About this time also he began to translate the simpler odes of Horace. One of these (viii. Bk. II.) long afterwards suggested to him the theme of his " Instans Tyrannus." It has been put on record that his sister remembers him, as a very little boy, walking round and round the dining-room table, and spanning out the scansion of his verses with his hand on the smooth

mahogany. He was scarce more than a child when,
one Guy Fawkes' day, he heard a woman singing an
unfamiliar song, whose burden was, "Following the
Queen of the Gipsies, O !" This refrain haunted him
often in the after years. That beautiful fantastic
romance, "The Flight of the Duchess," was born out
of an insistent memory of this woman's snatch of song,
heard in childhood. He was ten when, after several
passions malheureuses, this precocious Lothario plunged
into a love affair whose intensity was only equalled by its
hopelessness. A trifle of fifteen years' seniority and a
husband complicated matters, but it was not till after
the reckless expenditure of a Horatian ode upon an
unclassical mistress that he gave up hope. The outcome of this was what the elder Browning regarded as
a startling effusion of much Byronic verse. The young
Robert yearned for wastes of ocean and illimitable sands,
for dark eyes and burning caresses, for despair that
nothing could quench but the silent grave, and, in
particular, for hollow mocking laughter. His father
looked about for a suitable school, and decided to
entrust the boy's further education to Mr. Ready, of
Peckham.

Here he remained till he was fourteen. But already
he knew the dominion of dreams. His chief enjoyment, on holiday afternoons, was to gain an un-
frequented spot, where three huge elms re-echoed
the tones of incoherent human music borne thither-
ward by the west winds across the wastes of London.
Here he loved to lie and dream. Alas, those elms,
that high remote coign, have long since passed to
the "hidden way" whither the snows of yester year

have vanished. He would lie for hours looking upon
distant London—a golden city of the west literally
enough, oftentimes, when the sunlight came streaming
in long shafts from behind the towers of Westminster
and flashed upon the gold cross of St. Paul's. The
coming and going of the cloud-shadows, the sweeping
of sudden rains, the dull silvern light emanating from
the haze of mist shrouding the vast city, with the
added transitory gleam of troubled waters, the drifting
of fogs, at that distance seeming like gigantic veils
constantly being moved forward and then slowly withdrawn, as though some sinister creature of the atmosphere were casting a net among all the dross and
débris of human life for fantastic sustenance of its
own—all this endless, ever-changing, always novel
phantasmagoria had for him an extraordinary fascination.
One of the memorable nights of his boyhood was an eve
when he found his way, not without perturbation of spirit
because of the unfamiliar solitary dark, to his loved
elms. There, for the first time, he beheld London by
night. It seemed to him then more wonderful and
appalling than all the host of stars. There was something ominous in that heavy pulsating breath : visible, in
a waning and waxing of the tremulous, ruddy glow above
the black enmassed leagues of masonry ; audible, in the
low inarticulate moaning borne eastward across the
crests of Norwood. It was then and there that the
tragic significance of life first dimly awed and appealed
to his questioning spirit : that the rhythm of humanity
first touched deeply in him a corresponding chord.

CHAPTER II.

I T was certainly about this time, as he admitted once in one of his rare reminiscent moods, that Browning felt the artistic impulse stirring within him, like the rising of the sap in a tree. He remembered his mother's music, and hoped to be a musician : he recollected his father's drawings, and certain seductive landscapes and seascapes by painters whom he had heard called "the Norwich men," and he wished to be an artist : then reminiscences of the Homeric lines he loved, of haunting verse-melodies, moved him most of all.

> "I shall never, in the years remaining,
>   Paint you pictures, no, nor carve you statues,
>   Make you music that should all-express me :
>   . . . verse alone, one life allows me."

He now gave way to the compulsive Byronic vogue, with an occasional relapse to the polished artificialism of his father's idol among British poets. There were several ballads written at this time : if I remember aright, the poet specified the "Death of Harold" as the theme of one. Long afterwards he read these boyish forerunners of "Over the sea our galleys went," and "How they Brought the Good News from Ghent to Aix," and was amused by their derivative if delicate melodies. Mrs. Browning was very proud of

these early blooms of song, and when her twelve-year-old
son, tired of vain efforts to seduce a publisher from the
wary ways of business, surrendered in disgust his neatly
copied out and carefully stitched MSS., she lost no
opportunity—when Mr. Browning was absent—to expa-
tiate upon their merits. Among the people to whom
she showed them was a Miss Flower. This lady
took them home, perused them, discerned dormant
genius lurking behind the boyish handwriting, read
them to her sister (afterwards to become known
as Sarah Flower Adams), copied them out before
returning them, and persuaded the celebrated Rev.
William Johnson Fox to read the transcripts. Mr. Fox
agreed with Miss Flower as to the promise, but not
altogether as to the actual accomplishment, nor at all as
to the advisability of publication. The originals are
supposed to have been destroyed by the poet during the
eventful period when, owing to a fortunate gift, poetry
became a new thing for him : from a dream, vague, if
seductive, as summer-lightning, transformed to a dominating reality. Passing a bookstall one day, he
saw, in a box of second-hand volumes, a little book
advertised as "Mr. Shelley's Atheistical Poem: very
scarce." He had never heard of Shelley, nor did
he learn for a long time that the "Dæmon of the
World," and the miscellaneous poems appended thereto,
constituted a literary piracy. Badly printed, shamefully
mutilated, these discarded blossoms touched him to a
new emotion. Pope became further removed than ever :
Byron, even, lost his magnetic supremacy. From vague
remarks in reply to his inquiries, and from one or two
casual allusions, he learned that there really was a poet

called Shelley; that he had written several volumes; that he was dead.

Strange as it may seem, Browning declared once that the news of this unknown singer's death affected him more poignantly than did, a year or less earlier, the tidings of Byron's heroic end at Missolonghi. He begged his mother to procure him Shelley's works, a request not easily complied with, for the excellent reason that not one of the local booksellers had even heard of the poet's name. Ultimately, however, Mrs. Browning learned that what she sought was procurable at the Olliers' in Vere Street, London.

She was very pleased with the result of her visit. The books, it is true, seemed unattractive: but they would please Robert, no doubt. If that packet had been lost we should not have had "Pauline": we might have had a different Browning. It contained most of Shelley's writings, all in their first edition, with the exception of "The Cenci": in addition, there were three volumes by an even less known poet, John Keats, which kindly Mrs. Browning had been persuaded to include in her purchase on Mr. Ollier's assurance that they were the poetic kindred of Shelley's writings, and that Mr. Keats was the subject of the elegiac poem in the purple paper cover, with the foreign-looking type and the imprint "Pisa" at the foot of the title-page, entitled "Adonais." What an evening for the young poet that must have been. He told a friend it was a May night, and that in a laburnum, "heavy with its weight of gold," and in a great copper-beech at the end of a neighbour's garden, two nightingales strove one against the other. For a moment it is a pleasant fancy to imagine that

there the souls of Keats and Shelley uttered their enfranchised music, not in rivalry but in welcome. We
can realise, perhaps, something of the startled delight, of
the sudden electric tremors, of the young poet when, with
eager eyes, he turned over the pages of " Epipsychidion "
or " Prometheus Unbound," " Alastor " or " Endymion,"
or the Odes to a Nightingale, on Melancholy, on a
Grecian Urn.

More than once Browning alluded to this experience
as his first pervasive joy, his first free happiness in
outlook. Often in after life he was fain, like his "wise
thrush," to "recapture that first fine careless rapture."
It was an eventful eve.

> " And suddenly, without heart-wreck, I awoke
> As from a dream."

Thenceforth his poetic development was rapid, and continuous. Shelley enthralled him most. The fire and
spirit of the great poet's verse, wild and strange often,
but ever with an exquisiteness of music which seemed to
his admirer, then and later, supreme, thrilled him to a
very passion of delight. Something of the more richly
coloured, the more human rhythm of Keats affected
him also. Indeed, a line from the Ode to a Nightingale, in common with one of the loveliest passages in
"Epipsychidion," haunted him above all others: and
again and again in his poems we may encounter vague
echoes of those "remote isles" and "perilous seas"—
as, for example, in "the dim clustered isles of the blue
sea" of "Pauline," and the "some isle, with the sea's
silence on it—some unsuspected isle in the far seas!" of
" Pippa Passes."

But of course he had other matters for mental occu-
pation besides poetry. His education at Mr. Ready's
private academy seems to have been excellent so far as
it went. He remained there till he was fourteen.
Perhaps because of the few boarders at the school,
possibly from his own reticence in self-disclosure, he
does not seem to have impressed any school-mate
deeply. We hear of no one who "knew Browning at
school." His best education, after all, was at home.
His father and mother incidentally taught him as much
as Mr. Ready: his love of painting and music was
fostered, indirectly: and in the 'dovecot' bookshelf
above the fireplace in his bedroom, were the precious
volumes within whose sway and magic was his truest
life.

His father, for some reason which has not been made
public, but was doubtless excellent, and is, in the light
in which we now regard it, a matter for which to be
thankful, decided to send his son neither to a large public school, nor, later, to Oxford or Cambridge. A more
stimulative and wider training was awaiting him elsewhere.

For a time Robert's education was superintended by
a tutor, who came to the house in Camberwell for
several hours daily. The afternoons were mainly
devoted to music, to exercise, and occasionally to various
experimental studies in technical science. In the evenings, after his preparatory tasks were over, when he
was not in the entertaining company of his father, he
read and assiduously wrote. After poetry, he cared most
for history: but as a matter of fact, little came amiss
to his eager intellectual appetite. It was a period of

3

growth, with, it may be, a vague consciousness that his mind was expanding towards compulsive expression.

> " So as I grew, I rudely shaped my life
>   To my immediate wants, yet strong beneath
> Was a vague sense of powers folded up—
>   A sense that though those shadowy times were past,
>   Their spirit dwelt in me, and I should rule."

When Mr. Browning was satisfied that the tutor had fulfilled his duty he sent his son to attend a few lectures at University College, in Gower Street, then just founded. Robert Browning's name is on the registrar's books for the opening session, 1829-30. " I attended with him the Greek class of Professor Long" (wrote a friend, in the *Times*, Dec. 14 : '89), "and I well recollect the esteem and regard in which he was held by his fellow-students. He was then a bright, handsome youth, with long black hair falling over his shoulders." So short was his period of attendance, however, and so unimportant the instruction he there derived, that to all intents it may be said Browning had no University training.

Notwithstanding the fact that Mr. Browning but slightly appreciated his son's poetic idols and already found himself in an opposite literary camp, he had a profound sympathy with the boy's ideals and no little confidence in his powers. When the test came he acted wisely as well as with affectionate complaisance. In a word, he practically left the decision as to his course of life to Robert himself. The latter was helped thereto by the knowledge that his sister would be provided for, and that, if need be, there was sufficient for himself also.

There was of course but one way open to him. He would not have been a true poet, an artist, if he had hesitated. With a strange misconception of the artistic spirit, some one has awarded the poet great credit for his choice, because he had "the singular courage to decline to be rich." Browning himself had nothing of this bourgeois spirit : he was the last man to speak of an inevitable artistic decision as "singular courage." There are no doubt people who estimate his resolve as Mr. Barrett, so his daughter declared, regarded Horne when he heard of that poet having published "Orion" at a farthing: "Perhaps he is going to shoot the Queen, and is preparing evidence of monomania."

With Browning there never could have been two sides to the question : it were excusable, it were natural even, had his father wavered. The outcome of their delibera- tions was that Robert's further education should be obtained from travel, and intercourse with men and foreign literatures.

By this time the poet was twenty. His youth had been uneventful ; in a sense, more so than his boyhood. His mind, however, was rapidly unfolding, and great projects were casting a glory about the coming days. It was in his nineteenth year, I have been told on good authority, that he became ardently in love with a girl of rare beauty, a year or two older than himself, but other- wise, possibly, no inappropriate lover for this wooer. Why and when this early passion came to a close, or was rudely interrupted, is not known. What is certain is that it made a deep impression on the poet's mind. It may be that it, of itself, or wrought to a higher emotion by his hunger after ideal beauty, was the source of

" Pauline," that very unequal but yet beautiful first fruit of Browning's genius.

It was not till within the last few years that the poet spoke at all freely of his youthful life. Perhaps the earliest record of these utterances is that which appeared in the *Century Magazine* in 1881. From this source, and from what the poet himself said at various times and in various ways, we know that just about the time Balzac, after years of apparently waste labour, was beginning to forecast the Titanic range of the *Comédie Humaine*, Browning planned " a series of monodramatic epics, narratives of the life of typical souls —a gigantic scheme at which a Victor Hugo or a Lope de Vega would start back aghast."

Already he had set himself to the analysis of the human soul in its manifold aspects, already he had recognised that for him at least there was no other study worthy of a lifelong devotion. In a sense he has fulfilled this early dream: at any rate we have a unique series of monodramatic poems, illustrative of typical souls. In another sense, the major portion of Browning's life-work is, collectively, one monodramatic "epic." He is himself a type of the subtle, restless, curious, searching modern age of which he is the profoundest interpreter. Through a multitude of masks he, the typical soul, speaks, and delivers himself of a message which could not be presented emphatically enough as the utterance of a single individual. He is a true dramatic poet, though not in the sense in which Shakspere is. Shakspere and his kindred project themselves into the lives of their imaginary personages: Browning pays little heed to external life, or to the exigencies of action, and projects himself into the minds of his characters.

In a word, Shakspere's method is to depict a human soul in action, with all the pertinent play of circumstance, while Browning's is to portray the processes of its mental and spiritual development: as he said in his dedicatory preface to "Sordello," "little else is worth study." The one electrifies us with the outer and dominant actualities; the other flashes upon our mental vision the inner, complex, shaping potentialities. The one deals with life dynamically, the other with life as Thought. Both methods are compassed by art. Browning, who is above all modern writers the poet of dramatic situations, is surpassed by many of inferior power in continuity of dramatic sequence. His finest work is in his dramatic poems, rather than in his dramas. He realised intensely the value of quintessential moments, as when the Prefect in "The Return of the Druses" thrusts aside the arras, muttering that for the first time he enters without a sense of imminent doom, "no draught coming as from a sepulchre" saluting him, while that moment the dagger of the assassin plunges to his heart: or, further in the same poem, when Anael, coming to denounce Djabal as an impostor, is overmastered by her tyrannic love, and falls dead with the too bitter freight of her emotion, though not till she has proclaimed him the God by her single worshipping cry, *Hakeem!*—or, once more, in "The Ring and the Book," where, with the superbest close of any dramatic poem in our literature, the wretched Guido, at the point of death, cries out in the last extremity not upon God or the Virgin, but upon his innocent and

murdered wife—" Abate,—Cardinal,—Christ,—Maria,
—God, . . . Pompilia, will you let them murder me?"
Thus we can imagine Browning, with his characteristic perception of the profound significance of a
circumstance or a single word even, having written of
the knocking at the door in "Macbeth," or having
used, with all its marvellous cumulative effect, the word
'wrought' towards the close of "Othello," when the Moor
cries in his bitterness of soul, "But being wrought,
perplext in the extreme": we can imagine this, and yet
could not credit the suggestion that even the author
of "The Ring and the Book" could by any possibility
have composed the two most moving tragedies writ in
our tongue.

In the late autumn of 1832 Browning wrote a poem of
singular promise and beauty, though immature in thought
and crude in expression.[1] Thirty-four years later he
included "Pauline" in his "Poetical Works" with
reluctance, and in a note explained the reason of his
decision—namely, to forestall piratical reprints abroad.
"The thing was my earliest attempt at 'poetry always
dramatic in principle, and so many utterances of so
many imaginary persons, not mine,' which I have
since written according to a scheme less extrava-
gant, and scale less impracticable, than were ventured
upon in this crude preliminary sketch—a sketch that, on

[1] Probably from the fact of "Richmond" having been added to
the date at the end of the preface to "Pauline," have arisen the
frequent misstatements as to the Browning family having moved
west from Camberwell in or shortly before 1832. Mr. R. Barrett
Browning tells me that his father "never lived at Richmond, and
that that place was connected with 'Pauline,' when first printed,
as a mystification."

reviewal, appears not altogether wide of some hint of the characteristic features of that particular *dramatis persona* it would fain have reproduced : good draughtsmanship, however, and right handling were far beyond the artist at that time." These be hard words. No critic will ever adventure upon so severe a censure of "Pauline" : most capable judges agree that, with all its shortcomings, it is a work of genius, and therefore ever to be held treasurable for its own sake as well as for its significance.

On the fly-leaf of a copy of this initial work, the poet, six years after its publication, wrote : "Written in pursuance of a foolish plan I forget, or have no wish to remember; the world was never to guess that such an opera, such a comedy, such a speech proceeded from the same notable person. . . . Only this crab remains of the shapely Tree of Life in my fool's Paradise." It was in conformity with this plan that he not only issued "Pauline" anonymously, but enjoined secrecy upon those to whom he communicated the fact of his authorship.

When he read the poem to his parents, upon its conclusion, both were much impressed by it, though his father made severe strictures upon its lack of polish, its terminal inconcision, and its vagueness of thought. That he was not more severe was accepted by his son as high praise. The author had, however, little hope of seeing it in print. Mr. Browning was not anxious to provide a publisher with a present. So one day the poet was gratified when his aunt, handing him the requisite sum, remarked that she had heard he had written a fine poem, and that she wished to have the pleasure of seeing it in print.

To this kindly act much was due. Browning, of course, could not now have been dissuaded from the career he had forecast for himself, but his progress might have been retarded or thwarted to less fortunate grooves, had it not been for the circumstances resultant from his aunt's timely gift.

The MS. was forthwith taken to Saunders & Otley, of Conduit Street, and the little volume of seventy pages of blank verse, comprising only a thousand and thirty lines, was issued by them in January 1833. It seems to us, who read it now, so manifestly a work of exceptional promise, and, to a certain extent, of high accomplishment, that were it not for the fact that the public auditory for a new poet is ever extraordinarily limited, it would be difficult to understand how it could have been overlooked.

"Pauline" has a unique significance because of its autopsychical hints. The Browning whom we all know, as well as the youthful dreamer, is here revealed; here too, as well as the disciple of Shelley, we have the author of "The Ring and the Book." In it the long series culminating in "Asolando" is foreshadowed, as the oak is observable in the sapling. The poem is prefaced by a Latin motto from the *Occult Philosophy* of Cornelius Agrippa, and has also a note in French, set forth as being by Pauline, and appended to her lover's manuscript after his death. Probably Browning placed it in the mouth of Pauline from his rooted determination to speak dramatically and impersonally: and in French, so as to heighten the effect of verisimilitude.[1]

[1] "I much fear that my poor friend will not be always perfectly understood in what remains to be read of this strange fragment,

"Pauline" is a confession, fragmentary in detail but synthetic in range, of a young man of high impulses but weak determination. In its over-emphasis upon errors of judgment, as well as upon real if exaggerated misdeeds, it has all the crudeness of youth. An almost fantastic self-consciousness is the central motive: it is a matter of question if this be absolutely vicarious. To me it seems that the author himself was at the time confused by the complicated flashing of the lights of life.

The autobiographical and autopsychical lines and passages scattered through the poem are of immediate interest. Generously the poet repays his debt to Shelley, whom he apostrophises as "Sun-treader," and invokes in strains of lofty emotion—"Sun-treader—life and light

but it is less calculated than any other part to explain what of its nature can never be anything but dream and confusion. I do not know, moreover, whether in striving at a better connection of certain parts, one would not run the risk of detracting from the only merit to which so singular a production can pretend—that of giving a tolerably precise idea of the manner (*genre*) which it can merely indicate. This unpretending opening, this stir of passion, which first increases, and then gradually subsides, these transports of the soul, this sudden return upon himself, and above all, my friend's quite peculiar turn of mind, have made alterations almost impossible. The reasons which he elsewhere asserts, and others still more cogent, have secured my indulgence for this paper, which otherwise I should have advised him to throw into the fire. I believe none the less in the great principle of all composition—in that principle of Shakespeare, of Raphael, and of Beethoven, according to which concentration of ideas is due much more to their conception than to their execution; I have every reason to fear that the first of these qualities is still foreign to my friend, and I much doubt whether redoubled labour would enable him to acquire the second. It would be best to burn this, but what can I do?"—(*Mrs. Orr.*)

be thine for ever." The music of "Alastor," indeed, is audible ever and again throughout "Pauline." None the less is there a new music, a new poetic voice, in

> " Thou wilt remember one warm morn, when Winter
> Crept aged from the earth, and Spring's first breath
> Blew soft from the moist hills—the black-thorn boughs,
> So dark in the bare wood, when glistening
> In the sunshine were white with coming buds,
> Like the bright side of a sorrow—and the banks
> Had violets opening from sleep like eyes."

If we have an imaginary Browning, a Shelleyan phantasm, in

> " I seemed the fate from which I fled; I felt
> A strange delight in causing my decay;
> I was a fiend, in darkness chained for ever
> Within some ocean-wave:"

we have the real Browning in

> " So I will sing, on—fast as fancies come
> Rudely—the verse being as the mood it paints.
>
> .   .   .   .   .   .
>
> I am made up of an intensest life,"

and all the succeeding lines down to "Their spirit dwelt in me, and I should rule."

Even then the poet's inner life was animated by his love of the beautiful Greek literature. Telling how in "the first dawn of life," "which passed alone with wisest ancient books," Pauline's lover incorporated himself in whatsoever he read—was the god wandering after beauty, the giant standing vast against the sunset-light, the high-crested chief sailing with troops of friends to Tenedos—his second-self cries, " I tell you, nought has ever been so clear as the place, the time, the fashion of those lives." Never for him, then, had there been that alchemy of the soul which turns the inchoate drift of the world into golden ore, not then had come to him the electric awakening flash from "work of lofty art, nor woman's beauty, nor sweet nature's face"—

> " Yet, I say, never morn broke clear as those
> On the dim clustered isles in the blue sea:
> The deep groves, and white temples, and wet caves—
> And nothing ever will surprise me now—
> Who stood beside the naked Swift-footed,
> Who bound my forehead with Proserpine's hair."

Further, the allusion to Plato, and the more remote one to Agamemnon, the

> "old lore
> Loved for itself, and all it shows—the King
> Treading the purple calmly to his death,"

and the beautiful Andromeda passage, afford ample indication of how deeply Browning had drunk of that vital stream whose waters are the surest conserver of the ideal loveliness which we all of us, in some degree, cherish in various guises.

Yet, as in every long poem that he has written (and, it must be admitted, in too many of the shorter pieces of his later period) there is an alloy of prose, of something that is not poetry, so in " Pauline," written though it was in the first flush of his genius and under the inspiring stimulus of Shelley, the reader encounters prosaic passages, decasyllabically arranged. ""Twas in my plan to look on real life, which was all new to me; my theories were firm, so I left them, to look upon men,

and their cares, and hopes, and fears, and joys; and, as
I pondered on them all, I sought how best life's end
might be attained, an end comprising every joy."
Again: " Then came a pause, and long restraint
chained down my soul, till it was changed. I lost
myself, and were it not that I so loathe that time, I
could recall how first I learned to turn my mind against
itself . . . at length I was restored, yet long the influence
remained; and nought but the still life I led, apart from
all, which left my soul to seek its old delights, could e'er
have brought me thus far back to peace." No reader,
alert to the subtle and haunting music of rarefied blank
verse (and unless it be rarefied it should not be put
forward as poetry), could possibly accept these lines as
expressionally poetical. It would seem as though, from
the first, Browning's ear was keener for the apprehension
than for the sustained evocation of the music of verse.
Some flaw there was, somewhere. His heart, so to say,
beat too fast, and the singing in his ears from the o'er-
fevered blood confused the serene rhythm haunting the
far perspectives of the brain, "as Arab birds float sleep-
ing in the wind."

I have dwelt at this length upon " Pauline " partly
because of its inherent beauty and autopsychical significance, and partly because it is the least familiar of
Browning's poems, long overshadowed as it has been
by his own too severe strictures : mainly, however,
because of its radical importance to the student who
would arrive at a broad and true estimate of the power
and scope and shaping constituents of its author's genius.
Almost every quality of his after-verse may be found here,
in germ or outline. It is, in a word, more physiognomic

than any other single poem by Browning, and so must
ever possess a peculiar interest quite apart from its many
passages of haunting beauty.

To these the lover of poetry will always turn with
delight. Some will even regard them retrospectively
with alien emotion to that wherewith they strive to
possess their souls in patience over some one or other
of the barbarisms, the Titanic excesses, the poetic
banalities recurrent in the later volumes.

How many and how haunting these delicate oases are!
Those who know and love "Pauline" will remember
the passage where the poet, with that pantheistic ecstasy
which was possibly inspired by the singer he most
loved, tells how he can live the life of plants, content to
watch the wild bees flitting to and fro, or to lie absorbent
of the ardours of the sun, or, like the night-flowering
columbine, to trail up the tree-trunk and through its
rustling foliage " look for the dim stars ;" or, again, can
live the life of the bird, " leaping airily his pyramid of
leaves and twisted boughs of some tall mountain-tree ;"
or be a fish, breathing the morning air in the misty sun-
warm water. Close following this is another memorable
passage, that beginning " Night, and one single ridge of
narrow path ;" which has a particular interest for two
notes of a deeper and broader music to be evolved long
afterwards. For, as it seems to me, in

> " Thou art so close by me, the roughest swell
> Of wind in the tree-tops hides not the panting
> Of thy soft breasts——"

(where, by the way, should be noticed the subtle correspondence between the conceptive and the expressional

rhythm) we have a hint of that superb scene in "Pippa Passes," where, on a sinister night of July, a night of spiritual storm as well as of aerial tempest, Ottima and Sebald lie amid the lightning-scarcht forest, with "the thunder like a whole sea overhead." Again, in the lovely Turneresque, or rather Shelleyan picture of morning, over "the rocks, and valleys, and old woods," with the high boughs swinging in the wind above the sun-brightened mists, and the golden-coloured spray of the cataract amid the broken rocks, whereover the wild hawks fly to and fro, there is at least a suggestion, an outline, of the truly magnificent burst of morning music in the poet's penultimate volume, beginning—

> " But morning's laugh sets all the crags alight
> Above the baffled tempest : tree and tree
> Stir themselves from the stupor of the night,
> And every strangled branch resumes its right
> To breathe, shakes loose dark's clinging dregs, waves free
> In dripping glory.   Prone the runnels plunge,
> While earth, distent with moisture like a sponge,
> Smokes up, and leaves each plant its gem to see,
> Each grass-blade's glory-glitter," etc.

Who that has ever read "Pauline" will forget the masterful poetry descriptive of the lover's wild-wood retreat, the exquisite lines beginning "Walled in with a sloped mound of matted shrubs, tangled, old and green"?   There is indeed a new, an unmistakable voice here.

> " And tongues of bank go shelving in the waters,
> Where the pale-throated snake reclines his head,
> And old grey stones lie making eddies there;
> The wild mice cross them dry-shod " . . . .

What lovelier image in modern poetry than that depictive of the forest-pool in depths of savage woodlands, unvisited but by the shadows of passing clouds,—

> "the trees bend
> O'er it as wild men watch a sleeping girl."

How the passionate sexual emotion, always deep and true in Browning, finds lovely utterance in the lines where Pauline's lover speaks of the blood in her lips pulsing like a living thing, while her neck is as "marble misted o'er with love-breath," and

> ". . . her delicious eyes as clear as heaven,
> When rain in a quick shower has beat down mist,
> And clouds float white in the sun like broods of swans."

In the quotations I have made, and in others that might be selected (*e.g.*, "Her fresh eyes, and soft hair, and *lips which bleed like a mountain berry*"), it is easy to note how intimate an observer of nature the youthful poet was, and with what conscious but not obtrusive art he brings forward his new and striking imagery. Browning, indeed, is the poet of new symbols.

"Pauline" concludes with lines which must have been in the minds of many on that sad day when the tidings from Venice sent a thrill of startled, half-incredulous, bewildered pain throughout the English nations—

> "Sun-treader, I believe in God, and truth,
> And love ; . . .
> . . . but chiefly when I die . . .
> All in whom this wakes pleasant thoughts of me,
> Know my last state is happy—free from doubt,
> Or touch of fear."

Never again was Browning to write a poem with such conceptive crudeness, never again to tread the byways of thought so falteringly or so negligently : but never again, perhaps, was he to show so much over-rapturing joy in the world's loveliness, such Bacchic abandon to the ideal beauty which the true poet sees glowing upon the forlornest height and brooding in the shadow-haunted hollows of the hills. The Browning who might have been is here : henceforth the Browning we know and love stands unique among all the lords of song. But sometimes do we not turn longingly, wonderingly at least, to the young Dionysos upon whose forehead was the light of another destiny than that which descended upon him ? The Icelanders say there is a land where all the rainbows that have ever been, or are yet to be, forever drift to and fro, evanishing and reappearing, like immortal flowers of vapour. In that far country, it may be, are also the unfulfilled dreams, the visions too perfect to be fashioned into song, of the young poets who have gained the laurel.

We close the little book lovingly :

> " And I had dimly shaped my first attempt,
> And many a thought did I build up on thought,
> As the wild bee hangs cell to cell—in vain ;
> For I must still go on : my mind rests not."

CHAPTER III.

IT has been commonly asserted that "Pauline" was almost wholly disregarded, and swiftly lapsed into oblivion.

This must be accepted with qualification. It is like the other general assertion, that Browning had to live fifty years before he gained recognition—a statement as ludicrous when examined as it is unjust to the many discreet judges who awarded, publicly and privately, that intelligent sympathy which is the best sunshine for the flower of a poet's genius. If by "before he gained recognition" is meant a general and indiscriminate acclaim, no doubt Browning had, still has indeed, longer to wait than many other eminent writers have had to do: but it is absurd to assert that from the very outset of his poetic career he was met by nothing but neglect, if not scornful derision. None who knows the true artistic temperament will fall into any such mistake.

It is quite certain that neither Shakspere nor Milton ever met with such enthusiastic praise and welcome as Browning encountered on the publication of "Pauline" and "Paracelsus." Shelley, as far above Browning in poetic music as the author of so many parleyings with other people's souls is the superior in psychic

4

insight and intellectual strength, had throughout his too
brief life not one such review of praiseful welcome
as the Rev. W. J. Fox wrote on the publication of
"Pauline" (or, it may be added, as Allan Cunningham's
equally kindly but less able review in the *Athenæum*),
or as John Forster wrote in *The Examiner* concerning
"Paracelsus," and later in the *New Monthly Magazine,*
where he had the courage to say of the young and
quite unknown poet, "without the slightest hesitation
we name Mr. Robert Browning at once with Shelley,
Coleridge, Wordsworth." His plays even (which are
commonly said to have "fallen flat") were certainly not
failures. There is something effeminate, undignified,
and certainly uncritical, in this confusion as to what is
and what is not failure in literature. So enthusiastic
was the applause he encountered, indeed, that had his
not been too strong a nature to be thwarted by adula-
tion any more than by contemptuous neglect, he might
well have become spoilt—so enthusiastic, that were it
not for the heavy and prolonged counterbalancing dead
weight of public indifference, a huge amorphous mass
only of late years moulded into harmony with the
keenest minds of the century, we might well be
suspicious of so much and long-continued eulogium,
and fear the same reversal of judgment towards him
on the part of those who come after us as we ourselves have meted to many an one among the high
gods of our fathers.

Fortunately the deep humanity of his work in the
mass conserves it against the mere veerings of taste. A
reaction against it will inevitably come; but this will
pass : what, in the future, when the unborn readers of

Browning will look back with clear eyes untroubled by the dust of our footsteps, not to subside till long after we too are dust, will be the place given to this poet, we know not, nor can more than speculatively estimate. That it will, however, be a high one, so far as his weightiest (in bulk, it may possibly be but a relatively slender) accomplishment is concerned, we may rest well assured : for indeed " It lives, If precious be the soul of man to man."

So far as has been ascertained there were only three reviews or notices of " Pauline " : the very favourable article by Mr. Fox in the *Monthly Repository*, the kindly paper by Allan Cunningham in the *Athenæum*, and, in *Tait's Edinburgh Magazine*, the succinctly expressed impression of either an indolent or an incapable reviewer : " Pauline ; a Fragment of a Confession ; a piece of pure bewilderment"—a "criticism" which anticipated and thus prevented the insertion of a highly favourable review which John Stuart Mill voluntarily wrote.

Browning must have regarded his first book with mingled feelings. It was a bid for literary fortune, in one sense, but a bid so handicapped by the circumstances of its publication as to be almost certainly of no avail. Probably, however, he was well content that it should have mere existence. Already the fever of an abnormal intellectual curiosity was upon him : already he had schemed more potent and more vital poems : already, even, he had developed towards a more individualistic method. So indifferent was he to an easily gained reputation that he seems to have been really urgent upon his relatives and intimate acquaintances

not to betray his authorship. The Miss Flower, however, to whom allusion has already been made, could
not repress her admiration to the extent of depriving her
friend, Mr. Fox, of a pleasure similar to that she had
herself enjoyed. The result was the generous notice in
the *Monthly Repository.* The poet never forgot his
indebtedness to Mr. Fox, to whose sympathy and kind-
ness much direct and indirect good is traceable. The
friendship then begun was lifelong, and was continued
with the distinguished Unitarian's family when Mr. Fox
himself ended his active and beneficent career.

But after a time the few admirers of "Pauline" forgot
to speak about it: the poet himself never alluded to it:
and in a year or two it was almost as though it had
never been written. Many years after, when articles
upon Robert Browning were as numerous as they once
had been scarce, never a word betrayed that their
authors knew of the existence of "Pauline." There
was, however, yet another friendship to come out of
this book, though not until long after it was practically
forgotten by its author.

One day a young poet-painter came upon a copy of
the book in the British Museum Library, and was at
once captivated by its beauty. One of the earliest
admirers of Browning's poetry, Dante Gabriel Rossetti—
for it was he—felt certain that "Pauline" could be by
none other than the author of "Paracelsus." He himself informed me that he had never heard this authorship suggested, though some one had spoken to him of
a poem of remarkable promise, called "Pauline," which
he ought to read. If I remember aright, Rossetti told
me that it was on the forenoon of the day when the

"Burden of Nineveh" was begun, conceived rather, that he read this story of a soul by the soul's ablest historian. So delighted was he with it, and so strong his opinion it was by Browning, that he wrote to the poet, then in Florence, for confirmation, stating at the same time that his admiration for "Pauline" had led him to transcribe the whole of it.

Concerning this episode, Robert Browning wrote to me, some seven years ago, as follows :—

> "St. Pierre de Chartreuse,
>   Isère, France.

.   .   .   .

"Rossetti's 'Pauline' letter was addressed to me at Florence more than thirty years ago. I have preserved it, but, even were I at home, should be unable to find it without troublesome search-ing. It was to the effect that the writer, personally and altogether unknown to me, had come upon a poem in the British Museum, which he copied the whole of, from its being not otherwise pro-curable—that he judged it to be mine, but could not be sure, and wished me to pronounce in the matter—which I did. A year or two after, I had a visit in London from Mr. (William) Allingham and a friend—who proved to be Rossetti. When I heard he was a painter I insisted on calling on him, though he declared he had nothing to show me—which was far enough from the case. Subsequently, on another of my returns to London, he painted my portrait, not, I fancy, in oils, but water-colours, and finished it in Paris shortly after. This must have been in the year when Tennyson published 'Maud,' for I remember Tennyson reading the poem one evening while Rossetti made a rapid pen-and-ink sketch of him, very good, from one obscure corner of vantage, which I still possess, and duly value. This was before Rossetti's marriage." [1]

---

[1] The highly interesting and excellent portrait of Browning here alluded to has never been exhibited.

As a matter of fact, as recorded on the back of the original drawing, the eventful reading took place at 13 Dorset Street, Portman Square, on the 27th of September 1855, and those present, besides the Poet-Laureate, Browning, and Rossetti, were Mrs. E. Barrett Browning and Miss Arabella Barrett.

When, a year or two ago, the poet learned that a copy of his first work, which in 1833 could not find a dozen purchasers at a few shillings, went at a public sale for twenty-five guineas, he remarked that had his dear old aunt been living he could have returned to her, much to her incredulous astonishment, no doubt, he smilingly averred, the cost of the book's publication, less £3 15s. It was about the time of the publication of "Pauline" that Browning began to see something of the literary and artistic life for which he had such an inborn taste. For a brief period he went often to the British Museum, particularly the Library, and to the National Gallery. At the British Museum Reading Room he perused with great industry and research those works in philosophy and medical history which are the bases of "Paracelsus," and those Italian Records bearing upon the story of Sordello. Residence in Camberwell, in 1833, rendered night engagements often impracticable : but nevertheless he managed to mix a good deal in congenial society. It is not commonly known that he was familiar to these early associates as a musician and artist rather than as a poet. Among them, and they comprised many well-known workers in the several arts, were Charles Dickens and "Ion" Talfourd. Mr. Fox, whom Browning had met once or twice in his early youth, after the former had been shown the Byronic verses which had in one

way gratified and in another way perturbed the
poet's father, saw something more of his young friend
after the publication of " Pauline." He very kindly
offered to print in his magazine any short poems
the author of that book should see fit to send—an
offer, however, which was not put to the test for some
time.

Practically simultaneously with the publication of
"Pauline" appeared another small volume, containing
the "Palace of Art," " Œnone," "Mariana," etc. Those
early books of Tennyson and Browning have frequently,
and somewhat uncritically, been contrasted. Unquestionably, however, the elder poet showed a consummate and
continuous mastery of his art altogether beyond the
intermittent expressional power of Browning in his
most rhythmic emotion at any time of his life. To
affirm that there is more intellectual fibre, what Rossetti
called fundamental brain-work, in the product of the
younger poet, would be beside the mark. The insistence
on the supremacy of Browning over all poets since
Shakspere because he has the highest "message" to
deliver, because his intellect is the most subtle and
comprehensive, because his poems have this or that
dynamic effect upon dormant or sluggish or other
active minds, is to be seriously and energetically
deprecated. It is with presentment that the artist
has, fundamentally, to concern himself. If he cannot
present poetically then he is not, in effect, a poet,
though he may be a poetic thinker, or a great writer.
Browning's eminence is not because of his detachment
from what some one has foolishly called "the mere
handiwork, the furnisher's business, of the poet." It is

the delight of the true artist that the product of his
talent should be wrought to a high technique equally by
the shaping brain and the dexterous hand. Browning is
great because of his formative energy : because, despite
the excess of burning and compulsive thought—

> " Thoughts swarming thro' the myriad-chambered brain
>   Like multitudes of bees i' the innumerous cells,
>   Each staggering 'neath the undelivered freight——"

he strikes from t'ie _furor_ of words an electric flash so
transcendently illuminative that what is commonplace
becomes radiant with that light which dwells not in
nature, but only in the visionary eye of man.   Form
for the mere beauty of form, is a playing with the wind,
the acceptance of a shadow for the substance. If
nothing animate it, it may possibly be fair of aspect,
but only as the frozen smile upon a dead face.

We know little of Browning's inner or outer life in
1833 and 1834. It was a secretive, not a productive
period. One by one certain pinnacles of his fair snow-
mountain of Titanic aim melted away. He began to
realise the first disenchantment of the artist : the sense
of dreams never to be accomplished. That land of the
great unwritten poems, the great unpainted pictures :
what a heritance there for the enfranchised spirits of
great dreamers !

In the autumn of 1833 he went forth to his University,
that of the world of men and women. It was ever a
favourite answer of his, when asked if he had been
at either Oxford or Cambridge, — " Italy was my
University."

But first he went to Russia, and spent some time in
St. Petersburg, attracted thither by the invitation of a
friend. The country interested him, but does not seem
to have deeply or permanently engaged his attention.
That, however, his Russian experiences were not fruitless
is manifest from the remarkably picturesque and technically very interesting poem, "Iván Ivànovitch" (the
fourth of the *Dramatic Idyls*, 1879). Of a truth,
after his own race and country—readers will at once
think of "Home Thoughts from the Sea," or the
thrilling lines in "Home Thoughts from Abroad," beginning—

> " Oh, to be in England,
> Now that April's there ! "—

or perhaps, those lines in his earliest work—

> " I cherish most
> My love of England—how, her name, a word
> Of hers in a strange tongue makes my heart beat ! "

—it was of the mystic Orient or of the glowing South
that he oftenest thought and dreamed. With Heine he
might have cried: "O Firdusi ! O Ischami ! O Saadi !
How do I long after the roses of Schiraz !" As for
Italy, who of all our truest poets has not loved her : but
who has worshipped her with so manly a passion, so
loyal a love, as Browning? One alone indeed may be
mated with him here, she who had his heart of
hearts, and who lies at rest in the old Florentine
cemetery within sound of the loved waters of Arno.
Who can forget his lines in " De Gustibus,"

"Open my heart and you will see, graved inside of it, Italy."

It would be no difficult task to devote a volume larger than the present one to the descriptive analysis of none but the poems inspired by Italy, Italian personages and history, Italian Painting, Sculpture, Architecture, and Music. From Porphyria and her lover to Pompilia and all the direful Roman tragedy wherein she is as a moon of beauty above conflicting savage tides of passion, what an unparalleled gallery of portraits, what a brilliant phantasmagoria, what a movement of intensest life!

It is pleasant to know of one of them, "The Italian in England," that Browning was proud, because Mazzini told him he had read this poem to certain of his fellow-exiles in England to show how an Englishman could sympathise with them.

After leaving Russia the young poet spent the rest of his *Wanderjahr* in Italy. Among other places he visited was Asolo, that white little hill-town of the Veneto, whence he drew hints for "Sordello" and "Pippa Passes," and whither he returned in the last year of his life, as with unconscious significance he himself said, "on his way homeward."

In the summer of 1834, that is, when he was in his twenty-second year, he returned to Camberwell. "Sordello" he had in some fashion begun, but had set aside for a poem which occupied him throughout the autumn of 1834 and winter of 1835, "Paracelsus." In this period, also, he wrote some short poems, two of them of particular significance. The first of the series was a sonnet, which appeared above the signature 'Z' in the

August number of the *Monthly Repository* for 1834. It was never reprinted by the author, whose judgment it is impossible not to approve as well as to respect. Browning never wrote a good sonnet, and this earliest effort is not the most fortunate. It was in the *Repository* also, in 1835 and 1836, that the other poems appeared, four in all.

The song in "Pippa Passes," beginning "A King lived long ago," was one of these; and the lyric, "Still ailing, wind? Wilt be appeased or no?" afterwards revised and incorporated in "James Lee," was another. But the two which are much the most noteworthy are "Johannes Agricola" and "Porphyria." Even more distinctively than in "Pauline," in their novel sentiment, new method, and generally unique quality, is a new voice audible in these two poems. They are very remarkable as the work of so young a poet, and are interesting as showing how rapidly he had outgrown the influence of any other of his poetic kindred. "Johannes Agricola" is significant as being the first of those dramatic studies of warped religiosity, of strange self-sophistication, which have afforded so much matter for thought. In its dramatic concision, its complex psychological significance, and its unique, if to unaccustomed ears somewhat barbaric, poetic beauty, "Porphyria" is still more remarkable.

It may be of this time, though possibly some years later, that Mrs. Bridell-Fox writes:—"I remember him as looking in often in the evenings, having just returned from his first visit to Venice. I cannot tell the date for certain. He was full of enthusiasm for that Queen of Cities. He used to illustrate his glowing descriptions of its beauties, the palaces, the sunsets, the moonrises, by a most original kind of etching. Taking up a bit of stray notepaper, he would hold it over a lighted candle, moving the paper about gently till it was cloudily smoked over, and then utilising the darker smears for clouds, shadows, water, or what not, would etch with a dry pen the forms of lights on cloud and palace, on bridge or gondola on the vague and dreamy surface he had produced. My own passionate longing to see Venice dates from those delightful, well-remembered evenings of my childhood."

"Paracelsus," begun about the close of October or early in November 1834, was published in the summer of the following year. It is a poem in blank verse, about four times the length of "Pauline," with interspersed songs. The author divided it into five sections of unequal length, of which the third is the most extensive : "Paracelsus Aspires"; "Paracelsus Attains"; "Paracelsus"; "Paracelsus Aspires"; "Paracelsus Attains." In an interesting note, which was not reprinted in later editions of his first acknowledged poem, the author dissuades the reader from mistaking his performance for one of a class with which it has nothing in common, from judging it by principles on which it was not moulded, and from subjecting it to a standard to which it was never meant to conform. He then explains that he has composed a dramatic poem, and not a drama in the accepted sense; that he has not set forth the phenomena of the mind or the passions by the operation of persons and events, or by recourse to an external machinery of incidents to create and evolve the crisis sought to be produced. Instead of this, he remarks, "I have ventured to display somewhat minutely the mood itself in its rise and progress, and have suffered the agency, by which it is influenced and determined, to be generally discernible in its effects alone, and subordinate throughout, if not altogether excluded: and this for a reason. I have endeavoured to write a poem, not a drama." A little further, he states that a work like "Paracelsus" depends, for its success, immediately upon the intelligence and sympathy of the reader: "Indeed, were my scenes stars, it must be his co-operating fancy which, supplying all chasms, shall connect the scattered lights into one constellation—a Lyre or a Crown."

In the concluding paragraph of this note there is a point of interest—the statement of the author's hope that the readers of "Paracelsus" will not "be prejudiced against other productions which may follow in a more popular, and perhaps less difficult form." From this it might fairly be inferred that Browning had not definitively adopted his characteristic method: that he was far from unwilling to gain the general ear: and that he was alert to the difficulties of popularisation of poetry written on lines similar to those of "Paracelsus." Nor would this inference be wrong: for, as a matter of fact, the poet, immediately upon the publication of "Paracelsus," determined to devote himself to poetic work which should have so direct a contact with actual life that its appeal should reach even to the most uninitiate in the mysteries and delights of verse.

In his early years Browning had always a great liking for walking in the dark. At Camberwell he was wont to carry this love to the point of losing many a night's rest. There was, in particular, a wood near Dulwich, whither he was wont to go. There he would walk swiftly and

eagerly along the solitary and lightless byways, finding
a potent stimulus to imaginative thought in the happy
isolation thus enjoyed, with all the concurrent delights of
natural things, the wind moving like a spirit through the
tree-branches, the drifting of poignant fragrances, even
in winter-tide, from herb and sappy bark, imperceptible
almost by the alertest sense in the day's manifold
detachments.   At this time, too, he composed much
in the open air.   This he rarely, if ever, did in later life.
Not only many portions of "Paracelsus," but several
scenes in "Strafford," were enacted first in these midnight silences of the Dulwich woodland.   Here, too, as
the poet once declared, he came to know the serene
beauty of dawn : for every now and again, after having
read late, or written long, he would steal quietly from
the house, and walk till the morning twilight graded to
the pearl and amber of the new day.

As in childhood the glow of distant London had
affected him to a pleasure that was not without pain,
perhaps to a pain rather that was a fine delirium, so in
his early manhood the neighbourhood of the huge city,
felt in those midnight walks of his, and apprehended
more by the transmutive shudder of reflected glare
thrown fadingly upward against the stars, than by any
more direct vision or even far-borne indeterminate hum,
dominated his imagination.   At that distance, in those
circumstances, humanity became more human.   And
with the thought, the consciousness of this imperative
kinship, arose the vague desire, the high resolve to be no
curious dilettante in novel literary experiments, but to
compel an interpretative understanding of this complex
human environment.

Those who knew the poet intimately are aware of the loving regard he always had for those nocturnal experiences : but perhaps few recognise how much we owe to the subtle influences of that congenial isolation he was wont to enjoy on fortunate occasions.

It is not my intention—it would, obviously, be a futile one, if entertained—to attempt an analysis or elaborate criticism of the many poems, long and short, produced by Robert Browning. Not one volume, but several, of this size, would have to be allotted to the adequate performance of that end. Moreover, if readers are unable or unwilling to be their own expositors, there are several trustworthy hand-books which are easily procurable. Some one, I believe, has even, with unselfish consideration for the weaker brethren, turned " Sordello " into prose—a superfluous task, some scoffers may exclaim. Personally, I cannot but think this craze for the exposition of poetry, this passion for " dissecting a rainbow," is harmful to the individual as well as humiliating to the high office of Poetry itself, and not infrequently it is ludicrous.

I must be content with a few words anent the more important or significant poems, and in due course attempt an estimate by a broad synthesis, and not by cumulative critical analyses.

In the selection of Paracelsus as the hero of his first mature poem, Browning was guided first of all by his keen sympathy with the scientific spirit—the spirit of dauntless inquiry, of quenchless curiosity, of a searching enthusiasm. Pietro of Abano, Giordano Bruno, Galileo, were heroes whom he regarded with an admiration which would have been boundless but for the wise sympathy which enabled him to apprehend and understand their weaknesses as well as their lofty qualities. Once having come to the conclusion that Paracelsus was a great and much maligned man, it was natural for him to wish to portray aright the features he saw looming through the mists of legend and history. But over and above this, he half unwittingly, half consciously, felt the fascination of that mysticism associated with the name of the celebrated German scientist—a mysticism, in all its various phases, of which he is now acknowledged to be the subtlest poetic interpreter in our language, though, profound as its attraction always was for him, never was poet with a more exquisite balance of intellectual sanity.

Latest research has proved that whatsoever of a pretender Paracelsus may have been in certain respects, he was unquestionably a man of extraordinary powers : and, as a pioneer in a science of the first magnitude of importance, deserving of high honour. If ever the famous German attain a high place in the history of the modern intellectual movement in Europe, it will be primarily due to Browning's championship.

But of course the extent or shallowness of Paracelsus' claim is a matter of quite secondary interest. We are concerned with the poet's presentment of the man—of that strange soul whom he conceived of as having anticipated so far, and as having focussed all the vagrant speculations of the day into one startling beam of light, now lambently pure, now lurid with gross constituents.[1]

---

[1] Paracelsus has two particular claims upon our regard. He gave us laudanum, a discovery of incalculable blessing to mankind. And from his fourth baptismal name, which he inherited

Paracelsus, his friends Festus and his wife Michal, and Aprile, an Italian poet, are the characters who are the personal media through which Browning's already powerful genius found expression. The poem is, of a kind, an epic: the epic of a brave soul striving against baffling circumstance. It is full of passages of rare technical excellence, as well as of conceptive beauty: so full, indeed, that the sympathetic reader of it as a drama will be too apt to overlook its radical shortcomings, cast as it is in the dramatic mould. But it must not be forgotten that Browning himself distinctly stated he had attempted to write "a poem, not a drama": and in the light of this simple statement half the objections that have been made fall to the ground.

Paracelsus is the protagonist: the others are merely incidental. The poem is the soul-history of the great medical student who began life so brave of aspect and died so miserably at Salzburg: but it is also the history of a typical human soul, which can be read without any knowledge of actual particulars.

Aprile is a projection of the poet's own poetical ideal. He speaks, but he does not live as Festus lives, or even as Michal, who, by the way, is interesting as being the first in the long gallery of Browning's women—a gallery

from his father, we have our familiar term, 'bombast.' Readers interested in the known facts concerning the "master-mind, the thinker, the explorer, the creator," the forerunner of Mesmer and even of Darwin and Wallace, who began life with the sounding appellation "Philippus Aureolus Theophrastus Bombastus ab Hohenheim," should consult Browning's own learned appendical note, and Mr. Berdoe's interesting essay in the Browning Society Papers, No. xlix.

5

of superbly-drawn portraits, of noble and striking and
always intensely human women, unparalleled except in
Shakspere. Pauline, of course, exists only as an ab-
straction, and Porphyria is in no exact sense a portrait
from the life. Yet Michal can be revealed only to the
sympathetic eye, for she is not drawn, but again and
again suddenly silhouetted. We see her in profile always:
but when she exclaims at the last, " I ever did believe,"
we feel that she has withdrawn the veil partially hiding
her fair and generous spirit.

To the lover of poetry " Paracelsus" will always be
a Golconda. It has lines and passages of extraordinary
power, of a haunting beauty, and of a unique and
exquisite charm. It may be noted, in exemplification of
Browning's artistic range, that in the descriptive passages
he paints as well in the elaborate Pre-Raphaelite method
as with a broad synthetic touch: as in

> "One old populous green wall
> Tenanted by the ever-busy flies,
> Grey crickets and shy lizards and quick spiders,
> Each family of the silver-threaded moss—
> Which, look through near, this way, and it appears
> A stubble-field or a cane-brake, a marsh
> Of bulrush whitening in the sun. . . ."

But oftener he prefers the more succinct method of
landscape-painting, the broadest impressionism : as in

> " Past the high rocks the haunts of doves, the mounds
> Of red earth from whose sides strange trees grow out,
> Past tracks of milk-white minute blinding sand."

And where in modern poetry is there a superber union
of the scientific and the poetic vision than in this

magnificent passage—the quintessence of the poet's conception of the rapture of life:—

> " The centre-fire heaves underneath the earth,
>   And the earth changes like a human face;
>   The molten ore bursts up among the rocks,
>   Winds into the stone's heart, outbranches bright
>   In hidden mines, spots barren river-beds,
>   Crumbles into fine sand where sunbeams bask—
>   God joys therein. The wroth sea's waves are edged
>   With foam, white as the bitten lip of hate,
>   When in the solitary waste, strange groups
>   Of young volcanoes come up, cyclops-like,
>   Staring together with their eyes on flame—
>   God tastes a pleasure in their uncouth pride.
>   Then all is still; earth is a wintry clod:
>   But Spring-wind, like a dancing psaltress, passes
>   Over its breast to waken it, rare verdure
>   Buds tenderly upon rough banks, between
>   The withered tree-rests and the cracks of frost,
>   Like a smile striving with a wrinkled face;
>   The grass grows bright, the boughs are swoln with blooms
>   Like chrysalids impatient for the air,
>   The shining dorrs are busy, beetles run
>   Along the furrows, ants make their ado;
>   Above, birds fly in merry flocks, the lark
>   Soars up and up, shivering for very joy;
>   Afar the ocean sleeps; white fishing gulls
>   Flit where the strand is purple with its tribe
>   Of nested limpets; savage creatures seek
>   Their loves in wood and plain—and God renews
>   His ancient rapture."

In these lines, particularly in their close, is manifest the influence of the noble Hebraic poetry. It must have been at this period that Browning conned over and over with an exultant delight the simple but lordly diction of Isaiah and the other prophets, preferring this

Biblical poetry to that even of his beloved Greeks. There is an anecdote of his walking across a public park (**I am told Richmond**, but more probably it was Wimbledon Common) with his hat in his left hand and his right waving to and fro declamatorily, while the wind blew his hair around his head like a nimbus: so rapt in his ecstasy over the solemn sweep of the Biblical music that he did not observe a small following consisting of several eager children, expectant of thrilling stumporatory. He was just the man, however, to accept an anti-climax genially, and to dismiss his disappointed auditory with something more tangible than an address.

The poet-precursor of scientific knowledge is again and again manifest : as, for example, in

> " Hints and previsions of which faculties
> Are strewn confusedly everywhere about
> The inferior natures, and all lead up higher,
> All shape out dimly the superior race,
> The heir of hopes too fair to turn out false,
> And man appears at last." [1]

There are lines, again, which have a magic that cannot be defined. If it be not felt, no sense of it can be conveyed through another's words.

> " Whose memories were a solace to me oft,
> As mountain-baths to wild fowls in their flight."

---

[1] Readers interested in Browning's inspiration from, and treatment of, Science, should consult the excellent essay on him as "A Scientific Poet" by Mr. Edward Berdoe, F.R.C.S., and, in particular, compare with the originals the references given by Mr. Berdoe to the numerous passages bearing upon Evolution and the several sciences, from Astronomy to Physiology.

> " Ask the gier-eagle why she stoops at once
> Into the vast and unexplored abyss,
> What full-grown power informs her from the first,
> Why she not marvels, strenuously beating
> The silent boundless regions of the sky."

There is one passage, beautiful in itself, which has a pathetic significance henceforth. Gordon, our most revered hero, was wont to declare that nothing in all nonscriptural literature was so dear to him, nothing had so often inspired him in moments of gloom :—

> " I go to prove my soul !
> I see my way as birds their trackless way.
> I shall arrive ! What time, what circuit first,
> I ask not : but unless God send His hail
> Or blinding fireballs, sleet or stifling snow,
> In some time, His good time, I shall arrive :
> He guides me and the bird. In his good time."

As for the much misused 'Shaksperian' comparison, so often mistakenly applied to Browning, there is nothing in "Paracelsus" in the least way derivative. Because Shakspere is the greatest genius evolved from our race, it does not follow that every lofty intellect, every great objective poet, should be labelled "Shaksperian." But there is a certain quality in poetic expression which we so specify, because the intense humanity throbbing in it finds highest utterance in the greatest of our poets : and there is at least one instance of such poignant speech in "Paracelsus," worthy almost to be ranked with the last despairing cry of Guido calling upon murdered Pompilia :—

> " Festus, strange secrets are let out by death
> Who blabs so oft the follies of this world :

And 1 am death's familiar, as you know.
I helped a man to die, some few weeks since,
Warped even from his go-cart to one end—
The living on princes' smiles, reflected from
A mighty herd of favourites. No mean trick
He left untried, and truly well-nigh wormed
All traces of God's finger out of him :
Then died, grown old. And just an hour before,
Having lain long with blank and soulless eyes,
He sat up suddenly, and with natural voice
Said that in spite of thick air and closed doors
God told him it was June ; and he knew well
Without such telling, harebells grew in June;
And all that kings could ever give or take
Would not be precious as those blooms to him."

Technically, I doubt if Browning ever produced any finer long poem, except " Pippa Passes," which is a lyrical drama, and neither exactly a 'play' nor exactly a 'poem' in the conventional usage of the terms. Artistically, "Paracelsus" is disproportionate, and has faults, obtrusive enough to any sensitive ear : but in the main it has a beauty without harshness, a swiftness of thought and speech without tumultuous pressure of ideas or stammering. It has not, in like degree, the intense human insight of, say, "'The Inn Album," but it has that charm of sequent excellence too rarely to be found in many of Browning's later writings. It glides onward like a steadfast stream, the thought moving with the current it animates and controls, and throbbing eagerly beneath. When we read certain portions of " Paracelsus," and the lovely lyrics interspersed in it, it is difficult not to think of the poet as sometimes, in later life, stooping like the mariner in Roscoe's beautiful sonnet, striving to reclaim "some loved lost echo from the fleeting strand." But it is the fleeting shore of exquisite art, not of the far-reaching shadowy capes and promontories of "the poetic land."

Of the four interlusive lyrics the freer music is in the unique chant, "Over the sea our galleys went:" a song full of melody and blithe lilt. It is marvellously pictorial, and yet has a freedom that places it among the most delightful of spontaneous lyrics :—

> " We shouted, every man of us,
>   And steered right into the harbour thus,
>   With pomp and pæan glorious."

It is, however, too long for present quotation, and as an example of Browning's early lyrics I select rather the rich and delicate second of these "Paracelsus" songs, one wherein the influence of Keats is so marked, and yet where all is the poet's own :—

> " Heap cassia, sandal-buds and stripes
>   Of labdanum, and aloe-balls,
>   Smeared with dull nard an Indian wipes
>   From out her hair: such balsam falls
>   Down sea-side mountain pedestals,
>   From tree-tops where tired winds are fain,
>   Spent with the vast and howling main,
>   To treasure half their island-gain.

> " And strew faint sweetness from some old
>   Egyptian's fine worm-eaten shroud
>   Which breaks to dust when once unrolled;
>   Or shredded perfume, like a cloud
>   From closet long to quiet vowed,
>   With mothed and dropping arras hung,
>   Mouldering her lute and books among,
>   As when a queen, long dead, was young."

With this music in our ears we can well forgive some
of the prosaic commonplaces which deface " Paracelsus "
—some of those lapses from rhythmic energy to which
the poet became less and less sensitive, till he could be
so deaf to the vanishing "echo of the fleeting strand "
as to sink to the level of doggerel such as that which
closes the poem called " Popularity."

" Paracelsus " is not a great, but it is a memorable
poem : a notable achievement, indeed, for an author of
Browning's years. Well may we exclaim with Festus,
when we regard the poet in all the greatness of his
maturity—

> " The sunrise
> Well warranted our faith in this full noon ! "

CHAPTER IV.

THE *Athenæum* dismissed "Paracelsus" with a half contemptuous line or two. On the other hand, the *Examiner* acknowledged it to be a work of unequivocal power, and predicted for its author a brilliant career. The same critic who wrote this review contributed an article of about twenty pages upon "Paracelsus" to the *New Monthly Magazine*, under the heading, "Evidences of a New Dramatic Poetry." This article is ably written, and remarkable for its sympathetic insight. "Mr. Browning," the critic writes, "is a man of genius, he has in himself all the elements of a great poet, philosophical as well as dramatic."

The author of this enthusiastic and important critique was John Forster. When the *Examiner* review appeared the two young men had not met: but the encounter, which was to be the seed of so fine a flower of friendship, occurred before the publication of the *New Monthly* article. Before this, however, Browning had already made one of the most momentous acquaintanceships of his life.

His good friend and early critic, Mr. Fox, asked him to his house one evening in November, a few months after the publication of "Paracelsus." The chief guest of the occasion was Macready, then at the height of his great reputation. Mr. Fox had paved the way for the young poet, but the moment he entered he carried with him his best recommendation. Every one who met Browning in those early years of his buoyant manhood seems to have been struck by his comeliness and simple grace of manner. Macready stated that he looked more like a poet than any man he had ever met. As a young man he appears to have had a certain ivory delicacy of colouring, what an old friend perhaps somewhat exaggeratedly described to me as an almost flower-like beauty, which passed ere long into a less girlish and more robust complexion. He appeared taller than he was, for he was not above medium height, partly because of his rare grace of movement, and partly from a characteristic high poise of the head when listening intently to music or conversation. Even then he had that expressive wave o' the hand, which in later years was as full of various meanings as the *Ecco* of an Italian. A swift alertness pervaded him, noticeable as much in the rapid change of expression, in the deepening and illuming colours of his singularly expressive eyes, and in his sensitive mouth, with the upper lip ever so swift to curve or droop in response to the most fluctuant emotion, as in his greyhound-like apprehension, which so often grasped the subject in its entirety before its propounder himself realised its significance. A lady, who remembers Browning at that time, has told me that his hair—then of a brown so dark as to appear black—was so beautiful in its heavy sculpturesque waves as to attract frequent notice. Another, and more subtle, personal charm was his voice, then with a rare flute-like tone, clear, sweet, and resonant. Afterwards, though always with precise clarity, it became merely strong and hearty, a little too loud sometimes, and not infrequently as that of one simulating keen immediate interest while the attention was almost wholly detached.

Macready, in his Journal,[1] about a week later than the date of his first meeting with the poet, wrote—"Read 'Paracelsus,' a work of great daring, starred with poetry of thought, feeling, and diction, but occasionally obscure: the writer can scarcely fail to be a leading spirit of his time." The tragedian's house, whither he went at week-ends and on holidays, was at Elstree, a short distance to the northward of Hampstead: and there he invited Browning, among other friends, to come on the last day of December and spend New Year's Day (1836).[2] When alluding, in after years, to this visit, Browning always spoke of it as one of the red-letter days

[1] For many interesting particulars concerning Macready and Browning, and the production of "Strafford," etc., *vide* the *Reminiscences*, vol. i.

[2] It was for Macready's eldest boy, William Charles, that Browning wrote one of the most widely popular of his poems, "The Pied Piper of Hamelin." It is said to have been an impromptu performance, and to have been so little valued by the author that he hesitated about its inclusion in "Bells and Pomegranates." It was inserted at the last moment, in the third number, which was short of "copy." Some one (anonymous, but whom I take to be Mr. Nettleship) has publicly alluded to his possession of a rival poem (entitled, simply, "Hamelin") by Robert Browning the elder, and of a letter which he had sent to a friend along with the verses, in which he writes: "Before I knew that Robert had begun the story of the 'Rats' I had contemplated a tale on the same subject, and proceeded with it as far as you see, but, on hearing that Robert had a similar one on hand, I desisted." This

of his life. It was here he first met Forster, with whom he at once formed what proved to be an enduring friendship; and on this occasion, also, that he was urged by his host to write a poetic play.

Browning promised to consider the suggestion. Six weeks later, in company with Forster, with whom he had become intimate, he called upon Macready, to discuss the plot of a tragedy which he had pondered. He told the tragedian how deeply he had been impressed by his performance of "Othello," and how this had deflected his intention from a modern and European to an Oriental and ancient theme. "Browning said that I had *bit* him by my performance of 'Othello,' and I told him I hoped I should make the blood come." The "blood" had come in the guise of a drama-motive based on the crucial period in the career of Narses, the eunuch-general of Justinian. Macready liked the suggestion, though he demurred to one or two points in the outline: and before Browning left he eagerly pressed him to "go on with 'Narses.'" But whether Browning mistrusted his own interest in the theme, or was dubious as to the success with which Macready would realise his conception, or as to the reception a play of such a nature would win from an auditory no longer reverent of high dramatic ideals, he gave up the idea. Some three

must have been in 1842, for it was in that year that the third part of *Bells and Pomegranates* was published. In 1843, however, he finished it. Browning's "Pied Piper" has been translated into French, Russian, Italian, and German. The latter (or one German) version is in prose. It was made in 1880, for a special purpose, and occupied the whole of one number of the local paper of Hameln, which is a quaint townlet in Hanover.

months later (May 26th) he enjoyed another eventful evening. It was the night of the first performance of Talfourd's "Ion," and he was among the personal friends of Macready who were invited to the supper at Talfourd's rooms. After the fall of the curtain, Browning, Forster, and other friends sought the tragedian and congratulated him upon the success both of the play and of his impersonation of the chief character. They then adjourned to the house of the author of "Ion." To his surprise and gratification Browning found himself placed next but one to his host, and immediately opposite Macready, who sat between two gentlemen, one calm as a summer evening, and the other with a tempestuous youth dominating his sixty years, whom the young poet at once recognised as Wordsworth and Walter Savage Landor. Every one was in good spirits : the host perhaps most of all, who was celebrating his birthday as well as the success of "Ion." Possibly Macready was the only person who felt at all bored—unless it was Landor—for Wordsworth was not, at such a function, an entertaining conversationalist. There is much significance in the succinct entry in Macready's journal concerning the Lake-poet—"Wordsworth, who pinned me." . . . When Talfourd rose to propose the toast of "The Poets of England" every one probably expected that Wordsworth would be named to respond. But with a kindly grace the host, after flattering remarks upon the two great men then honouring him by sitting at his table, coupled his toast with the name of the youngest of the poets of England—"Mr. Robert Browning, the author of 'Paracelsus.'" It was a very proud moment for Browning, singled out among that brilliant

company : and it is pleasant to know, on the authority
of Miss Mitford, who was present, that "he performed
his task with grace and modesty," looking, the amiable
lady adds, even younger than he was. Perhaps, however, he was prouder still when Wordsworth leaned
across the table, and with stately affability said, "I am
proud to drink your health, Mr. Browning : " when
Landor, also, with a superbly indifferent and yet kindly
smile, also raised his glass to his lips in courteous
greeting.

Of Wordsworth Browning saw not a little in the
ensuing few years, for on the rare visits the elderly poet
paid to London, Talfourd never failed to ask the author
of "Paracelsus," for whom he had a sincere admiration,
to meet the great man. It was not in the nature of things
that the two poets could become friends, but though
the younger was sometimes annoyed by the elder's
pooh-poohing his republican sympathies, and contemptu-
ously waiving aside as a mere nobody no less an individual than Shelley, he never failed of respect and even
reverence. With what tenderness and dignity he has
commemorated the great poet's falling away from his
early ideals, may be seen in "The Lost Leader," one of
the most popular of Browning's short poems, and likely
to remain so. For several reasons, however, it is best
as well as right that Wordsworth should not be more
than merely nominally identified with the Lost Leader.
Browning was always imperative upon this point.

Towards Landor, on the other hand, he entertained a
sentiment of genuine affection, coupled with a profound
sympathy and admiration : a sentiment duly recipro-
cated. The care of the younger for the elder, in the old

age of the latter, is one of the most beautiful incidents in a beautiful life.

But the evening was not to pass without another memorable incident, one to which we owe "Strafford," and probably "A Blot on the 'Scutcheon." Just as the young poet, flushed with the triumphant pleasure of the evening, was about to leave, Macready arrested him by a friendly grip of the arm. In unmistakable earnestness he asked Browning to write him a play. With a simplicity equal to the occasion, the poet contented himself with replying, "Shall it be historical and English? What do you say to a drama on Strafford?"

Macready was pleased with the idea, and hopeful that his friend would be more successful with the English statesman than with the eunuch Narses.

A few months elapsed before the poet, who had set aside the long work upon which he was engaged ("Sordello"), called upon Macready with the manuscript of "Strafford." The latter hoped much from it. In March the MS. was ready. About the end of the month Macready took it to Covent Garden Theatre, and read it to Mr. Osbaldiston, "who caught at it with avidity, and agreed to produce it without delay."

It was an eventful first of May—an eventful twelvemonth, indeed, for it was the initial year of the Victorian era, notable, too, as that wherein the Electric Telegraph was established, and, in letters, wherein a new dramatic literature had its origin. For "Strafford," already significant of a novel movement, and destined, it seems to me, to be still more significant in that great dramatic period towards which we are fast converging, was not less important to the Drama in

England, as a new departure in method and radically
indicative of a fresh standpoint, than "Hernani" was
in France. But in literary history the day itself is
doubly memorable, for in the forenoon Carlyle gave the
first of his lectures in London. The play was a success,
despite the shamefully inadequate acting of some of
those entrusted with important parts. There was once,
perhaps there were more occasions than one, where
success poised like the soul of a Mohammedan on
the invisible thread leading to Paradise, but on either
side of which lies perdition. There was none to cry
Timbul save Macready, except Miss Helen Faucit,
who gained a brilliant triumph as Lady Carlisle.
The part of Charles I. was enacted so execrably that
damnation for all was again and again within measur-
able distance. "The Younger Vane" ranted so that a
hiss, like an embodied scorn, vibrated on vagrant wings
throughout the house. There was not even any extraneous aid to a fortunate impression. The house was in
ill repair: the seats dusty, the "scenery" commonplace
and sometimes noticeably inappropriate, the costumes
and accessories almost sordid. But in the face of
all this, a triumph was secured. For a brief while
Macready believed that the star of regeneration had
arisen. Unfortunately 'twas, in the words of a contemporary dramatic poet, "a rising sorrow splendidly
forlorn." The financial condition of Covent Garden
Theatre was so ruinous that not even the most successful
play could have restored its doomed fortunes.

After the fifth night one of the leading actors, having received a better offer elsewhere, suddenly with-
drew.

This was the last straw. A collapse forthwith occurred. In the scramble for shares in the few remaining funds every one gained something, except the author, who was to have received £12 for each performance for the first twenty-five nights, and £10 each for ten nights further. This disaster was a deep disappointment to Browning, and a by no means transitory one, for three or four years later he wrote (*Advt.* of "Bells and Pomegranates"): "Two or three years ago I wrote a play, about which the chief matter I much care to recollect at present is, that a pitful of good-natured people applauded it. Ever since, I have been desirous of doing something in the same way that should better reward their attention." But, except in so far as its abrupt declension from the stage hurt its author in the eyes of the critics, and possibly in those of theatrical managers, "Strafford" was certainly no failure. It has the elements of a great acting play. Everything, even the language (and here was a stumbling-block with most of the critics and criticasters), was subordinated to dramatic exigencies : though the subordination was in conformity with a novel shaping method. "Strafford" was not, however, allowed to remain unknown to those who had been unable to visit Covent Garden Theatre.[1] Browning's name had

---

[1] "It is time to deny a statement that has been repeated *ad nauseam* in every notice that professes to give an account of Mr. Browning's career. Whatever is said or not said, it is always that his plays have 'failed' on the stage. In point of fact, the three plays which he has brought out have all succeeded, and have owed it to fortuitous circumstances that their tenure on the boards has been comparatively short."—E. W. GOSSE, in article in *The Century Magazine.*

quite sufficient literary repute to justify a publisher in
risking the issue of a drama by him, one, at any rate, that
had the advantage of association with Macready's name.
The Longmans issued it, and the author had the pleasure
of knowing that his third poetic work was not produced
at the expense of a relative, but at that of the publishers.
It had but an indifferent reception, however.

Most people who saw the performance of "Strafford"
given in 1886, under the auspices of the Browning
Society, were surprised as well as impressed: for few,
apparently, had realised from perusal the power of the
play as made manifest when acted. The secret of this
is that the drama, when privily read, seems hard if not
heavy in its diction, and to be so inornate, though by no
means correspondingly simple, as to render any comparison between it and the dramatic work of Shakspere
out of the question. But when acted, the artistry of the
play is revealed. Its intense naturalness is due in great
part to the stern concision of the lines, where no word is
wasted, where every sentence is fraught with the utmost
it can convey. The outlines which disturbed us by
their vagueness become more clear: in a word, we all
see in enactment what only a few of us can discern in
perusal. The play has its faults, but scarcely those of
language, where the diction is noble and rhythmic,
because it is, so to speak, the genuine rind of the fruit
it envelops. But there are dramatic faults—primarily,
in the extreme economy of the author in the presentment of his *dramatis personæ*, who are embodied abstrac-
tions—monomaniacs of ideas, as some one has said
of Hugo's personages—rather than men as we are,
with manifold complexities in endless friction or fusion.

One cardinal fault is the lack of humour, which to
my mind is the paramount objection to its popular
acceptance. Another, is the misproportionate length
of some of the speeches. Once again, there is, as in
the greater portion of Browning's longer poems and
dramas, a baneful equality of emphasis. The conception of Charles I. is not only obviously weak, but
strangely prejudiced adversely for so keen an analyst of
the soul as Browning. For what a fellow-dramatist calls
this "Sunset Shadow of a King," no man or woman could
abase every hope and energy. Shakspere would never
have committed the crucial mistake of making Charles
the despicable deformity he is in Browning's drama.
Strafford himself disappears too soon : in the fourth act
there is the vacuum abhorred of dramatic propriety.

When he again comes on the scene, the charm is
partly broken. But withal the play is one of remarkable
vigour and beauty. It seems to me that too much has
been written against it on the score of its metrical rude-
ness. The lines are beat out by a hammer, but in the
process they are wrought clear of all needless alloy. To
urge, as has been lately urged, that it lacks all human
touch and is a mere intellectual fanfaronade, and that
there is not once a line of poignant insight, is altogether
uncritical. Readers of this mind must have forgotten or
be indifferent to those lines, for example, where the
wretched Charles stammeringly excuses himself to his
loyal minister for his death-warrant, crying out that it
was wrung from him, and begging Strafford not to curse
him : or, again, that wonderfully significant line, so full
of a too tardy knowledge and of concentrated scorn,
where Strafford first begs the king to "be good to his

children," and then, with a contempt that is almost
sublime, implores, "Stay, sir, do not promise, do not
swear!" The whole of the second scene in the fifth act
is pure genius. The reader, or spectator, knows by this
time that all hope is over: that Strafford, though all
unaware, is betrayed and undone. It is a subtle dramatic
ruse, that of Browning's representing him sitting in his
apartment in the Tower with his young children, William
and Anne, blithely singing.

Can one read and ever forget the lines giving the gay
Italian rhyme, with the boy's picturesquely childish
prose-accompaniment? Strafford is seated, weary and
distraught :—

> " *O bell' andare*
> *Per barca in mare,*
> *Verso la sera*
> *Di Primavera !*

William. The boat's in the broad moonlight all this while—
> *Verso la sera*
> *Di Primavera !*

And the boat shoots from underneath the moon
Into the shadowy distance ; only still
You hear the dipping oar—
> *Verso la sera,*

And faint, and fainter, and then all's quite gone,
Music and light and all, like a lost star.

Anne. But you should sleep, father : you were to sleep.

Strafford. I do sleep, Anne ; or if not—you must know
There's such a thing as . . .

William.   You're too tired to sleep.

Strafford. It will come by-and-by and all day long,
In that old quiet house I told you of :
We sleep safe there.

Anne.   Why not in Ireland ?

Strafford.   No !
Too many dreams !—"

To me this children's-song and the fleeting and now plaintive echo of it, as " Voices from Within "—" *Verso la sera, Di Primavera*"—in the terrible scene where Strafford learns his doom, is only to be paralleled by the song of Mariana in " Measure for Measure," wherein, likewise, is abduced in one thrilling poignant strain the quintessential part of the tense life of the whole play.

So much has been written concerning the dramas of Robert Browning—though indeed there is still room for a volume of careful criticism, dealing solely with this theme—that I have the less regret in having so in-adequately to pass in review works of such poetic magnitude as those enumerated above.

But it would be impossible, in so small a book as this, to examine them in detail without incurring a just charge of misproportion. The greatness and the shortcomings of the dramas and dramatic poems must be noted as succinctly as practicable ; and I have dwelt more liber-ally upon " Pauline," " Paracelsus," and " Strafford," partly because (certainly without more than one excep-tion, " Sordello ") these are the three least read of Browning's poems, partly because they indicate the sweep and reach of his first orient eagle-flight through new morning-skies, and mainly because in them we already find Browning at his best and at his weakest, because in them we hear not only the rush of his sunlit pinions, but also the low earthward surge of dullard wings.

Browning is foreshadowed in his earliest writings, as perhaps no other poet has been to like extent. In the "Venus and Adonis," and the "Rape of Lucrece," we have but the dimmest foreview of the author of " Hamlet," " Othello," and " Macbeth "; had Shakspere died prematurely none could have predicted, from the exquisite blossoms of his adolescence, the immortal fruit of his maturity. But, in Browning's three earliest works, we clearly discern him, as the sculptor of Melos previsioned his Venus in the rough-hewn block.

Thenceforth, to change the imagery, he developed rapidly upon the same lines, or doubled upon himself in intricate revolutions; but already his line of life, his poetic parallel, was definitely established.

In the consideration of Browning's dramas it is needful to be sure of one's vantage for judgment. The first step towards this assurance is the ablation of the chronic Shaksperian comparison. Primarily, the shaping spirit of the time wrought Shakspere and Browning to radically divergent methods of expression, but each to a method in profound harmony with the dominant sentiment of the age in which he lived. Above all others, the Elizabethan era was rich in romantic adventure, of the mind as well as of the body, and above all others, save that of the Renaissance in Italy, animated by a passionate curiosity. So, too, supremely, the Victorian era has been prolific of novel and vast Titanic struggles of the human spirit to reach those Gates of Truth whose lowest steps are the scarce discernible stars and furthest suns we scan, by piling Ossas of searching speculation upon Pelions of hardly-won positive knowledge. The highest exemplar of the former is Shakspere, Browning the profoundest interpreter of the latter. To achieve supremacy the one had to create a throbbing actuality, a world of keenest living, of acts and intervolved situations and episodes: the other to fashion a mentality so passionately alive that

its manifold phases should have all the reality of concrete individualities. The one reveals individual life to
us by the play of circumstance, the interaction of
events, the correlative eduction of personal characteristics: the other by his apprehension of that quintessential movement or mood or phase wherein the soul
is transitorily visible on its lonely pinnacle of light. The
elder poet reveals life to us by the sheer vividness of his
own vision: the younger, by a newer, a less picturesque
but more scientific abduction, compels the complex
rayings of each soul-star to a singular simplicity, as
by the spectrum analysis. The one, again, fulfils his
aim by a broad synthesis based upon the vivid observ-
ance and selection of vital details: the other by an
extraordinary acute psychic analysis. In a word,
Shakspere works as with the clay of human action:
Browning as with the clay of human thought.

As for the difference in value of the two methods
it is useless to dogmatise. The psychic portraiture
produced by either is valuable only so far as it is
convincingly true.

The profoundest insight cannot reach deeper than its
own possibilities of depth. The physiognomy of the
soul is never visible in its entirety, barely ever even its
profile. The utmost we can expect to reproduce, perhaps even to perceive in the most quintessential moment,
is a partially faithful, partially deceptive silhouette. As
no human being has ever seen his or her own soul,
in all its rounded completeness of good and evil, of
strength and weakness, of what is temporal and perishable
and what is germinal and essential, how can we expect
even the subtlest analyst to adequately depict other souls

than his own. It is Browning's high distinction that he has this soul-depictive faculty—restricted as even in his instance it perforce is—to an extent unsurpassed by any other poet, ancient or modern. As a sympathetic critic has remarked, " His stage is not the visible phenomenal England (or elsewhere) of history; it is a point in the spiritual universe, where naked souls meet and wrestle, as they play the great game of life, for counters, the true value of which can only be realised in the bullion of a higher life than this." No doubt there is "a certain crudeness in the manner in which these naked souls are presented," not only in "Strafford" but elsewhere in the plays. Browning markedly has the defects of his qualities.

As part of his method, it should be noted that his real trust is upon monologue rather than upon dialogue. To one who works from within outward—in contradistinction to the Shaksperian method of striving to win from outward forms " the passion and the life whose fountains are within"—the propriety of this dramatic means can scarce be gainsaid. The swift complicated mental machinery can thus be exhibited infinitely more coherently and comprehensibly than by the most electric succinct dialogue. Again and again Browning has nigh foundered in the morass of monologue, but, broadly speaking, he transcends in this dramatic method.

At the same time, none must take it for granted that the author of the " Blot on the 'Scutcheon," " Luria," " In a Balcony," is not dramatic in even the most conventional sense. Above all, indeed—as Mr. Walter Pater has said—his is the poetry of situations. In each

of the *dramatis personæ*, one of the leading characteristics
is loyalty to a dominant ideal. In Strafford's case it is
that of unswerving devotion to the King: in Mildred's
and in Thorold's, in the "Blot on the 'Scutcheon," it is
that of subservience respectively to conventional morality
and family pride (Lord Tresham, it may be added, is the
most hopelessly monomaniacal of all Browning's "monomaniacs"): in Valence's, in "Colombe's Birthday," to
chivalric love: in Charles, in "King Victor and King
Charles," to kingly and filial duty: in Anael's and
Djabal's, in "The Return of the Druses," respectively
to religion and unscrupulous ambition modified by
patriotism: in Chiappino's, in "A Soul's Tragedy," to
purely sordid ambition: in Luria's, to noble steadfastness:
and in Constance's, in "In a Balcony," to self-denial. Of
these plays, "The Return of the Druses" seems to me
the most picturesque, "Luria" the most noble and
dignified, and "In a Balcony" the most potentially a
great dramatic success. The last is in a sense a
fragment, but, though the integer of a great un-
accomplished drama, is as complete in itself as the
Funeral March in Beethoven's *Eroica* Symphony. The
"Blot on the 'Scutcheon" has the radical fault characteristic of writers of sensational fiction, a too pro-
miscuous "clearing the ground" by syncope and suicide.
Another is the juvenility of Mildred: — a serious
infraction of dramatic law, where the mere tampering
with history, as in the circumstances of King Victor's
death in the earlier play, is at least excusable by high
precedent. More disastrous, poetically, is the ruinous
banality of Mildred's anticlimax when, after her brother
reveals himself as her lover's murderer, she, like the

typical young *Miss Anglaise* of certain French novelists,
betrays her incapacity for true passion by exclaiming,
in effect, "What, you've murdered my lover! Well, tell
me all. Pardon? Oh, well, I pardon you: at least
I *think* I do. Thorold, my dear brother, how very
wretched you must be!"

I am unaware if this anticlimax has been pointed out
by any one, but surely it is one of the most appalling
lapses of genius which could be indicated. Even the
beautiful song in the third scene of the first act, "There's
a woman like a dew-drop, she's so purer than the purest,"
is, in the circumstances, nearly over the verge which
divides the sublime from the ridiculous. No wonder
that, on the night the play was first acted, Mertoun's
song, as he clambered to his mistress's window, caused
a sceptical laugh to ripple lightly among the tolerant
auditory. It is with diffidence I take so radically
distinct a standpoint from that of Dickens, who declared
he knew no love like that of Mildred and Mertoun, no
passion like it, no moulding of a splendid thing after its
conception, like it; who, further, at a later date, affirmed
that he would rather have written this play than any
work of modern times: nor with less reluctance, that I
find myself at variance with Mr. Skelton, who speaks
of the drama as "one of the most perfectly conceived
and perfectly executed tragedies in the language." In
the instance of Luria, that second Othello, suicide has
all the impressiveness of a plenary act of absolution:
the death of Anael seems as inevitable as the flash of
lightning after the concussion of thunder-clouds. But
Thorold's suicide is mere weakness, scarce a perverted
courage; and Mildred's broken heart was an ill not

beyond the healing of a morally robust physician. "Colombe's Birthday" has a certain remoteness of interest, really due to the reader's more or less acute perception of the radical divergence, for all Valence's greatness of mind and spirit, between the fair young Duchess and her chosen lover : a circumstance which must surely stand in the way of its popularity. Though " A Soul's Tragedy " has the saving quality of humour, it is of too grim a kind to be provocative of laughter.

In each of these plays[1] the lover of Browning will recall passage after passage of superbly dramatic effect. But supreme in his remembrance will be the wonderful scene in " The Return of the Druses," where the Prefect, drawing a breath of relief, is almost simultaneously assassinated ; and that where Anael, with every nerve at tension in her fierce religious resolve, with a poignant, life-surrendering cry, hails Djabal as *Hakeem*—as Divine —and therewith falls dead at his feet. Nor will he forget that where, in the " Blot on the 'Scutcheon," Mildred, with a dry sob in her throat, stammeringly utters—

> " I—I—was so young !
> Besides I loved him, Thorold—and I had
> No mother ; God forgot me : so I fell——"

or that where, "at end of the disastrous day," Luria takes the phial of poison from his breast, muttering—

> "Strange ! This is all I brought from my own land
> To help me."

---

[1] " Strafford," 1837 ; " King Victor and King Charles," 1842 ; " The Return of the Druses," and " A Blot on the 'Scutcheon," 1843 ; " Colombe's Birthday," 1844 ; " Luria," and " A Soul's Tragedy," 1845.

Before passing on from these eight plays to Browning's most imperishable because most nearly immaculate dramatic poem, " Pippa Passes," and to "Sordello," that colossal derelict upon the ocean of poetry, I should like—out of an embarrassing quantity of alluring details —to remind the reader of two secondary matters of interest, pertinent to the present theme.   One is that the song in " A Blot on the 'Scutcheon," "'There's a woman like a dew-drop," written several years before the author's meeting with Elizabeth Barrett, is so closely in the style of " Lady Geraldine's Courtship," and other ballads by the sweet singer who afterwards became a partner in the loveliest marriage of which we have record in literary history, that, even were there nothing to substantiate the fact, it were fair to infer that Mertoun's song to Mildred was the electric touch which compelled to its metric shape one of Mrs. Browning's best-known poems.

The further interest lies in the lordly acknowledgment of the dedication to him of " Luria," which Landor sent to Browning—lines pregnant with the stateliest music of his old age :—

> " Shakespeare is not our poet but the world's,
> Therefore on him no speech ! and brief for thee,
> Browning ! Since Chaucer was alive and hale
> No man has walked along our roads with step
> So active, so enquiring eye, or tongue
> So varied in discourse.   But warmer climes
> Give brighter plumage, stronger wing : the breeze
> Of Alpine heights thou playest with, borne on
> Beyond Sorrento and Amalfi, where
> The Siren waits thee, singing song for song."

CHAPTER V

IN my allusion to " Pippa Passes," towards the close of the preceding chapter, as the most imperishable because the most nearly immaculate of Browning's dramatic poems, I would not have it understood that its pre-eminence is considered from the standpoint of technical achievement, of art, merely. It seems to me, like all simple and beautiful things, profound enough for the searching plummet of the most curious explorer of the depths of life. It can be read, re-read, learned by heart, and the more it is known the wider and more alluring are the avenues of imaginative thought which it discloses. It has, more than any other long composition by its author, that quality of symmetry, that *symmetria prisca* recorded of Leonardo da Vinci in the Latin epitaph of Platino Piatto; and, as might be expected, its mental basis, what Rossetti called fundamental brain-work, is as luminous, depth within depth, as the morning air. By its side, the more obviously " profound " poems, Bishop Blougram and the rest, are mere skilled dialectics.

The art that is most profound and most touching must ever be the simplest. Whenever Æschylus, Dante, Shakspere, Milton, are at white heat they require no exposition, but meditation only—the meditation akin to the sentiment of little children who listen, intent upon every syllable, and passionately eager of soul, to hearthside tragedies. The play of genius is like the movement of the sea. It has its solemn rhythm : its joy, irradiate of the sun ; its melancholy, in the patient moonlight: its surge and turbulence under passing tempests : below all, the deep oceanic music. There are, of course, many to whom the sea is but a waste of water, at best useful as a highway and as the nursery of the winds and rains. For them there is no hint " of the incommunicable dream " in the curve of the rising wave, no murmur of the oceanic undertone in the short leaping sounds, invisible things that laugh and clap their hands for joy and are no more. To them it is but a desert: obscure, imponderable, a weariness. The " profundity " of Browning, so dear a claim in the eyes of the poet's fanatical admirers, exists, in their sense, only in his inferior work. There is more profound insight in Blake's Song of Innocence, "Piping down the valleys wild," or in Wordsworth's line, "Thoughts that do often lie too deep for tears," or in Keats' single verse, "There is a budding morrow in midnight," or in this quatrain on Poetry, by a young living poet—

> " She comes like the husht beauty of the night,
>   But sees too deep for laughter;
>   Her touch is a vibration and a light
>   From worlds before and after——"

there is more " profundity " in any of these than in libraries of " Sludge the Medium " literature. Mere hard thinking does not involve profundity, any more than neurotic excitation involves spiritual ecstasy. *De profundis*, indeed, must the poet come: there must the deep rhythm of life have electrified his "volatile essence" to a living rhythmic joy. In this deep sense, and this only, the poet is born, not made. He may learn to fashion anew that which he hath seen: the depth of his insight depends upon the depth of his spiritual heritage. If wonder dwell not in his eyes and soul there can be no "far ken" for him. Here it seems apt to point out that Browning was the first writer of our day to indicate this transmutive, this inspired and inspiring wonder-spirit, which is the deepest motor in the evolution of our modern poetry. Characteristically, he puts his utterance into the mouth of a dreamy German student, the shadowy Schramm who is but metaphysics embodied, metaphysics finding apt expression in tobacco-smoke: "Keep but ever looking, whether with the body's eye or the mind's, and you will soon find something to look on! Has a man done wondering at women?—there follow men, dead and alive, to wonder at. Has he done wondering at men?—there's God to wonder at: and the faculty of wonder may be, at the same time, old and tired enough with respect to its first object, and yet young and fresh sufficiently, so far as concerns its novel one."

This wonder is akin to that 'insanity' of the poet which is but impassioned sanity. Plato sums the matter when he says, "He who, having no touch of the Muse's madness in his soul, comes to the door and thinks he will get into the temple by the help of Art—he, I say, and his poetry, are not admitted."

In that same wood beyond Dulwich to which allusion

has already been made, the germinal motive of "Pippa
Passes" flashed upon the poet.   No wonder this resort
was for long one of his sacred places, and that he
lamented its disappearance as fervently as Ruskin
bewailed the encroachment of the ocean of bricks
and mortar upon the wooded privacies of Denmark
Hill.

Save for a couple of brief visits abroad, Browning spent
the years, between his first appearance as a dramatic
writer and his marriage, in London and the neighbourhood.   Occasionally he took long walks into the country.
One particular pleasure was to lie beside a hedge,
or deep in meadow-grasses, or under a tree, as circumstances and the mood concurred, and there to give
himself up so absolutely to the life of the moment
that even the shy birds would alight close by, and
sometimes venturesomely poise themselves on suspicious
wings for a brief space upon his recumbent body.   I
have heard him say that his faculty of observation at that
time would not have appeared despicable to a Seminole
or an Iroquois : he saw and watched everything, the bird
on the wing, the snail dragging its shell up the pendulous
woodbine, the bee adding to his golden treasure as he
swung in the bells of the campanula, the green fly
darting hither and thither like an animated seedling, the
spider weaving her gossamer from twig to twig, the wood-
pecker heedfully scrutinising the lichen on the gnarled
oak-bole, the passage of the wind through leaves or
across grass, the motions and shadows of the clouds, and
so forth.   These were his golden holidays.   Much of
the rest of his time, when not passed in his room
in his father's house, where he wrote his dramas and

early poems, and studied for hours daily, was spent in the Library of the British Museum, in an endless curiosity into the more or less unbeaten tracks of literature. These London experiences were varied by whole days spent at the National Gallery, and in communion with kindred spirits. At one time he had rooms, or rather a room, in the immediate neighbourhood of the Strand, whither he could go when he wished to be in town continuously for a time, or when he had any social or theatrical engagement.

Browning's life at this period was distraught by more than one episode of the heart. It would be strange were it otherwise. He had in no ordinary degree a rich and sensuous nature, and his responsiveness was so quick that the barriers of prudence were apt to be as shadowy to him as to the author of " The Witch of Atlas." But he was the earnest student for the most part, and, above all, the poet. His other pleasure, in his happy vagrant days, was to join company with any tramps, gipsies, or other wayfarers, and in good fellowship gain much knowledge of life that was useful at a later time. Rustic entertainments, particularly peripatetic " Theatres Royal," had a singular fascination for him, as for that matter had rustic oratory, whether of the alehouse or the pulpit. At one period he took the keenest interest in sectaries of all kinds : and often he incurred a gentle reproof from his mother because of his nomad propensities in search of *"pastors* new." There was even a time when he seriously deliberated whether he should not combine literature and religious ministry, as Faraday combined evangelical fervour with scientific enthusiasm. "'Twas a girl with eyes like two dreams of night" that

7

saved him from himself, and defrauded the Church Independent of a stalwart orator.

It was, as already stated, while he strolled through
Dulwich Wood one day that the thought occurred to him
which was to find development and expression in "Pippa
Passes." "The image flashed upon him," writes his
intimate friend, Mrs. Sutherland Orr, "of some one
walking thus alone through life; one apparently too
obscure to leave a trace of his or her passage, yet exer-
cising a lasting though unconscious influence at every
step of it; and the image shaped itself into the little
silk-winder of Asolo, Felippa or Pippa."

It has always seemed to me a radical mistake to
include "Pippa Passes" among Browning's dramas.
Not only is it absolutely unactable, but essentially
undramatic in the conventional sense. True dramatic
writing concerns itself fundamentally with the apt
conjunction of events, and the more nearly it approxi-
mates to the verity of life the more likely is it
to be of immediate appeal. There is a *vraie vérité*
which only the poet, evolving from dramatic concepts
rather than attempting to concentrate these in a quick,
moving verisimilitude, can attempt. The passing hither
and thither of Pippa, like a beneficent Fate, a wandering
chorus from a higher amid the discordant medley of a
lower world, changing the circumstances and even the
natures of certain more or less heedless listeners by the
wild free lilt of her happy song of innocence, is of this
vraie vérité. It is so obviously true, spiritually, that it is
unreal in the commonplace of ordinary life. Its very
effectiveness is too apt for the dramatist, who can ill
afford to tamper further with the indifferent banalities

of actual existence. The poet, unhampered by the exigencies of dramatic realism, can safely, and artistically, achieve an equally exact, even a higher verisimilitude, by means which are, or should be, beyond adoption by the dramatist proper.

But over and above any ' nice discrimination,' " Pippa Passes " is simply a poem, a lyrical masque with interspersed dramatic episodes, and subsidiary interludes in prose. The suggestion recently made that it should be acted is a wholly errant one. The finest part of it is unrepresentable. The rest would consist merely of a series of tableaux, with conversational accompaniment.

The opening scene, "the large mean airy chamber," where Pippa, the little silk-winder from the mills at Asolo, springs from bed, on her New Year's Day *festa,* and soliloquises as she dresses, is as true as it is lovely when viewed through the rainbow glow of the poetic atmosphere: but how could it succeed on the stage ? It is not merely that the monologue is too long: it is too inapt, in its poetic richness, for its purpose. It is the poet, not Pippa, who evokes this sweet sunrise music, this strain of the "long blue solemn hours serenely flowing." The dramatic poet may occupy himself with that deeper insight, and the wider expression of it, which is properly altogether beyond the scope of the playwright. In a word, he may irradiate his theme with the light that never was on sea or land, nor will he thereby sacrifice aught of essential truth : but his comrade must see to it that he is content with the wide liberal air of the common day. The poetic alchemist may turn a sword into pure gold: the playwright will concern himself with the due usage of the weapon as we know it, and attribute to it no transcendent value, no miraculous properties. What is permissible to Blake, painting Adam and Eve among embowering roses and lilies, while the sun, moon, and stars simultaneously shine, is impermissible to the portrait-painter or the landscapist, who has to idealise actuality to the point only of artistic realism, and not to transmute it at the outset from happily-perceived concrete facts to a glorified abstract concept.

In this opening monologue the much-admired song, "All service ranks the same with God," is no song at all, properly, but simply a beautiful short poem. From the dramatist's point of view, could anything be more shaped for disaster than the second of the two stanzas?—

> " Say not 'a small event !' Why 'small'?
> Costs it more pain than this, ye call
> A 'great event,' should come to pass,
> Than that?   Untwine me from the mass
> Of deeds which make up life, one deed
> Power shall fall short in or exceed !"

The whole of this lovely prologue is the production of a dramatic poet, not of a poet writing a drama. On the other hand, I cannot agree with what I read somewhere recently—that Sebald's song, at the opening of the most superb dramatic writing in the whole range of Victorian literature, is, in the circumstances, wholly inappropriate. It seems to me entirely consistent with the character of Ottima's reckless lover. He is akin to the gallant in one of Dumas' romances, who lingered atop of the wall of the prison whence he was escaping in order to whistle the concluding bar of a blithe chanson of freedom. What is, dramatically, disastrous in the instance of Mertoun singing "There's a woman like a dewdrop," when he ought to be seeking Mildred's presence in profound stealth and silence, is, dramatically, electrically startling in the mouth of Sebald, among the geraniums of the shattered shrub-house, where he has passed the night with Ottima, while her murdered husband lies stark in the adjoining room.

It must, however, be borne in mind that this thrilling dramatic effect is fully experienced only in retrospection, or when there is knowledge of what is to follow.

A conclusive objection to the drama as an actable play is that three of the four main episodes are fragmentary. We know nothing of the fate of Luigi: we can but surmise the future of Jules and Phené : we know not how or when Monsignor will see Pippa righted. Ottima and Sebald reach a higher level in voluntary death than they ever could have done in life.

It is quite unnecessary, here, to dwell upon this exquisite flower of genius in detail. Every one who knows Browning at all knows "Pippa Passes." Its lyrics have been unsurpassed, for birdlike spontaneity and a rare high music, by no other Victorian poet: its poetic insight is such as no other poet than the author of "The Ring and the Book" and "The Inn Album" can equal. Its technique, moreover, is superb. From the outset of the tremendous episode of Ottima and Sebald, there is a note of tragic power which is almost overwhelming. Who has not known what Jakob Boehme calls "the shudder of a divine excitement" when Luca's murderer replies to his paramour,

> " morning ?
> It seems to me a night with a sun added."

How deep a note, again, is touched when Sebald
exclaims, in allusion to his murder of Luca, that he
was so " wrought upon," though here, it may be, there
is an unconscious reminiscence of the tenser and more
culminative cry of Othello, "but being wrought, perplext in the extreme." Still more profound a touch
is that where Ottima, daring her lover to the " one
thing that must be done ; you know what thing : Come
in and help to carry," says, with affected lightsomeness,
" This dusty pane might serve for looking-glass," and
simultaneously exclaims, as she throws them rejectingly
from her nervous fingers, " Three, four—four grey
hairs ! " then with an almost sublime coquetry of horror
turns abruptly to Sebald, saying with a voice striving
vainly to be blithe—

> " Is it so you said
> A plait of hair should wave across my neck ?
> No—this way."

Who has not been moved by the tragic grandeur of
the verse, as well as by the dramatic intensity of the
episode of the lovers' " crowning night " ?

> " *Ottima.*   The day of it too, Sebald !
> When heaven's pillars seemed o'erbowed with heat,
> Its black-blue canopy suffered descend
> Close on us both, to weigh down each to each,
> And smother up all life except our life.
> So lay we till the storm came.
>   *Sebald.*   How it came !
>   *Ottima.* Buried in woods we lay, you recollect ;
> Swift ran the searching tempest overhead ;

> And ever and anon some bright white shaft
> Burned thro' the pine-tree roof, here burned and there,
> As if God's messenger thro' the close wood screen
> Plunged and replunged his weapon at a venture,
> Feeling for guilty thee and me: then broke
> The thunder like a whole sea overhead——"

Surely there is nothing in all our literature more poignantly dramatic than this first part of " Pippa Passes." The strains which Pippa sings here and throughout are as pathetically fresh and free as a thrush's song in the heart of a beleaguered city, and as with the same unconsidered magic. There is something of the mavis-note, liquid falling tones, caught up in a moment in joyous caprice, in

> " *Give her but a least excuse to love me !*
> *When—where——*"

No one of these songs, all acutely apt to the time and the occasion, has a more overwhelming effect than that which interrupts Ottima and Sebald at the perilous summit of their sin, beyond which lies utter darkness, behind which is the narrow twilit backward way.

> "*Ottima.*   Bind it thrice about my brow;
>   Crown me your queen, your spirit's arbitress,
>   Magnificent in sin. Say that !
> *Sebald.*   I crown you
>   My great white queen, my spirit's arbitress,
>   Magnificent . . .
>
>   [*From without is heard the voice of* PIPPA *singing*—]
>   The year's at the spring,
>   And day's at the morn;
>   Morning's at seven;
>   The hill-side's dew-pearled;

> The lark's on the wing;
> The snail's on the thorn:
> God's in his heaven—
> All's right with the world!
>
> [PIPPA *passes.*
>
> *Sebald.* God's in his heaven! Do you hear that?
> Who spoke?"

This sweet voice of Pippa reaches the guilty lovers,
reaches Luigi in his tower, hesitating between love and
patriotic duty, reaches Jules and Phené when all the
happiness of their unborn years trembles in the balance,
reaches the Prince of the Church just when his conscience is sore beset by a seductive temptation, reaches
one and all at a crucial moment in the life of each.
The ethical lesson of the whole poem is summed up in

> " All service ranks the same with God—
> With God, whose puppets, best and worst,
> Are we: there is no last nor first,"

and in

> " God's in his heaven—
> All's right with the world!"

"With God there is no lust of Godhood," says Rossetti
in "Hand and Soul": *Und so ist der blaue Himmel
grosser als jedes Gewölk darin, und dauerhafter dazu,*
meditates Jean Paul: "There can be nothing good, as
we know it, nor anything evil, as we know it, in the eye
of the Omnipresent and the Omniscient," utters the
Oriental mystic.

It is interesting to know that many of the nature touches
were indirectly due to the poet's solitary rambles, by
dawn, sundown, and "dewy eve," in the wooded districts
south of Dulwich, at Hatcham, and upon Wimbledon
Common, whither he was often wont to wander and to

ramble for hours, and where he composed one day the well-known lines upon Shelley, with many another unrecorded impulse of song. Here, too, it was, that Carlyle, riding for exercise, was stopped by 'a beautiful youth,' who introduced himself as one of the philosopher's profoundest admirers.

' It was from the Dulwich wood that, one afternoon in March, he saw a storm glorified by a double rainbow of extraordinary beauty; a memorable vision, recorded in an utterance of Luigi to his mother: here too that, in autumnal dusks, he saw many a crescent moon with " notched and burning rim." He never forgot the bygone " sunsets and great stars " he saw in those days of his fervid youth. Browning remarked once that the romance of his life was in his own soul; and on another occasion I heard him smilingly add, to some one's vague assertion that in Italy only was there any romance left, " Ah, well, I should like to include poor old Camberwell!" Perhaps he was thinking of his lines in " Pippa Passes," of the days when that masterpiece came ebullient from the fount of his genius—

> " May's warm slow yellow moonlit summer nights—
> Gone are they, but I have them in my soul ! "

There is all the distinction between " Pippa Passes " and " Sordello" that there is between the Venus of Milos and a gigantic Theban Sphinx. The latter is, it is true, proportionate in its vastness ; but the symmetry of mere bulk is not the *symmetria prisca* of ideal sculpture. I have already alluded to it as a derelict upon the ocean of poetry. This, indeed, it still seems to me, notwithstanding the well-meaning suasion of certain admirers of the

poem who have hoped "I should do it justice," thereby
meaning that I should eulogise it as a masterpiece. It
is a gigantic effort, of a kind; so is the sustained throe
of a wrestling Titan. That the poem contains much
which is beautiful is undeniable, also that it is surcharged
with winsome and profound thoughts and a multitude of
will-o'-the-wisp-like fancies which all shape towards high
thinking.

But it is monotonous as one of the enormous
American inland seas to a lover of the ocean, to whom
the salt brine is as the breath of delight. The fatal
facility of the heroic couplet to lapse into diffuseness,
has, coupled with a warped anxiety for irreducible
concision, been Browning's ruin here.

There is one charge even yet too frequently made
against "Sordello," that of "obscurity." Its interest
may be found remote, its treatment verbose, its intricacies
puzzling to those unaccustomed to excursions from the
familiar highways of old usage, but its motive thought is
not obscure. It is a moonlit plain compared with the
" *silva oscura* " of the " Divina Commedia."

Surely this question of Browning's obscurity was
expelled to the Limbo of Dead Stupidities when Mr.
Swinburne, in periods as resplendent as the whirling
wheels of Phœbus Apollo's chariot, wrote his famous
incidental passage in his " Essay on Chapman."

Too probably, in the dim disintegrating future which
will reduce all our o'ertoppling extremes, "Sordello" will
be as little read as "The Faerie Queene," and, similarly,
only for the gleam of the quenchless lamps amid its long
deserted alleys and stately avenues. Sadly enough, for
to poets it will always be an unforgotten land—a continent

with amaranth-haunted Vales of Tempe, where, as Spenser says in one of the Aeclogues of "The Shepherd's Calendar," they will there oftentimes "sitten as drouned in dreme."

It has, for those who are not repelled, a charm all its own. I know of no other poem in the language which is at once so wearisome and so seductive. How can one explain paradoxes? There is a charm, or there is none : that is what it amounts to, for each individual. *Tutti ga i so gusti, e mi go i mii*—" everybody follows his taste, and I follow mine," as the Venetian saying, quoted by Browning at the head of his Rawdon Brown sonnet, has it.

All that need be known concerning the framework of "Sordello," and of the real Sordello himself, will be found in the various Browning hand-books, in Mr. Nettleship's and other dissertations, and, particularly, in Mrs. Dall's most circumspect and able historical essay. It is sufficient here to say that while the Sordello and Palma of the poet are traceable in the Cunizza and the strange comet-like Sordello of the Italian and Provençal Chronicles (who has his secure immortality, by Dante set forth in leonine guise—*a guisa di leon quando si posa*—in the "Purgatorio"), both these are the most shadowy of prototypes. The Sordello of Browning is a typical poetic soul: the narrative of the incidents in the development of this soul is adapted to the historical setting furnished by the aforesaid Chronicles. Sordello is a far more profound study than Aprile in "Paracelsus," in whom, however, he is obviously foreshadowed. The radical flaw in his nature is that indicated by Goethe of Heine, that "he had no heart." The poem is the narrative of his transcendent aspirations, and more or less futile accomplishment.

It would be vain to attempt here any adequate excerption of lines of singular beauty. Readers familiar with the poem will recall passage after passage—among which there is probably none more widely known than the grandiose sunset lines :—

> " That autumn eve was stilled:
> A last remains of sunset dimly burned
> O'er the far forests,—like a torch-flame turned
> By the wind back upon its bearer's hand
> In one long flare of crimson ; as a brand,
> The woods beneath lay black." . . .

What haunting lines there are, every here and there—such as those of Palma, with her golden hair like spilt sunbeams, or those on Elys, with her

> " Few fine locks
> Coloured like honey oozed from topmost rocks
> Sun-blanched the livelong summer," . . .

or these,
> " Day by day
> New pollen on the lily-petal grows,
> And still more labyrinthine buds the rose——"

or, once more,
> " A touch divine—
> And the sealed eyeball owns the mystic rod ;
> Visibly through his garden walketh God——"

But, though sorely tempted, I must not quote further, save only the concluding lines of the unparalleled and impassioned address to Dante :—

> " Dante, pacer of the shore
> Where glutted hell disgorgeth filthiest gloom,
> Unbitten by its whirring sulphur-spume,
> Or whence the grieved and obscure waters slope
> Into a darkness quieted by hope ;
> Plucker of amaranths grown beneath God's eye
> In gracious twilights where his chosen lie——"

. . . . . .

It is a fair land, for those who have lingered in its byways : but, alas, a troubled tide of strange metres, of desperate rhythms, of wild conjunctions, of panic-stricken collocations, oftentimes overwhelms it. "Sordello" grew under the poet's fashioning till, like the magic vapour of the Arabian wizard, it passed beyond his control, "voluminously vast."

It is not the truest admirers of what is good in it who will refuse to smile at the miseries of conscientious but baffled readers. Who can fail to sympathise with Douglas Jerrold when, slowly convalescent from a serious illness, he found among some new books sent him by a friend a copy of "Sordello." Thomas Powell, writing in 1849, has chronicled the episode. A few lines, he says, put Jerrold in a state of alarm. Sentence after sentence brought no consecutive thought to his brain. At last the idea occurred to him that in his illness his mental faculties had been wrecked. The perspiration rolled from his forehead, and smiting his head he sank back on the sofa, crying, "O God, I *am* an idiot!" A little later, adds Powell, when Jerrold's wife and sister entered, he thrust "Sordello" into their hands, demanding what they thought of it. He watched them intently while they read. When at last Mrs. Jerrold remarked, "I don't understand what this man means; it is gibberish," her delighted husband gave a sigh of relief and exclaimed, "Thank God, I am *not* an idiot!"

Many friends of Browning will remember his recounting this incident almost in these very words, and his enjoyment therein: though he would never admit justification for such puzzlement.

But more illustrious personages than Douglas Jerrold were puzzled by the poem. Lord Tennyson manfully tackled it, but he is reported to have admitted in bitterness of spirit: "There were only two lines in it that I understood, and they were both lies; they were the opening and closing lines, ' *Who will may hear Sordello's story told,*' and ' *Who would has heard Sordello's story told!*'" Carlyle was equally candid: "My wife," he writes, "has read through 'Sordello' without being able to make out whether 'Sordello' was a man, or a city, or a book."

In an article on this poem, in a French magazine, M. Odysse Barot quotes a passage where the poet says "God gave man two faculties"—and adds, "I wish while He was about it (*pendant qu'il était en train*) God had supplied another—viz., the power of understanding Mr. Browning."

And who does not remember the sad experience of generous and delightful Gilead P. Beck, in "The Golden Butterfly": how, after "Fifine at the Fair," frightful symptoms set in, till in despair he took up "Red Cotton Nightcap Country," and fell for hours into a dull comatose misery. "His eyes were bloodshot, his hair was pushed in disorder about his head, his cheeks were flushed, his hands were trembling, the nerves in his face were twitching. Then he arose, and solemnly cursed Robert Browning. And then he took all his volumes, and, disposing them carefully in the fireplace, set light to them. 'I wish,' he said, 'that I could put the poet there too.'" One other anecdote of the kind was often, with evident humorous appreciation, recounted by the poet. On his introduction to the Chinese Ambassador, as a "brother-poet," he asked that dignitary what kind of poetic expression he particularly affected. The great man deliberated, and then replied that his poetry might be defined as "enigmatic." Browning at once admitted his fraternal kinship.

That he was himself aware of the shortcomings of "Sordello" as a work of art is not disputable. In 1863, Mrs. Orr says, he considered the advisability of "rewriting it in a more transparent manner, but concluded that the labour would be disproportionate to the result, and contented himself with summarising the contents of each 'book' in a continuous heading, which represents the main thread of the story."

The essential manliness of Browning is evident in the famous dedication to the French critic Milsand, who was among his early admirers. "My own faults of expression were many; but with care for a man or book such would be surmounted, and without it what avails the faultlessness of either? I blame nobody, least of all myself, who did my best then and since."

Whatever be the fate of "Sordello," one thing pertinent to it shall survive: the memorable sentence in the dedicatory preface—"My stress lay on the incidents in the development of a soul: little else is worth study."

The poem has disastrous faults, but is a magnificent failure. "Vast as night," to borrow a simile from Victor Hugo, but, like night, innumerously starred.

CHAPTER VI.

"PIPPA PASSES," "The Ring and the Book," "The Inn Album," these are Browning's three great dramatic poems, as distinct from his poetic plays. All are dramas in the exact sense, though the three I have named are dramas for mental and not for positive presentation. Each reader must embody for himself the images projected on his brain by the electric quality of the poet's genius: within the ken of his imagination he may perceive scenes not less moving, incidents not less thrilling, complexities of motive and action not less intricately involved, than upon the conventional stage.

The first is a drama of an idea, the second of the immediate and remote consequences of a single act, the third of the tyranny of the passions.

I understand the general opinion among lovers and earnest students of Browning's poetry to be that the highest peaks of his genius tower from the vast tableland of "The Ring and the Book"; that thenceforth there was declension. But Browning is not to be measured by common estimates. It is easy to indicate, in the instances of many poets, just where the music reached its sweetest, its noblest, just where the extreme glow wanes, just where the first shadows come leaping

S

like greyhounds, or steal almost imperceptibly from slow-closing horizons.

But with Browning, as with Shakspere, as with Victor Hugo, it is difficult for our vision to penetrate the glow irradiating the supreme heights of accomplishment. Like Balzac, like Shakspere again, he has revealed to us a territory so vast, that while we bow down before the sun westering athwart distant Andes, the gold of sunrise is already flashing behind us, upon the shoulder of Atlas.

It is certain that "The Ring and the Book" is unique. Even Goethe's masterpiece had its forerunners, as in Marlowe's "Faustus," and its ambitious offspring, as in Bailey's "Festus." But is it a work of art? Here is the only vital question which at present concerns us.

It is altogether useless to urge, as so many admirers of Browning do, that "The Ring and the Book" is as full of beauties as the sea is of waves. Undeniably it is, having been written in the poet's maturity. But, to keep to the simile, has this epical poem the unity of ocean? Does it consist of separate seas, or is it really one, as the wastes which wash from Arctic to Antarctic, through zones temperate and equatorial, are yet one and indivisible? If it have not this unity it is still a stupendous accomplishment, but it is not a work of art. And though art is but the handmaiden of genius, what student of Comparative Literature will deny that nothing has survived the ruining breath of Time—not any intellectual greatness nor any spiritual beauty, that is not clad in perfection, be it absolute or relative— for relative perfection there is, despite the apparent paradox.

The mere bulk of "The Ring and the Book" is, in

point of art, nothing. One day, after the publication of this poem, Carlyle hailed the author with enthusiastic praise in which lurked damning irony: "What a wonderful fellow you are, Browning: you have written a whole series of 'books' about what could be summed up in a newspaper paragraph !" Here, Carlyle was at once right and wrong. The theme, looked at dispassionately, is unworthy of the monument in which it is entombed for eternity. But the poet looked upon the central incident as the inventive mechanician regards the tiny pivot remote amid the intricate maze of his machinery. Here, as elsewhere, Browning's real subject is too often confounded with the accidents of the subject. His triumph is not that he has created so huge a literary monument, but rather that, notwithstanding its bulk, he has made it shapely and impressive. Stress has frequently been laid on the greatness of the achievement in the writing of twelve long poems in the exposition of one theme. Again, in point of art, what significance has this? None. There is no reason why it should not have been in nine or eleven parts; no reason why, having been demonstrated in twelve, it should not have been expanded through fifteen or twenty. Poetry ever looks askance at that gipsy-cousin of hers, "Tour-de-force."

Of the twelve parts—occupying in all about twenty-one thousand lines—the most notable as poetry are those which deal with the plea of the implicated priest, Caponsacchi, with the meditation of the Pope, and with the pathetic utterance of Pompilia. It is not a dramatic poem in the sense that "Pippa Passes" is, for its ten Books (the first and twelfth are respectively introductory and appendical) are monologues. "The Ring and the

Book," in a word, consists, besides the two extraneous parts, of ten monodramas, which are as ten huge facets to a poetic Koh-i-Noor.

The square little Italian volume, in its yellow parchment and with its heavy type, which has now found a haven in Oxford, was picked up by Browning for a *lira* (about eightpence), on a second-hand bookstall in the Piazza San Lorenzo at Florence, one June day, 1865. Therein is set forth, in full detail, all the particulars of the murder of his wife Pompilia, for her supposed adultery, by a certain Count Guido Franceschini; and of that noble's trial, sentence, and doom. It is much the same subject matter as underlies the dramas of Webster, Ford, and other Elizabethan poets, but subtlety of insight rather than intensity of emotion and situation distinguishes the Victorian dramatist from his predecessors. The story fascinated Browning, who, having in this book and elsewhere mastered all the details, conceived the idea of writing the history of the crime in a series of monodramatic revelations on the part of the individuals more or less directly concerned. The more he considered the plan the more it shaped itself to a great accomplishment, and early in 1866 he began the most ambitious work of his life.

An enthusiastic admirer has spoken of the poem as "one of the most extraordinary feats of which we have any record in literature." But poetry is not mental gymnastics. All this insistence upon "extraordinary feats" is to be deprecated: it presents the poet as Hercules, not as Apollo: in a word, it is not criticism. The story is one of vulgar fraud and crime, romantic to us only because the incidents occurred in Italy, in the

picturesque Rome and Arezzo of two centuries ago. The
old bourgeois couple, Pietro and Violante Comparini,
manage to wed their thirteen-year-old putative daughter
to a middle-aged noble of Arezzo. They expect the
exquisite repute of an aristocratic connection, and other
tangible advantages. He, impoverished as he is, looks
for a splendid dowry. No one thinks of the child-wife,
Pompilia. She becomes the scapegoat, when the gross
selfishness of the contracting parties stands revealed.
Count Guido has a genius for domestic tyranny. Pompilia
suffers. When she is about to become a mother she
determines to leave her husband, whom she now dreads
as well as dislikes. Since the child is to be the inheritor
of her parents' wealth, she will not leave it to the tender
mercies of Count Guido. A young priest, a canon of
Arezzo, Giuseppe Caponsacchi, helps her to escape. In
due course she gives birth to a son. She has scarce time
to learn the full sweetness of her maternity ere she is
done to death like a trampled flower. Guido, who has
held himself thrall to an imperative patience, till his
hold upon the child's dowry should be secure, hires four
assassins, and in the darkness of night betakes himself to
Rome. He and his accomplices enter the house of Pietro
Comparini and his wife, and, not content with slaying
them, also murders Pompilia. But they are discovered,
and Guido is caught red-handed. Pompilia's evidence
alone is damnatory, for she was not slain outright, and
lingers long enough to tell her story. Franceschini is
not foiled yet, however. His plea is that he simply
avenged the wrong done to him by his wife's adulterous
connection with the priest Caponsacchi. But even in
the Rome of that evil day justice was not extinct.

Guido's motive is proved to be false; he himself is condemned to death.   An appeal to the Pope is futile. Finally, the wretched man pays the too merciful penalty of his villainy.

There is nothing grand, nothing noble here : at most only a tragic pathos in the fate of the innocent child-wife Pompilia.   It is clear, therefore, that the greatness of "The Ring and the Book" must depend even less upon its subject, its motive, than upon its being "an extraordinary feat" in the gymnastics of verse.

In a sense, Browning's longest work is akin to that of his wife.   Both "The Ring and the Book" and "Aurora Leigh" are metrical novels.   The one is discursive in episodes and spiritual experiences : the other in intricacies of evidence.   But there the parallel ends.   If "The Ring and the Book" were deflowered of its blooms of poetry and rendered into a prose narrative, it might interest a barrister "getting up" a criminal case, but it would be much inferior to, say, "The Moonstone"; its author would be insignificant beside the ingenious M. Gaboriau.   The extraordinariness of the feat would then be but indifferently commented upon.

As neither its subject, nor its extraordinariness as a feat, nor its method, will withstand a searching exami-nation, we must endeavour to discern if transcendent poetic merit be discoverable in the treatment.   To arrive at a just estimate it is needful to free the mind not merely from preconceptions, but from that niggard-liness of insight which can perceive only the minor flaws and shortcomings almost inevitable to any vast literary achievement, and be blind to the superb merits.   One must prepare oneself to listen to a new musician, with mind and body alert to the novel harmonies, and oblivious of what other musicians have done or refrained from doing.

"The Ring and the Book," as I have said, was not begun in the year of its imagining.[1] It is necessary to anticipate the biographical narrative, and state that the finding of the parchment-booklet happened in the fourth year of the poet's widowerhood, for his happy married period of less than fifteen years came to a close in 1861.

On the afternoon of the day on which he made his purchase he read the book from end to end. "A Spirit laughed and leapt through every limb." The midsummer heats had caused thunder-clouds to con-

[1] The title is explained as follows : — "The story of the Franceschini case, as Mr. Browning relates it, forms a circle of evidence to its one central truth ; and this circle was constructed in the manner in which the worker in Etruscan gold prepares the ornamental circlet which will be worn as a ring. The pure metal is too soft to bear hammer or file; it must be mixed with alloy to gain the necessary power of resistance. The ring once formed and embossed, the alloy is disengaged, and a pure gold ornament remains. Mr. Browning's material was also inadequate to his purpose, though from a different cause. It was too *hard*. It was 'pure crude fact,' secreted from the fluid being of the men and women whose experience it had formed. In its existing state it would have broken up under the artistic attempt to weld and round it. He supplied an alloy, the alloy of fancy, or—as he also calls it—of one fact more : this fact being the echo of those past existences awakened within his own. He breathed into the dead record the breath of his own life ; and when his ring of evidence had re-formed, first in elastic then in solid strength, here delicately incised, there broadly stamped with human thought and passion, he could cast fancy aside, and bid his readers recognise in what he set before them unadulterated human truth."—*Mrs. Orr.*

gregate above Vallombrosa and the whole valley of
Arno: and the air in Florence was painfully sultry.
The poet stood by himself on his terrace at Casa Guidi,
and as he watched the fireflies wandering from the
enclosed gardens, and the sheet-lightnings quivering
through the heated atmosphere, his mind was busy in
refashioning the old tale of loveless marriage and crime.

> " Beneath
> I' the street, quick shown by openings of the sky
> When flame fell silently from cloud to cloud,
> Richer than that gold snow Jove rained on Rhodes,
> The townsmen walked by twos and threes, and talked,
> Drinking the blackness in default of air—
> A busy human sense beneath my feet:
> While in and out the terrace-plants, and round
> One branch of tall datura, waxed and waned
> The lamp-fly lured there, wanting the white flower."

Scene by scene was re-enacted, though of course only
in certain essential details. The final food for the
imagination was found in a pamphlet of which he came
into possession of in London, where several important
matters were given which had no place in the volume
he had picked up in Florence.

Much, far the greater part, of the first "book" is
—interesting! It is mere verse. As verse, even, it is
often so involved, so musicless occasionally, so banal
now and again, so inartistic in colour as well as in form,
that one would, having apprehended its explanatory
interest, pass on without regret, were it not for the noble
close—the passionate, out-welling lines to "the truest
poet I have ever known," the beautiful soul who had
given her all to him, whom, but four years before he

wrote these words, he had laid to rest among the
cypresses and ilexes of the old Florentine garden of the
dead.

> "O lyric Love, half angel and half bird
> And all a wonder and a wild desire,—
> Boldest of hearts that ever braved the sun,
> Took sanctuary within the holier blue,
> And sang a kindred soul out to his face,—
> Yet human at the red-ripe of the heart—
> When the first summons from the darkling earth
> Reached thee amid thy chambers, blanched their blue,
> And bared them of the glory—to drop down,
> To toil for man, to suffer or to die,—
> This is the same voice: can thy soul know change?
> Hail then, and hearken from the realms of help!
> Never may I commence my song, my due
> To God who best taught song by gift of thee,
> Except with bent head and beseeching hand—
> That still, despite the distance and the dark,
> What was, again may be; some interchange
> Of grace, some splendour once thy very thought,
> Some benediction anciently thy smile:
> —Never conclude, but raising hand and head
> Thither where eyes, that cannot reach, yet yearn
> For all hope, all sustainment, all reward,
> Their utmost up and on,—so blessing back
> In those thy realms of help, that heaven thy home,
> Some whiteness which, I judge, thy face makes proud,
> Some wanness where, I think, thy foot may fall!"

Thereafter, for close upon five thousand words, the
poem descends again to the level of a versified tale. It
is saved from ruin by subtlety of intellect, striking dramatic verisimilitude, an extraordinary vigour, and occasional lines of real poetry. Retrospectively, apart from
the interest, often strained to the utmost, most readers,

I fancy, will recall with lingering pleasure only the opening of :" The Other Half Rome," the description of Pompilia, " with the patient brow and lamentable smile," with flower-like body, in white hospital array—a child with eyes of infinite pathos, "whether a flower or weed, ruined : who did it shall account to Christ."

In these three introductory books we have the view of the matter taken by those who side with Count Guido, of those who are all for Pompilia, and of the "superior person," impartial because superciliously indifferent, though sufficiently interested to " opine."

In the ensuing three books a much higher poetic level is reached. In the first, Guido speaks ; in the second, Caponsacchi ; the third, that lustrous opal set midway in the " Ring," is Pompilia's narrative. Here the three protagonists live and move before our eyes. The sixth book may be said to be the heart of the whole poem. The extreme intellectual subtlety of Guido's plea stands quite unrivalled in poetic literature. In comparing it, for its poetic beauty, with other sections, the reader must bear in mind that in a poem of a dramatic nature the dramatic proprieties must be dominant. It would be obviously inappropriate to make Count Guido Franceschini speak with the dignity of the Pope, with the exquisite pathos of Pompilia, with the ardour, like suppressed molten lava, of Caponsacchi. The self-defence of the latter is a superb piece of dramatic writing. Once or twice the flaming volcano of his heart bursts upward uncontrollably, as when he cries—

> " No, sirs, I cannot have the lady dead !
> That erect form, flashing brow, fulgurant eye,

> That voice immortal (oh, that voice of hers!) —
> That vision of the pale electric sword
> Angels go armed with—that was not the last
> O' the lady. Come, I see through it, you find,
> Know the manœuvre! Also herself said
> I had saved her: do you dare say she spoke false ?
> Let me see for myself if it be so ! "

Than the poignant pathos and beauty of " Pompilia," there is nothing more exquisite in our literature. It stands alone. Here at last we have the poet who is the Lancelot to Shakspere's Arthur. It takes a supreme effort of genius to be as simple as a child. How marvellously, after the almost sublime hypocrisy of the end of Guido's defence, after the beautiful dignity of Caponsacchi's closing words, culminating abruptly in the heart-wrung cry, "O great, just, good God! miserable me!"—how marvellously comes upon the reader the delicate, tearful tenderness of the innocent child-wife—

> " I am just seventeen years and five months old,
>   And, if I lived one day more, three full weeks ;
>   'Tis writ so in the church's register,
>   Lorenzo in Lucina, all my names
>   At length, so many names for one poor child,
>   —Francesca Camilla Vittoria Angela
>   Pompilia Comparini—laughable ! "

Only two writers of our age have depicted women with that imaginative insight which is at once more comprehensive and more illuminative than women's own invision of themselves—Robert Browning and George Meredith, but not even the latter, most subtle and delicate of all analysts of the tragi-comedy of human life, has surpassed " Pompilia." The meeting and the swift uprising of love between Lucy and Richard, in "The Ordeal of Richard Feveral," is, it is true, within the highest reach of prose romance : but between even the loftiest height of prose romance and the altitudes of poetry, there is an impassable gulf.

And as it is with simplicity so it is with tenderness. Only the sternly strong can be supremely tender. And infinitely tender is the poetry of " Pompilia "—

> " Oh, how good God is that my babe was born,
> —Better than born, baptised and hid away
> Before this happened, safe from being hurt !
> That had been sin God could not well forgive :
> *He was too young to smile and save himself*——"

or the lines which tell how as a little girl she gave her roses not to the spick and span Madonna of the Church, but to the poor, dilapidated Virgin, " at our street-corner in a lonely niche," with the babe that had sat upon her knees broken off : or that passage, with its exquisite naïveté, where Pompilia relates why she called her boy Gaetano, because she wished " no old name for sorrow's sake," so chose the latest addition to the saints, elected only twenty-five years before—

> " So, carefuller, perhaps,
> To guard a namesake than those old saints grow,
> Tired out by this time,—see my own five saints ! "

or these—

> " Thus, all my life,
> I touch a fairy thing that fades and fades.
> —Even to my babe ! I thought, when he was born,
> Something began for once that would not end,
> Nor change into a laugh at me, but stay
> For evermore, eternally quite mine——"

once more—

> " One cannot judge
> Of what has been the ill or well of life
> The day that one is dying. . . .
> Now it is over, and no danger more . . .
> To me at least was never evening yet
> But seemed far beautifuller than its day,
> For past is past——"

Lovely, again, are the lines in which she speaks of the first "thrill of dawn's suffusion through her dark," the "light of the unborn face sent long before : " or those unique lines of the starved soul's Spring (ll. 1512-27): or those, of the birth of her little one—

> " A whole long fortnight; in a life like mine
> A fortnight filled with bliss is long and much.
> All women are not mothers of a boy. . . .
> I never realised God's birth before—
> How he grew likest God in being born.
> This time I felt like Mary, had my babe
> Lying a little on my breast like hers."

When she has weariedly, yet with surpassing triumph, sighed out her last words—

> " God stooping shows sufficient of His light
> For us i' the dark to rise by. And I rise——

who does not realise that to life's end he shall not forget that plaintive voice, so poignantly sweet, that ineffable dying smile, those wistful eyes with so much less of earth than heaven ?

But the two succeeding " books " are more tiresome and more unnecessary than the most inferior of the

three opening sections—the first of the two, indeed, is
intolerably wearisome, a desolate boulder-strewn gorge
after the sweet air and sunlit summits of " Caponsacchi "
and "Pompilia." In the next "book" Innocent XII.
is revealed. All this section has a lofty serenity,
unsurpassed in its kind. It must be read from first to
last for its full effect, but I may excerpt one passage, the
high-water mark of modern blank-verse :—

> " For the main criminal I have no hope
> Except in such a suddenness of fate.
> I stood at Naples once, a night so dark
> I could have scarce conjectured there was earth
> Anywhere, sky or sea or world at all:
> But the night's black was burst through by a blaze——
> Thunder struck blow on blow, earth groaned and bore,
> Through her whole length of mountain visible:
> There lay the city thick and plain with spires,
> And, like a ghost disshrouded, white the sea.
> So may the truth be flashed out by one blow,
> And Guido see, one instant, and be saved."

Finally comes that throbbing, terrible last "book"
where the murderer finds himself brought to bay and
knows that all is lost. Who can forget its unparalleled
close, when the wolf-like Guido suddenly, in his supreme
agony, transcends his lost manhood in one despairing
cry—

> " Abate,—Cardinal,—Christ,—Maria,—God, . . .
> Pompilia, will you let them murder me ? "

Lastly, the Epilogue rounds off the tale. But is this
Epilogue necessary ? Surely the close should have come
with the words just quoted ?

It will not be after a first perusal that the reader will be able to arrive at a definite conviction. No individual or collective estimate of to-day can be accepted as final. Those who come after us, perhaps not the next generation, nor the next again, will see "The Ring and the Book" free of all the manifold and complex considerations which confuse our judgment. Meanwhile, each can only speak for himself. To me it seems that "The Ring and the Book" is, regarded as an artistic whole, the most magnificent failure in our literature. It enshrines poetry which no other than our greatest could have written; it has depths to which many of far inferior power have not descended. Surely the poem must be judged by the balance of its success and failure? It is in no presumptuous spirit, but out of my profound admiration of this long-loved and often-read, this superb poem, that I, for one, wish it comprised but the Prologue, the Plea of Guido, "Caponsacchi," "Pompilia," "The Pope," and Guido's last Defence. I cannot help thinking that this is the form in which it will be read in the years to come. Thus circumscribed, it seems to me to be rounded and complete, a great work of art void of the dross, the mere *débris* which the true artist discards. But as it is, in all its lordly poetic strength and flagging impulse, is it not, after all, the true climacteric of Browning's genius?

"The Inn Album," a dramatic poem of extraordinary power, has so much more markedly the defects of his qualities that I take it to be, at the utmost, the poise of the first gradual refluence. This analogy of the tidal ebb and flow may be observed with singular aptness in Browning's life-work—the tide that first moved shoreward in the loveliness of " Pauline," and, with " long withdrawing roar," ebbed in slow, just perceptible lapse to the poet's penultimate volume. As for " Asolando," I would rather regard it as the gathering of a new wave—nay, again rather, as the deep sound of ocean which the outward surge has reached.

But for myself I do not accept " The Inn Album " as the first hesitant swing of the tide. I seem to hear the resilient undertone all through the long slow poise of " The Ring and the Book." Where then is the full splendour and rush of the tide, where its culminating reach and power ?

I should say in " Men and Women " ; and by " Men and Women " I mean not merely the poems comprised in the collection so entitled, but all in the " Dramatic Romances," " Lyrics," and the " Dramatis Personæ," all the short pieces of a certain intensity of note and quality of power, to be found in the later volumes, from " Pacchiarotto " to " Asolando."

And this because, in the words of the poet himself when speaking of Shelley, I prefer to look for the highest attainment, not simply the high—and, seeing it, to hold by it. Yet I am not oblivious of the mass of Browning's lofty achievement, " to be known enduringly among men,"—an achievement, even on its secondary level, so high, that around its imperfect proportions, "the most elaborated productions of ordinary art must arrange themselves as inferior illustrations."

How am I to convey concisely that which it would take a volume to do adequately—an idea of the richest efflorescence of Browning's genius in these unfading blooms which we will agree to include in " Men and

Women"? How better—certainly it would be impossible to be more succinct—than by the enumeration of the contents of an imagined volume, to be called, say "Transcripts from Life"?

It would be to some extent, but not rigidly, arranged chronologically. It would begin with that masterpiece of poetic concision, where a whole tragedy is burned in upon the brain in fifty-six lines, "My Last Duchess." Then would follow "In a Gondola," that haunting lyrical drama *in petto*, where the lover is stabbed to death as his heart is beating against that of his mistress; "Cristina," with its keen introspection; those delightfully stirring pieces, the "Cavalier-Tunes," "Through the Metidja to Abd-el-Kadr," and "The Pied Piper of Hamelin"; "The Flower's Name"; "The Flight of the Duchess"; "The Tomb at St. Praxed's," the poem which educed Ruskin's enthusiastic praise for its marvellous apprehension of the spirit of the Middle Ages; "Pictor Ignotus," and "The Lost Leader." But as there is not space for individual detail, and as many of the more important are spoken of elsewhere in this volume, I must take the reader's acquaintance with the poems for granted. So, following those first mentioned, there would come "Home Thoughts from Abroad"; "Home Thoughts from the Sea"; "The Confessional"; "The Heretic's Tragedy"; "Earth's Immortalities"; "Meeting at Night: Parting at Morning"; "Saul"; "Karshish"; "A Death in the Desert"; "Rabbi Ben Ezra"; "A Grammarian's Funeral"; "Love Among the Ruins"; *Song*, "Nay but you"; "A Lover's Quarrel"; "Evelyn Hope"; "A Woman's Last Word"; "Fra Lippo

Lippi"; "By the Fireside"; "Any Wife to Any Husband"; "A Serenade at the Villa"; "My Star"; "A Pretty Woman"; "A Light Woman"; "Love in a Life"; "Life in a Love"; "The Last Ride Together"; "A Toccata of Galuppi's"; "Master Hugues of Saxe Gotha"; "Abt Vogler"; "Memorabilia"; "Andrea Del Sarto"; "Before"; "After"; "In Three Days"; "In a Year"; "Old Pictures in Florence"; "De Gustibus"; "Women and Roses"; "The Guardian Angel"; "Cleon"; "Two in the Campagna"; "One Way of Love"; "Another Way of Love"; "Misconceptions"; "May and Death"; "James Lee's Wife"; "Dîs Aliter Visum"; "Too Late"; "Confessions"; "Prospice"; "Youth and Art"; "A Face"; "A Likeness"; "Apparent Failure." Epilogue to Part I.—"O Lyric Voice," etc., from end of First Part of "The Ring and the Book." Part II.—"Hervé Riel"; "Amphibian"; "Epilogue to Fifine"; "Pisgah Sights"; "Natural Magic"; "Magical Nature"; "Bifurcation"; "Numpholeptos"; "Appearances"; "St. Martin's Summer"; "A Forgiveness"; Epilogue to Pacchiarotto volume; Prologue to "La Saisiaz"; Prologue to "Two Poets of Croisic"; "Epilogue"; "Pheidippides"; "Halbert and Hob"; "Iván Ivànovitch"; "Echetlos"; "Muléykeh"; "Pan and Luna"; "Touch him ne'er so lightly"; Prologue to "Jocoseria"; "Cristina and Monaldeschi"; "Mary Wollstonecraft and Fuseli"; "Ixion"; "Never the Time and the Place"; *Song*, "Round us the wild creatures"; *Song*, "Wish no word unspoken"; *Song*, "You groped your way"; *Song*, "Man I am"; *Song*, "Once I saw"; "Verse-making"; "Not with my Soul Love"; "Ask not one least word of praise"; "Why from the world"; "The Round of Day" (Pts. 9, 10, 11, 12 of Gérard de Lairesse); Prologue to "Asolando"; "Rosny"; "Now"; "Poetics"; "Summum Bonum"; "A Pearl"; "Speculative"; "Inapprehensiveness"; "The Lady and the Painter;" "Beatrice Signorini"; "Imperante Augusto"; "Rephan"; "Reverie"; Epilogue to "Asolando" (in all, 122).

But having drawn up this imaginary anthology, possibly with faults of commission and probably with worse errors of omission, I should like to take the reader into my confidence concerning a certain volume, originally compiled for my own pleasure, though not without thought of one or two dear kinsmen of a scattered Brotherhood—a volume half the size of the projected Transcripts, and rare as that star in the tip of the moon's horn of which Coleridge speaks.

Flower o' the Vine, so it is called, has for double-motto these two lines from the Epilogue to the Pacchi-arotto volume—

> " Man's thoughts and loves and hates !
> Earth is my vineyard, these grew there——"

and these words, already quoted, from the Shelley Essay, " I prefer to look for the highest attainment, not simply the high."

1. From "Pauline"[1]—1. "Sun-treader, life and light be thine for ever ! " 2. The Dawn of Beauty ; 3. Andromeda ; 4. Morning. 11. "Heap Cassia, Sandal-buds,"

---

[1] The first, from the line quoted, extends through 55 lines—" To see thee for a moment as thou art." No. 2 consists of the xviii ll. beginning, " They came to me in my first dawn of life." No. 3, the xi ll. of the Andromeda picture. No. 4, the lix ll. beginning, " Night, and one single ridge of narrow path " (to "delight").

etc. (song from " Paracelsus "). III. "Over the Sea our
Galleys went " (song from " Paracelsus "). IV. The Joy
of the World (" Paracelsus ").[1] V. From " Sordello "—
1. Sunset;[2] 2. The Fugitive Ethiop;[3] 3. Dante.[4] VI.
Ottima and Sebald (Pt. i., " Pippa Passes "). VII. Jules
and Phene (Pt. ii., " Pippa Passes "). VIII. My Last
Duchess. IX. In a Gondola. X. Home Thoughts from
Abroad (i. and ii.). XI. Meeting at Night : Parting at
Morning. XII. A Grammarian's Funeral. XIII. Saul.
XIV. Rabbi Ben Ezra. XV. Love among the Ruins.
XVI. Evelyn Hope. XVII. My Star. XVIII. A Toccata
of Galuppi's. XIX. Abt Vogler. XX. Memorabilia. XXI.
Andrea del Sarto. XXI. Two in the Campagna. XXII.
James Lee's Wife. XXIII. Prospice. XXIV. From "The
Ring and the Book"—1. O Lyric Love (The Invoca-
tion : 26 lines); 2. Caponsacchi (ll. 2069 to 2103); 3.
Pompilia (ll. 181 to 205); 4. Pompilia (ll. 1771 to
1845); 5. The Pope (ll. 2017 to 2228); 6. Count Guido
(Book XI., ll. 2407 to 2427). XXV. Prologue to "La
Saisiaz." XXVI. Prologue to "Two Poets of Croisic."
XXVII. Epilogue to "Two Poets of Croisic." XXVIII.
Never the Time and Place. XXIX. "Round us the
Wild Creatures," etc. (song from " Ferishtah's Fancies").
XXX. "The Walk" (Pts. ix., x., xi., xii., of "Gérard de
Lairesse." XXXI. "One word more" (To E. B. B.).[5]

[1] No. IV. comprises the xxix ll. beginning, "The centre fire
heaves underneath the earth," down to "ancient rapture."

[2] No. V. The vi. ll. beginning, "That autumn ere has stilled."

[3] The xxii ll. beginning, " As, shall I say, some Ethiop."

[4] The xxix ll. beginning, " For he,—for he."

[5] To these XXXI selections there must now be added "Now,"
"Summum Bonum," "Reverie," and the "Epilogue," from
"Asolando."

It is here—I will not say in *Flower o' the Vine*, nor even venture to restrictively affirm it of that larger and fuller compilation we have agreed, for the moment, to call "Transcripts from Life"—it is here, in the worthiest poems of Browning's most poetic period, that, it seems to me, his highest greatness is to be sought. In these "Men and Women" he is, in modern times, an unparalleled dramatic poet. The influence he exercises through these, and the incalculably cumulative influence which will leaven many generations to come, is not to be looked for in individuals only, but in the whole thought of the age, which he has moulded to new form, animated anew, and to which he has imparted a fresh stimulus. For this a deep debt is due to Robert Browning. But over and above this shaping force, this manipulative power upon character and thought, he has enriched our language, our literature, with a new wealth of poetic diction, has added to it new symbols, has enabled us to inhale a more liberal if an unfamiliar air, has, above all, raised us to a fresh standpoint, a standpoint involving our construction of a new definition.

Here, at least, we are on assured ground : here, at any rate, we realise the scope and quality of his genius. But, let me hasten to add, he, at his highest, not being of those who would make Imagination the handmaid of the Understanding, has given us also a Dorado of pure poetry, of priceless worth. Tried by the severest tests, not merely of substance, but of form, not merely of the melody of high thinking, but of rare and potent verbal music, the larger number of his "Men and Women" poems are as treasurable acquisitions, in kind, to our literature, as the shorter poems of Milton, of Shelley, of Keats, and of Tennyson.   But once again, and finally, let me repeat that his primary importance—not greatness, but importance—is in having forced us to take up a novel standpoint, involving our construction of a new definition.

The removal of the Barrett household to Gloucester Place, in Western London, was a great event. Here, invalid though she was, she could see friends occasionally and get new books constantly. Her name was well known and became widely familiar when her "Cry of the Children" rang like a clarion throughout the country. The poem was founded upon an official report by Richard Hengist Horne, the friend whom some years previously she had won in correspondence, and with whom she had become so intimate, though without personal acquaintance, that she had agreed to write a drama in collaboration with him, to be called "Psyche Apocalypté," and to be modelled on "Greek instead of modern tragedy."

Horne—a poet of genius, and a dramatist of remarkable power—was one of the truest friends she ever had, and, so far as her literary life is concerned, came next in influence only to her poet-husband. Among the friends she saw much of in the early forties was a distant "cousin," John Kenyon — a jovial, genial, gracious, and altogether delightful man, who acted the part of Providence to many troubled souls, and, in particular, was "a fairy godfather" to Elizabeth Barrett and to "the other poet," as he used to call Browning. It was to Mr. Kenyon—"Kenyon, with the face of a Bendectine monk, but the most jovial of good fellows," as a friend has recorded of him ; "Kenyon the Magnificent," as he was called by Browning—that Miss Barrett owed her first introduction to the poetry of her future husband.

Browning's poetry had for her an immediate appeal. With sure insight she discerned the special quality of the

poetic wealth of the "Bells and Pomegranates," among
which she then and always cared most for the penultimate volume, the "Dramatic Romances and Lyrics."
Two years before she met the author she had written,
in "Lady Geraldine's Courtship "—

" Or from Browning some ' Pomegranate' which, if cut deep down
   the middle,
   Shows a heart within blood-tinctured, of a veined humanity."

A little earlier she had even, unwittingly on either side,
been a collaborateur with "the author of ' Paracelsus.'"
She gave Horne much aid in the preparation of his
"New Spirit of the Age," and he has himself told us
"that the mottoes, which are singularly happy and
appropriate, were for the most part supplied by Miss
Barrett and Robert Browning, then unknown to each
other." One thing and another drew them nearer and
nearer. Now it was a poem, now a novel expression,
now a rare sympathy.

An intermittent correspondence ensued, and both
poets became anxious to know each other. "We artists
—how well praise agrees with us," as Balzac says.

A few months later, in 1846, they came to know one
another personally. The story of their first meeting,
which has received a wide acceptance, is apocryphal.
The meeting was brought about by Kenyon. This
common friend had been a schoolfellow of Browning's
father, and so it was natural that he took a more than
ordinary interest in the brilliant young poet, perhaps all
the more so that the reluctant tide of popularity which
had promised to set in with such unparalleled sweep and
weight had since experienced a steady ebb.

And so the fates brought these two together. The younger was already far the stronger, but he had an unbounded admiration for Miss Barrett. To her, he was even then the chief living poet. She perceived his ultimate greatness; as early as 1845 had "a full faith in him as poet and prophet."

As Browning admitted to a friend, the love between them was almost instantaneous, a thing of the eyes, mind, and heart—each striving for supremacy, till all were gratified equally in a common joy. They had one bond of sterling union : passion for the art to which both had devoted their lives.

To those who love love for love's sake, who *se passionnent pour la passion,* as Prosper Merimée says, there could scarce be a more sacred spot in London than that fiftieth house in unattractive Wimpole Street, where these two poets first met each other ; and where, in the darkened room, "Love quivered, an invisible flame." Elizabeth Barrett was indeed, in her own words, "as sweet as Spring, as Ocean deep." She, too, was always, as she wrote of Harriet Martineau, in a hopeless anguish of body and serene triumph of spirit. As George Sand says of one of her fictitious personages, she was an "artist to the backbone ; that is, one who feels life with frightful intensity." To this too keen intensity of feeling must be attributed something of that longing for repose, that deep craving for rest from what is too exciting from within, which made her affirm the exquisite appeal to her of such Biblical passages as "The Lord of peace Himself give you peace," and "He giveth His Beloved Sleep," which, as she says in one of her numerous letters to Miss Mitford, "strike upon the disquieted earth with such a *foreignness* of heavenly music."

Nor was he whom she loved as a man, as well as revered as a poet, unworthy of her. His was the robustest poetic intellect of the century; his the serenest outlook; his, almost the sole unfaltering footsteps along the perilous ways of speculative thought. A fair life, irradiate with fairer ideals, conserved his native integrity from that incongruity between practice and precept so commonly exemplified. Comely in all respects, with his black-brown wavy hair, finely-cut features, ready and winsome smile, alert luminous eyes, quick, spontaneous, expressive gestures—an inclination of the head, a lift of the eyebrows, a modulation of the lips, an assertive or deprecatory wave of the hand, conveying so much—and a voice at that time of a singular penetrating sweetness, he was, even without that light of the future upon his forehead which she was so swift to discern, a man to captivate any woman of kindred nature and sympathies. Over and above these advantages, he possessed a rare quality of physical magnetism. By virtue of this he could either attract irresistibly or strongly repel.

I have several times heard people state that a handshake from Browning was like an electric shock. Truly enough, it did seem as though his sterling nature rang in his genially dominant voice, and, again, as though his voice transmitted instantaneous waves of an electric current through every nerve of what, for want of a better phrase, I must perforce call his intensely alive hand. I remember once how a lady, afflicted with nerves, in the dubious enjoyment of her first experience of a "literary afternoon," rose hurriedly and, in reply to her hostess' inquiry as to her motive, explained that she could not sit any longer beside the elderly gentleman who was talking to Mrs. So-and-so, as his near presence made her quiver all over, "like a mild attack of pins-and-needles," as she phrased it. She was chagrined to learn that she had been discomposed not by 'a too exuberant financier,' as she had surmised, but by, as "Waring" called Browning, the "subtlest assertor of the Soul in song."

With the same quick insight as she had perceived Robert Browning's poetic greatness, Elizabeth Barrett discerned his personal worth. He was essentially manly in all respects : so manly, that many frail souls of either sex philandered about his over-robustness. From the twilight gloom of an æsthetic clique came a small voice belittling the great man as "quite too 'loud,' painfully excessive." Browning was manly enough to laugh at all ghoulish cries of any kind whatsoever. Once in a way the lion would look round and by a raised breath make the jackals wriggle ; as when the poet wrote to a correspondent, who had drawn his attention to certain abusive personalities in some review or newspaper : "Dear Sir—I am sure you mean very kindly, but I have had too long an experience of the inability of the human goose to do other than cackle when benevolent and hiss when malicious, and no amount of goose criticism shall make me lift a heel against what waddles behind it."

Herself one whose happiest experiences were in dreamland, Miss Barrett was keenly susceptible to the strong humanity of Browning's song, nor less keenly attracted by his strenuous and fearless outlook, his poetic practicality, and even by his bluntness of insight in certain matters. It was no slight thing to her that she could, in Mr. Lowell's words, say of herself and of him—

> " We, who believe life's bases rest
> Beyond the probe of chemic test."

She rejoiced, despite her own love for remote im-aginings, to know that he was of those who (to quote again from the same fine poet)

> " . . . wasted not their breath in schemes
> Of what man might be in some bubble-sphere,
> As if he must be other than he seems
> Because he was not what he should be here,
> Postponing Time's slow proof to petulant dreams ; "

that, in a word, while ' he could believe the promise of to-morrow,' he was at the same time supremely conscious of ' the wondrous meaning of to-day.'

Both, from their youth onward, had travelled ' on trails divine of unimagined laws.' It was sufficient for her that he kept his eyes fixed on the goal beyond the way he followed : it did not matter that he was blind to the dim adumbrations of novel byways, of strange Calvarys by the wayside, so often visible to her.

Their first meeting was speedily followed by a second —by a third—and then? When we know not, but ere long, each found that happiness was in the bestowal of the other.

The secret was for some time kept absolutely private. From the first Mr. Barrett had been jealous of his beloved daughter's new friend. He did not care much for the man, he with all the prejudices and baneful conservatism of the slave-owning planter, the other

with ardent democratic sentiments and a detestation
of all forms of iniquity. Nor did he understand the
poet. He could read his daughter's flowing verse with
pleasure, but there was to his ear a mere jumble of
sound and sense in much of the work of the author of
"The Tomb at St. Praxed's" and "Sibrandus Schafnaburgensis." Of a selfishly genial but also of a violent
and often sullen nature, he resented more and more
any friendship which threatened to loosen the chain
of affection and association binding his daughter to
himself.

Both the lovers believed that an immediate marriage
would, from every point of view, be best. It was not
advisable that it should be long delayed, if to happen
at all, for the health of Miss Barrett was so poor that
another winter in London might, probably would, mean
irretrievable harm.

Some time before this she had become acquainted
with Mrs. Jameson, the eminent art-writer. The regard,
which quickly developed to an affectionate esteem, was
mutual. One September morning Mrs. Jameson called,
and after having dwelt on the gloom and peril of another
winter in London, dwelt on the magic of Italy, and
concluded by inviting Miss Barrett to accompany her in
her own imminent departure for abroad. The poet was
touched and grateful, but, pointing to her invalid sofa,
and gently emphasising her enfeebled health and other
difficult circumstances, excused herself from acceptance
of Mrs. Jameson's generous offer.

In the "Memoirs of Mrs. Jameson" that lady's niece,
Mrs. Macpherson, relates how on the eve of her and her
aunt's departure, a little note of farewell arrived from

Miss Barrett, "deploring the writer's inability to come in person and bid her friend good-bye, as she was 'forced to be satisfied with the sofa and silence.'"

It is easy to understand, therefore, with what amazement Mrs. Jameson, shortly after her arrival in Paris, received a letter from Robert Browning to the effect that he *and his wife* had just come from London, on their way to Italy. "My aunt's surprise was something almost comical," writes Mrs. Macpherson, "so startling and entirely unexpected was the news." And duly married indeed the two poets had been!

From the moment the matter was mooted to Mr. Barrett, he evinced his repugnance to the idea. To him even the most foolish assertion of his own was a sacred pledge. He called it "pride in his word": others recognised it as the very arrogance of obstinacy. He refused to countenance the marriage in any way, refused to have Browning's name mentioned in his presence, and even when his daughter told him that she had definitely made up her mind, he flatly declined to acknowledge as even possible what was indeed very imminent.

Nor did he ever step down from his ridiculous pinnacle of wounded self-love. Favourite daughter though she had been, Mr. Barrett never forgave her, held no communication with her even when she became a mother, and did not mention her in his will. It is needless to say anything more upon this subject. What Mr. and Mrs. Browning were invariably reticent upon can well be passed over with mere mention of the facts.

At the last moment there had been great hurry and confusion. But nevertheless, on the forenoon of the

12th of September 1846, Robert Browning and Elizabeth Barrett had unceremoniously stepped into St. Mary-
le-bone Church and there been married. So secret had
the matter been kept that even such old friends as
Richard Hengist Horne and Mr. Kenyon were in
ignorance of the event for some time after it had actually
occurred.

Mrs. Jameson made all haste to the hotel where the
Brownings were, and ultimately persuaded them to leave
the hotel for the quieter *pension* in the Rue Ville
d'Evêque, where she and Mrs. Macpherson were staying. Thereafter it was agreed that, as soon as a fortnight
had gone by, they should journey to Italy together.

Truly enough, as Mrs. Macpherson says, the journey
must have been "enchanting, made in such companionship." Before departing from Paris, Mrs. Jameson, in
writing to a friend, alluded to her unexpected companions, and added, "Both excellent: but God help
them! for I know not how the two poet heads and
poet hearts will get on through this prosaic world."
This kindly friend was not the only person who experienced similar doubts. One acquaintance, no other than
the Poet-Laureate, Wordsworth, added: "So, Robert
Browning and Elizabeth Barrett have gone off together!
Well, I hope they may understand each other—nobody
else could!"

As a matter of fact they did, and to such good intent
that they seem never to have had one hour of dissatis-
faction, never one jar in the music of their lives.

What a happy wayfaring through France that must
have been! The travelling had to be slow, and with
frequent interruptions, on account of Mrs. Browning's

10

health : yet she steadily improved, and was almost from the start able to take more exercise, and to be longer in the open air than had for long been her wont. They passed southward, and after some novel experiences in *diligences*, reached Avignon, where they rested for a couple of days. Thence a little expedition, a poetical pilgrimage, was made to Vaucluse, sacred to the memory of Petrarch and Laura. There, as Mrs. Macpherson has told us, at the very source of the "chiare, fresche e dolce acque," Browning took his wife up in his arms, and, carrying her across through the shallow curling waters, seated her on a rock that rose throne-like in the middle of the stream. Thus, indeed, did love and poetry take a new possession of the spot immortalised by Petrarch's loving fancy.

Three weeks passed happily before Pisa, the Brownings' destination, was reached. But even then the friends were unwilling to part, and Mrs. Jameson and her niece remained in the deserted old city for a score of days longer. So wonderful was the change wrought in Mrs. Browning by happiness, and by all the enfranchisement her marriage meant for her, that, as her friend wrote to Miss Mitford, "she is not merely improved but transformed." In the new sunshine which had come into her life, she blossomed like a flower-bud long delayed by gloom and chill. Her heart, in truth, was like a lark when wafted skyward by the first spring-wind.

At last to her there had come something of that peace she had longed for, and though, in the joy of her new life, her genius "like an Arab bird slept floating in the wind," it was with that restful hush which precedes the creative storm. There is something deeply pathetic in her conscious joy. So little actual experience of life had been hers that in many respects she was as a child : and she had all the child's yearning for those unsullied hours that never come when once they are missed. But it was not till love unfastened the inner chambers of her heart and brain that she realised to the full, what she had often doubted, how supreme a thing mere life is. It was in some such mood that she wrote the lovely forty-second of the "Sonnets from the Portuguese," closing thus—

> " Let us stay
> Rather on earth, Belovèd,—where the unfit
> Contrarious moods of men recoil away
> And isolate pure spirits, and permit
> A place to stand and love in for a day,
> With darkness and the death-hour rounding it."

As for Browning's love towards his wife, nothing more tender and chivalrous has ever been told of ideal lovers in an ideal romance. It is so beautiful a story that one often prefers it to the sweetest or loftiest poem that came from the lips of either. That love knew no soilure in the passage of the years. Like the flame of oriental legend, it was perennially incandescent though fed not otherwise than by sunlight and moonshine. If it alone survive, it may resolve the poetic fame of either into one imperishable, luminous ray of white light : as the uttered song fused in the deathless passion of Sappho gleams star-like down the centuries from the high steep of Leucadoe.

It was here, in Pisa, I have been told on indubitable authority, that Browning first saw in manuscript those "Sonnets from the Portuguese" which no poet of

Portugal had ever written, which no man could have written, which no other woman than his wife could have composed. From the time when it had first dawned upon her that love was to be hers, and that the laurel of poetry was not to be her sole coronal, she had found expression for her exquisite trouble in these short poems, which she thinly disguised from 'inner publicity' when she issued them as "from the Portuguese."

It is pleasant to think of the shy delight with which the delicate, flower-like, almost ethereal poet-wife, in those memorable Pisan evenings—with the wind blowing soundingly from the hills of Carrara, or quiescent in a deep autumnal calm broken only by the slow wash of Arno along the sea-mossed long-deserted quays—showed her love-poems to her husband. With what love and pride he must have read those outpourings of the most sensitive and beautiful nature he had ever met, vials of lovely thought and lovelier emotion, all stored against the coming of a golden day.

> " How do I love thee?   Let me count the ways.
> I love thee to the depth and breadth and height
> My soul can reach, when feeling out of sight
> For the ends of Being and ideal Grace.
> I love thee to the level of every day's
> Most quiet need, by sun and candle light.
> I love thee freely, as men strive for Right ;
> I love thee purely, as they turn from Praise.
> I love thee with the passion put to use
> In my old griefs, and with my childhood's faith.
> I love thee with a love I seemed to lose
> With my lost saints,—I love thee with the breath,
> Smiles, tears, of all my life !—and, if God choose,
> I shall but love thee better after Death ! "

Even such heart-music as this cannot have thrilled him more than these two exquisite lines, with their truth almost too poignant to permit of serene joy—

" I yield the grave for thy sake, and exchange
My near sweet view of heaven for earth with thee ! "

Their Pisan home was amid sacred associations. It was situate in an old palazzo built by Vasari, within sight of the Leaning Tower and the Duomo. There, in absolute seclusion, they wrote and planned. Once and again they made a pilgrimage to the Lanfranchi Palace "to walk in the footsteps of Byron and Shelley": occasionally they went to Vespers in the Duomo, and listened, rapt, to the music wandering spirally through the vast solitary building: once they were fortunate in hearing the impressive musical mass for the dead, in the Campo Santo. They were even reminded often of their distant friend Horne, for every time they crossed one of the chief piazzas they saw the statue of Cosimo de Medici looking down upon them.

In this beautiful old city, so full of repose as it lies "asleep in the sun," Mrs. Browning's health almost leapt, so swift was her advance towards vigour. " She is getting better every day," wrote her husband, " stronger, better wonderfully, and beyond all our hopes."

That happy first winter they passed "in the most secluded manner, reading Vasari, and dreaming dreams of seeing Venice in the summer." But early in April, when the swallows had flown inland above the pines of Viareggio, and Shelley's favourite little Aziola was hooting silverly among the hollow vales of Carrara, the two poets prepared to leave what the frailer of them called "this perch of Pisa."

But with all its charm and happy associations, the little city was dull. "Even human faces divine are quite *rococo* with me," Mrs. Browning wrote to a friend. The change to Florence was a welcome one to both. Browning had already been there, but to his wife it was as the fulfilment of a dream. They did not at first go to that romantic old palace which will be for ever sociate with the author of "Casa Guidi Windows," but found accommodation in a more central locality.

When the June heats came, husband and wife both declared for Ancona, the picturesque little town which dreams out upon the Adriatic. But though so close to the sea, Ancona is in summer time almost insufferably hot. Instead of finding it cooler than Florence, it was as though they had leapt right into a cauldron. Alluding to it months later, Mrs. Browning wrote to Horne, "The heat was just the fiercest fire of your imagination, and I *seethe* to think of it at this distance.

It was a memorable journey all the same. They went to Ravenna, and at four o'clock one morning stood by Dante's tomb, moved deeply by the pathetic inscription and by all the associations it evoked. All along the coast from Ravenna to Loretto was new ground to both, and endlessly fascinating; in the passing and repassing of the Apennines they had 'wonderful visions of beauty and glory.' At Ancona itself, notwithstanding the heat, they spent a happy season. Here Browning wrote one of the loveliest of his short poems, "The Guardian Angel," which had its origin in Guercino's picture in the chapel at Fano. By the allusions in the sixth and

eighth stanzas it is clear that the poem was inscribed to
Alfred Domett, the poet's well-loved friend immortalised
as " Waring." Doubtless it was written for no other
reason than the urgency of song, for in it are the loving
allusions to his wife, " *my* angel with me too," and " my
love is here." Three times they went to the chapel, he
tells us in the seventh stanza, to drink in to their souls'
content the beauty of " dear Guercino's " picture.
Browning has rarely uttered the purely personal note
of his inner life. It is this that affords a peculiar value
to " The Guardian Angel," over and above its technical
beauty. In the concluding lines of the stanzas I am
about to quote he gives the supreme expression to what
was his deepest faith, his profoundest song-motive.

> " I would not look up thither past thy head
>   Because the door opes, like that child, I know,
> For I should have thy gracious face instead,
>   Thou bird of God! And wilt thou bend me low
> Like him, and lay, like his, my hands together,
> And lift them up to pray, and gently tether
>   Me, as thy lamb there, with thy garment's spread?
>
> .   .   .   .
>
> " How soon all worldly wrong would be repaired!
>   I think how I should view the earth and skies
> And sea, when once again my brow was bared
>   After thy healing, with such different eyes.
> O world, as God has made it! All is beauty:
> And knowing this, is love, and love is duty.
>   What further may be sought for or declared? "

After the Adriatic coast was left, they hesitated as to
returning to Florence, the doctors having laid such
stress on the climatic suitability of Pisa for Mrs.

Browning. But she felt so sure of herself in her new strength that it was decided to adventure upon at least one winter in the queen-city. They were fortunate in obtaining a residence in the old palace called Casa Guidi, in the Via Maggiore, over against the church of San Felice, and here, with a few brief intervals, they lived till death separated them.

On the little terrace outside there was more noble verse fashioned in the artist's creative silence than we can ever be aware of: but what a sacred place it must ever be for the lover of poetry! There, one ominous sultry eve, Browning, brooding over the story of a bygone Roman crime, foreshadowed "The Ring and the Book," and there, in the many years he dwelt in Casa Guidi, he wrote some of his finer shorter poems. There, also, "Aurora Leigh" was born, and many a lyric fresh with the dew of genius. Who has not looked at the old sunworn house and failed to think of that night when each square window of San Felice was aglow with festival lights, and when the summer lightnings fell silently in broad flame from cloud to cloud: or has failed to hear, down the narrow street, a little child go singing, 'neath Casa Guidi windows by the church, *O bella libertà, O bella !*

Better even than these, for happy dwelling upon, is the poem the two poets lived. Morning and day were full of work, study, or that pleasurable idleness which for the artist is so often his best inspiration. Here, on the little terrace, they used to sit together, or walk slowly to and fro, in conversation that was only less eloquent than silence. Here one day they received a letter from Horne. There is nothing of particular note in Mrs. Browning's

reply, and yet there are not a few of her poems we
would miss rather than these chance words—delicate
outlines left for the reader to fill in : "We were reading
your letter, together, on our little terrace—walking up and
down reading it—I mean the letter to Robert—and then,
at the end, suddenly turning, lo, just at the edge of the
stones, just between the balustrades, and already fluttering in a breath of wind and about to fly away over San
Felice's church, we caught a glimpse of the feather of a
note to E. B. B.   How near we were to the loss of it, to
be sure ! ".

Happier still must have been the quiet evenings in
late spring and summer, when, the one shrouded against
possible chills, the other bare-headed and with loosened
coat, walked slowly to and fro in the dark, conscious
of "a busy human sense" below, but solitary on their
balcony beyond the lamplit room.

> " While in and out the terrace-plants, and round
>   One branch of tall datura, waxed and waned
>   The lamp-fly lured there, wanting the white flower. "

An American friend has put on record his impressions
of the two poets, and their home at this time.   He had
been called upon by Browning, and by him invited to
take tea at Casa Guidi the same evening.   There the
visitor saw, "seated at the tea-table of the great room
of the palace in which they were living, a very small,
very slight woman, with very long curls drooping forward,
almost across the eyes, hanging to the bosom, and quite
concealing the pale, small face, from which the piercing
inquiring eyes looked out sensitively at the stranger.
Rising from her chair, she put out cordially the thin

white hand of an invalid, and in a few moments they were pleasantly chatting, while the husband strode up and down the room, joining in the conversation with a vigour, humour, eagerness, and affluence of curious lore which, with his trenchant thought and subtle sympathy, make him one of the most charming and inspiring of companions."

In the autumn the same friend, joined by one or two other acquaintances, went with the Brownings to Vallombrosa for a couple of days, greatly to Mrs. Browning's delight, for whom the name had had a peculiar fascination ever since she had first encountered it in Milton.

She was conveyed up the steep way towards the monastery in a great basket, without wheels, drawn by two oxen : though, as she tells Miss Mitford, she did not get into the monastery after all, she and her maid being turned away by the monks " for the sin of womanhood." She was too much of an invalid to climb the steeper heights, but loved to lie under the great chestnuts upon the hill-slopes near the convent. At twilight they went to the little convent-chapel, and there Browning sat down at the organ and played some of those older melodies he loved so well.

It is, strangely enough, from Americans that we have the best account of the Brownings in their life at Casa Guidi : from R. H. Stoddart, Bayard Taylor, Nathaniel Hawthorne, George Stillman Hillard, and W. W. Story. I can find room, however, for but one excerpt :—

"Those who have known Casa Guidi as it was, could hardly enter the loved rooms now, and speak above a whisper. They who have been so favoured, can never forget the square anteroom, with

its great picture and pianoforte, at which the boy Browning passed
many an hour—the little dining-room covered with tapestry, and
where hung medallions of Tennyson, Carlyle, and Robert Browning
—the long room filled with plaster-casts and studies, which was
Mrs. Browning's retreat—and, dearest of all, the large drawing-
room where *she* always sat. It opens upon a balcony filled with
plants, and looks out upon the iron-grey church of Santa Felice.
There was something about this room that seemed to make it a
proper and especial haunt for poets. The dark shadows and sub-
dued light gave it a dreary look, which was enhanced by the
tapestry-covered walls, and the old pictures of saints that looked
out sadly from their carved frames of black wood. Large bookcases constructed of specimens of Florentine carving selected by
Mr. Browning were brimming over with wise-looking books.
Tables were covered with more gaily-bound volumes, the gifts of
brother authors. Dante's grave profile, a cast of Keats's face and
brow taken after death, a pen-and-ink sketch of Tennyson, the
genial face of John Kenyon, Mrs. Browning's good friend and
relative, little paintings of the boy Browning, all attracted the eye
in turn, and gave rise to a thousand musings. A quaint mirror,
easy-chairs and sofas, and a hundred nothings that always add an
indescribable charm, were all massed in this room. But the glory of
all, and that which sanctified all, was seated in a low arm-chair near
the door. A small table, strewn with writing-materials, books, and
newspapers, was always by her side. . . . After her death, her
husband had a careful water-colour drawing made of this room,
which has been engraved more than once. It still hangs in his
drawing-room, where the mirror and one of the quaint chairs
above named still are. The low arm-chair and small table are in
Browning's study—with his father's desk, on which he has written
all his poems."—(*W. W. Story.*)

To Mr. and Mrs. Hawthorne, Mr. Hillard, and Mr.
Story, in particular, we are indebted for several delightful glimpses into the home-life of the two poets. We
can see Mrs. Browning in her "ideal chamber," neither
a library nor a sitting-room, but a happy blending of

both, with the numerous old paintings in antique Florentine frames, easy-chairs and lounges, carved bookcases
crammed with books in many languages, bric-a-brac in
any quantity, but always artistic, flowers everywhere, and
herself the frailest flower of all.

Mr. Hillard speaks of the happiness of the Brownings'
home and their union as perfect: he, full of manly power,
she, the type of the most sensitive and delicate womanhood.   This much-esteemed friend was fascinated by
Mrs. Browning.   Again and again he alludes to her
exceeding spirituality: "She is a soul of fire enclosed
in a shell of pearl:" her frame "the transparent veil
for a celestial and mortal spirit:" and those fine words
which prove that he too was of the brotherhood of the
poets, "Her tremulous voice often flutters over her
words like the flame of a dying candle over the wick."

CHAPTER VIII.

WITH the flower-tide of spring in 1849 came a new happiness to the two poets: the son who was born on the 9th of March. The boy was called Robert Wiedemann Barrett, the second name, in remembrance of Browning's much-loved mother, having been substituted for the "Sarianna" wherewith the child, if a girl, was to have been christened. Thereafter their "own young Florentine" was an endless joy and pride to both: and he was doubly loved by his father for his having brought a renewal of life to her who bore him.

That autumn they went to the country, to the neighbourhood of Vallombrosa, and then to the Bagni di Lucca. There they wandered content in chestnut-forests, and gathered grapes at the vintage.

Early in the year Browning's "Poetical Works" were published in two volumes. Some of the most beautiful of his shorter poems are to be found therein. What a new note is struck throughout, what range of subject there is! Among them all, are there any more treasurable than two of the simplest, "Home Thoughts from Abroad" and "Night and Morning"?

> " Oh, to be in England
> Now that April's there,
> And whoever wakes in England
> Sees, some morning, unaware,

That the lowest boughs and the brushwood sheaf
Round the elm-tree bole are in tiny leaf,
While the chaffinch sings on the orchard bough
In England—now !

And after April, when May follows,
And the whitethroat builds, and all the swallows !
Hark, where my blossomed pear-tree in the hedge
Leans to the field and scatters on the clover
Blossoms and dewdrops—at the bent spray's edge—
That's the wise thrush ; he sings each song twice over,
Lest you should think he never could recapture
The first fine careless rapture ! "

A more significant note is struck in " Meeting at
Night " and " Parting at Morning."

MEETING.

I.

The grey sea and the long black land ;
And the yellow half-moon large and low ;
And the startled little waves that leap
In fiery ringlets from their sleep,
As I gain the cove with pushing prow,
And quench its speed i' the slushy sand.

II.

Then a mile of warm sea-scented beach ;
Three fields to cross till a farm appears ;
A tap at the pane, the quick sharp scratch
And blue spurt of a lighted match,
And a voice less loud, through its joys and fears,
Than the two hearts beating each to each !

PARTING.

Round the cape of a sudden came the sea,
And the sun looked over the mountain's rim :
And straight was a path of gold for him,
And the need of a world of men for me.

The following winter, when they were again at their Florentine home, Browning wrote his "Christmas Eve and Easter Day," that remarkable *apologia* for Christianity, and close-reasoned presentation of the religious thought of the time. It is, however, for this reason that it is so widely known and admired: for it is ever easier to attract readers by dogma than by beauty, by intellectual argument than by the seduction of art. Coincidently, Mrs. Browning wrote the first portion of "Casa Guidi Windows."

In the spring of 1850 husband and wife spent a short stay in Rome. I have been told that the poem entitled 'Two in the Campagna' was as actually personal as the already quoted "Guardian Angel." But I do not think stress should be laid on this and kindred localisations. Exact or not, they have no literary value. To the poet, the dramatic poet above all, locality and actuality of experience are, so to say, merely fortunate coigns of outlook, for the winged genius to temporally inhabit. To the imaginative mind, truth is not simply actuality. As for 'Two in the Campagna': it is too universally true to be merely personal. There is a gulf which not the profoundest search can fathom, which not the strongest-winged love can overreach: the gulf of individuality. It is those who have loved most deeply who recognise most acutely this always pathetic and often terrifying isolation of the soul. None save the weak can believe in the absolute union of two spirits. If this were demonstrable, immortality would be a palpable fiction. The moment individuality can lapse to fusion, that moment the tide has ebbed, the wind has fallen, the dream has been dreamed. So

long as the soul remains inviolate amid all shock of
time and change, so long is it immortal. No man, no
poet assuredly, could love as Browning loved, and fail
to be aware, often with vague anger and bitterness, no
doubt, of this insuperable isolation even when spirit
seemed to leap to spirit, in the touch of a kiss, in the
evanishing sigh of some one or other exquisite moment.
The poem tells us how the lovers, straying hand in
hand one May day across the Campagna, sat down
among the seeding grasses, content at first in the idle
watching of a spider spinning her gossamer threads from
yellowing fennel to other vagrant weeds. All around
them

> " The champaign with its endless fleece
>   Of feathery grasses everywhere !
> Silence and passion, joy and peace,
>   An everlasting wash of air— . . .
>
> " Such life here, through such length of hours,
>   Such miracles performed in play,
> Such primal naked forms of flowers,
>   Such letting nature have her way." . . .

Let us too be unashamed of soul, the poet-lover says,
even as earth lies bare to heaven. Nothing is to be
overlooked. But all in vain : in vain " I drink my fill at
your soul's springs."

> " Just when I seemed about to learn !
>   Where is the thread now ? off again !
> The old trick ! Only I discern—
>   Infinite passion, and the pain
> Of finite hearts that yearn."

It was during this visit to Rome that both were

gratified by the proposal in the leading English literary weekly, that the Poet-Laureateship, vacant by the death of Wordsworth, should be conferred upon Mrs. Browning: though both rejoiced when they learned that the honour had devolved upon one whom each so ardently admired as Alfred Tennyson. In 1851 a visit was paid to England, not one very much looked forward to by Mrs. Browning, who had never had cause to yearn for her old home in Wimpole Street, and who could anticipate no reconciliation with her father, who had persistently refused even to open her letters to him, and had forbidden the mention of her name in his home circle.

Bayard Taylor, in his travel-sketches published under the title "At Home and Abroad," has put on record how he called upon the Brownings one afternoon in September, at their rooms in Devonshire Street, and found them on the eve of their return to Italy.

In his cheerful alertness, self-possession, and genial suavity Browning impressed him as an American rather than as an Englishman, though there can be no question but that no more thorough Englishman than the poet ever lived. It is a mistake, of course, to speak of him as a typical Englishman : for typical he was not, except in a very exclusive sense. Bayard Taylor describes him in reportorial fashion as being apparently about seven-and-thirty (a fairly close guess), with his dark hair already streaked with grey about the temples : with a fair complexion, just tinged with faintest olive : eyes large, clear, and grey, and nose strong and well-cut, mouth full and rather broad, and chin pointed, though not prominent : about the medium height, strong in the shoulders, but slender at the waist, with movements expressive of a combination of vigour and elasticity. With due allowance for the passage of five-and-thirty years, this description would not be inaccurate of Browning the septuagenarian.

They did not return direct to Italy after all, but wintered in Paris with Robert Browning the elder, who had retired to a small house in a street leading off the Champs Élysées. The pension he drew from the Bank of England was a small one, but, with what he otherwise had, was sufficient for him to live in comfort. The old gentleman's health was superb to the last, for he died in 1866 without ever having known a day's illness.

Spring came out and found them still in Paris, Mrs. Browning enthusiastic about Napoleon III. and interested in spiritualism : her husband serenely sceptical concerning both. In the summer they again went to London : but they appear to have seen more of Kenyon and other intimate friends than to have led a busy social life. Kenyon's friendship and good company never ceased to have a charm for both poets. Mrs. Browning loved him almost as a brother : her husband told Bayard Taylor, on the day when that good poet and charming man called upon them, and after another visitor had departed—a man with a large rosy face and rotund body, as Taylor describes him—" there goes one of the most splendid men living—a man so noble in his friendship, so lavish in his hospitality, so large-hearted and benevolent, that he deserves to be known all over the world as Kenyon the Magnificent."

In the early autumn a sudden move towards Italy was again made, and after a few weeks in Paris and on the way the Brownings found themselves at home once more in Casa Guidi.

But before this, probably indeed before they had left Paris for London, Mr. Moxon had published the now notorious Shelley forgeries. These were twenty-five spurious letters, but so cleverly manufactured that they at first deceived many people. In the preceding November Browning had been asked to write an introduction to them. This he had gladly agreed to do, eager as he was for a suitable opportunity of expressing his admiration for Shelley. When the letters reached him, he found that, genuine or not, though he never suspected they were forgeries, they contained nothing of particular import, nothing that afforded a just basis for what he had intended to say. Pledged as he was, however, to write something for Mr. Moxon's edition of the Letters, he set about the composition of an Essay, of a general as much as of an individual nature. This he wrote in Paris, and finished by the beginning of December. It dealt with the objective and subjective poet; on the relation of the latter's life to his work; and upon Shelley in the light of his nature, art, and character. Apart from the circumstance that it is the only independent prose writing of any length from Browning's pen, this is an exceptionally able and interesting production.

Dr. Furnivall deserves general gratitude for his obtaining the author's leave to re-issue it, and for having published it as one of the papers of the Browning Society. As that enthusiastic student and good friend of the poet says in his "foretalk" to the reprint, the essay is noteworthy, not merely as a signal service to Shelley's fame and memory, but for Browning's statement of his own aim in his own work, both as objective and subjective poet. The same clear-sightedness and impartial sympathy, which are such distinguishing characteristics of his dramatic studies of human thought and emotion, are obvious in Browning's Shelley essay. "It would be idle to enquire," he writes, "of these two kinds of poetic faculty in operation, which is the higher or even rarer endowment. If the subjective might seem to be the ultimate requirement of every age, the objective in the strictest state must still retain its original value. For it is with this world, as starting-point and basis alike, that we shall always have to concern ourselves; the world is not to be learned and thrown aside, but reverted to and reclaimed."

Of its critical subtlety—the more remarkable as by a poet-critic who revered Shelley the poet and loved and believed in Shelley the man—the best example, perhaps, is in those passages where he alludes to the charge against the poet's moral nature—"charges which, if substantiated to their wide breadth, would materially disturb, I do not deny, our reception and enjoyment of his works, however wonderful the artistic qualities of these. For we are not sufficiently supplied with instances of genius of his order to be able to pronounce certainly how many of its constituent parts have been tasked and strained to the production of a given lie, and how high and pure a mood of the creative mind may be dramatically simulated as the poet's habitual and exclusive one."

The large charity, the liberal human sympathy, the keen critical acumen of this essay, make one wish that

the author had spared us a "Sludge the Medium" or
a "Pacchiarotto," or even a "Prince Hohenstiel-
Schwangau," and given us more of such honourable
work in "the other harmony."

Glad as the Brownings were to be home again at
Casa Guidi, they could not enjoy the midsummer heats
of Florence, and so went to the Baths of Lucca. It
was a delight for them to ramble among the chestnut-
woods of the high Tuscan forests, and to go among
the grape-vines where the sunburnt vintagers were busy.
Once Browning paid a visit to that remote hill-stream
and waterfall, high up in a precipitous glen, where, more
than three-score years earlier, Shelley had been wont
to amuse himself by sitting naked on a rock in the
sunlight, reading *Herodotus* while he cooled, and
then plunging into the deep pool beneath him—
to emerge, further up stream, and then climb
through the spray of the waterfall till he was like
a glittering human wraith in the middle of a dissolving
rainbow.

Those Tuscan forests, that high crown of Lucca,
must always have special associations for lovers of
poetry. Here Shelley lived, rapt in his beautiful
dreams, and translated the *Symposium* so that his wife
might share something of his delight in Plato. Here,
ten years later, Heine sneered, and laughed and wept,
and sneered again—drank tea with "la belle Irlandaise,"
flirted with Francesca "la ballerina," and wrote alternately with a feathered quill from the breast of a
nightingale and with a lancet steeped in aquafortis:
and here, a quarter of a century afterward, Robert and
Elizabeth Browning also laughed and wept and "joyed

i' the sun," dreamed many dreams, and touched chords of beauty whose vibration has become incorporated with the larger rhythm of all that is high and enduring in our literature.

On returning to Florence (Browning with the MS. of the greater part of his splendid fragmentary tragedy, "In a Balcony," composed mainly while walking alone through the forest glades), Mrs. Browning found that the chill breath of the *tramontana* was affecting her lungs, so a move was made to Rome, for the passing of the winter (1853-4). In the spring their little boy, their beloved "Pen,"[1] became ill with malaria. This delayed their return to Florence till well on in the summer. During this stay in Rome Mrs. Browning rapidly proceeded with "Aurora Leigh," and Browning wrote several of his "Men and Women," including the exquisite 'Love among the Ruins,' with its novel metrical music; 'Fra Lippo Lippi,' where the painter, already immortalised by Landor, has his third warrant of perpetuity; the 'Epistle of Karshish' (in part); 'Memorabilia' (composed on the Campagna); 'Saul,' a portion of which had been written and published ten years previously, that noble and lofty utterance, with its trumpet-like note of the

---

[1] So-called, it is asserted, from his childish effort to pronounce a difficult name (Wiedemann). But despite the good authority for this statement, it is impossible not to credit rather the explanation given by Nathaniel Hawthorne, who, moreover, affords the practically definite proof that the boy was at first, as a term of endearment, called "Pennini," which was later abbreviated to "Pen." The cognomen, Hawthorne states, was a diminutive of "Apennino," which was bestowed upon the boy in babyhood because he was very small, there being a statue in Florence of colossal size called "Apennino."

regnant spirit; the concluding part of "In a Balcony;"
and 'Holy Cross Day'—besides, probably, one or two
others. In the late spring (April 27th) also, he wrote the
short dactylic lyric, 'Ben Karshook's Wisdom.' This
little poem was given to a friend for appearance in one of
the then popular *Keepsakes*—literally given, for Browning
never contributed to magazines. The very few exceptions to this rule were the result of a kindliness stronger
than scruple: as when (1844), at request of Lord
Houghton (then Mr. Monckton Milnes), he sent
'Tokay,' the 'Flower's Name,' and 'Sibrandus Schafnaburgensis,' to "help in making up some magazine
numbers for poor Hood, then at the point of death
from hemorrhage of the lungs, occasioned by the
enlargement of the heart, which had been brought
on by the wearing excitement of ceaseless and excessive
literary toil." As 'Ben Karshook's Wisdom,' though it
has been reprinted in several quarters, will not be found
in any volume of Browning's works, and was omitted
from "Men and Women" by accident, and from further
collections by forgetfulness, it may be fitly quoted here.
Karshook, it may be added, is the Hebraic word for
a thistle.

I.

" ' Would a man 'scape the rod ' ?—
Rabbi Ben Karshook saith,
' See that he turns to God
The day before his death.'

' Ay, could a man inquire
When it shall come !' I say.
The Rabbi's eye shoots fire—
' Then let him turn to-day!'

II.

Quoth a young Sadducee,—
  ' Reader of many rolls,
Is it so certain we
  Have, as they tell us, souls?'—

' Son, there is no reply!'
  The Rabbi bit his beard:
' Certain, a soul have *I*——
  We may have none,' he sneer'd.

Thus Karshook, the Hiram's-Hammer,
  The Right-Hand Temple column,
Taught babes their grace in grammar,
  And struck the simple, solemn."

It was in this year (1855) that "Men and Women" was published. It is difficult to understand how a collection comprising poems such as "Love among the Ruins," "Evelyn Hope," "Fra Lippo Lippi," "A Toccata of Galuppi's," "Any Wife to any Husband," "Master Hugues of Saxe-Gotha," "Andrea del Sarto," "In a Balcony," "Saul," "A Grammarian's Funeral," to mention only ten now almost universally known, did not at once obtain a national popularity for the author. But lovers of literature were simply enthralled: and the two volumes had a welcome from them which was perhaps all the more ardent because of their disproportionate numbers. Ears alert to novel poetic music must have thrilled to the new strain which sounded first—"Love among the Ruins," with its Millet-like opening—

  " Where the quiet-coloured end of evening smiles,
    Miles and miles
  On the solitary pastures where our sheep
    Half asleep

Tinkle homeward through the twilight, stray or stop
          As they crop—
    Was the site once of a city great and gay . . ."

Soon after the return to Florence, which, hot as it was, was preferable in July to Rome, Mrs. Browning wrote to her frequent correspondent Miss Mitford, and mentioned that about four thousand lines of " Aurora Leigh " had been written. She added a significant passage : that her husband had not seen a single line of it up to that time —significant, as one of the several indications that the union of Browning and his wife was indeed a marriage of true minds, wherein nothing of the common bane of matrimonial life found existence. Moreover, both were artists, and, therefore, too full of respect for themselves and their art to bring in any way the undue influence of each other into play.

By the spring of 1856, however, the first six " books " were concluded : and these, at once with humility and pride, Mrs. Browning placed in her husband's hands. The remaining three books were written, in the summer, in John Kenyon's London house.

It was her best, her fullest answer to the beautiful dedicatory poem, "One Word More," wherewith her husband, a few months earlier, sent forth his " Men and Women," to be for ever associated with " E. B. B."

I.

" There they are, my fifty men and women
    Naming me the fifty poems finished !
    Take them, Love, the book and me together :
    Where the heart lies, let the brain lie also.

  .   .   .   .   .   .

XVIII.

This I say of me, but think of you, Love!
This to you—yourself my moon of poets!
Ah, but that's the world's side, there's the wonder,
Thus they see you, praise you, think they know you!
There, in turn I stand with them and praise you—
Out of my own self, I dare to phrase it.
But the best is when I glide from out them,
Cross a step or two of dubious twilight,
Come out on the other side, the novel
Silent silver lights and darks undreamed of,
Where I hush and bless myself with silence."

The transference from Florence to London was made in May. In the summer " Aurora Leigh " was published, and met with an almost unparalleled success : even Landor, most exigent of critics, declared that he was "half drunk with it," that it had an imagination germane to that of Shakspere, and so forth.

The poem was dedicated to Kenyon, and on their homeward way the Brownings were startled and shocked to hear of his sudden death. By the time they had arrived at Casa Guidi again they learned that their good friend had not forgotten them in the disposition of his large fortune. To Browning he bequeathed six thousand, to Mrs. Browning four thousand guineas. This loss was followed early in the ensuing year (1857) by the death of Mr. Barrett, steadfast to the last in his refusal of reconciliation with his daughter.

Winters and summers passed happily in Italy—with one period of feverish anxiety, when the little boy lay for six weeks dangerously ill, nursed day and night by his father and mother alternately—with pleasant occasionings, as the companionship for a season of Nathaniel

Hawthorne and his family, or of weeks spent at Siena with valued and lifelong friends, W. W. Story, the poet-sculptor, and his wife.

So early as 1858 Mrs. Hawthorne believed she saw the heralds of death in Mrs. Browning's excessive pallor and the hectic flush upon the cheeks, in her extreme fragility and weakness, and in her catching, fluttering breath. Even the motion of a visitor's fan perturbed her. But "her soul was mighty, and a great love kept her on earth a season longer. She was a seraph in her flaming worship of heart." "She lives so ardently," adds Mrs. Hawthorne, "that her delicate earthly vesture must soon be burnt up and destroyed by her soul of pure fire."

Yet, notwithstanding, she still sailed the seas of life, like one of those fragile argonauts in their shells of foam and rainbow-mist which will withstand the rude surge of winds and waves. But slowly, gradually, the spirit was o'erfretting its tenement. With the waning of her strength came back the old passionate longing for rest, for quiescence from that "excitement from within," which had been almost over vehement for her in the calm days of her unmarried life.

It is significant that at this time Browning's genius was relatively dormant. Its wings were resting for the long-sustained flight of "The Ring and the Book," and for earlier and shorter though not less royal aerial journeyings. But also, no doubt, the prolonged comparatively unproductive period of eight or nine years (1855-1864), between the publication of "Men and Women" and "Dramatis Personæ," was due in some measure to the poet's incessant and anxious care for his wife, to the deep sorrow of witnessing her slow but

visible passing away, and to the profound grief occasioned by her death. However, barrenness of imaginative creative activity can be only very relatively
affirmed, even of so long a period, of years wherein
were written such memorable and treasurable poems
as 'James Lee's Wife,' among Browning's writings
what 'Maud' is among Lord Tennyson's; 'Gold Hair:
a Legend of Pornic;' 'Dîs Aliter Visum ;' 'Abt Vogler,'
the most notable production of its kind in the language;
'A Death in the Desert,' that singular and impressive
study; 'Caliban upon Setebos,' in its strange potency
of interest and stranger poetic note, absolutely unique;
'Youth and Art;' 'Apparent Failure;' 'Prospice,' that
noble lyrical defiance of death; and the supremely
lofty and significant series of weighty stanzas, 'Rabbi
Ben Ezra,' the most quintessential of all the distinctively
psychical monologues which Browning has written. It
seems to me that if these two poems only, "Prospice"
and "Rabbi Ben Ezra," were to survive to the day of
Macaulay's New Zealander, the contemporaries of that
meditative traveller would have sufficient to enable them
to understand the great fame of the poet of "dim
ancestral days," as the more acute among them could
discern something of the real Shelley, though time had
preserved but the three lines—

> " Yet now despair itself is mild,
> Even as the winds and waters are ;
> I could lie down like a tired child " . . .

something of the real Catullus, through the mists of
remote antiquity, if there had not perished the single
passionate cry—

" Lesbia illa,
  Illa Lesbia, quam Catullus unam
  Plus quam se, atque suos amavit omnes ! "

At the beginning of July (1858), the Brownings left Florence for the summer and autumn, and by easy stages travelled to Normandy. Here the invalid benefited considerably at first : and here, I may add, Browning wrote his 'Legend of Pornic,' 'Gold-Hair.' This poem of twenty-seven five-line stanzas (which differs only from that in more recent " Collected Works," and " Selections," in its lack of the three stanzas now numbered xxi., xxii., and xxiii.) was printed for limited private circulation, though primarily for the purpose of securing American copyright. Browning several times printed single poems thus, and for the same reasons— that is, either for transatlantic copyright, or when the verses were not likely to be included in any volume for a prolonged period. These leaflets or half-sheetlets of 'Gold Hair' and 'Prospice,' of 'Cleon' and 'The Statue and the Bust'— together with the "Two Poems by Elizabeth Barrett and Robert Browning," published, for benefit of a charity, in 1854—are among the rarest "finds" for the collector, and are literally worth a good deal more than their weight in gold.

In the tumultuous year of 1859 all Italy was in a ferment. No patriot among the Nationalists was more ardent in her hopes than the delicate, too fragile, dying poetess, whose flame of life burned anew with the great hopes that animated her for her adopted country. Well indeed did she deserve, among the lines which the poet Tommaseo wrote and the Florence municipality caused to be engraved in gold upon a white marble slab, to be placed upon Casa Guidi, the words *fece del suo verso aureo anello fra Italia e Inghilterra*—" who of her Verse made a golden link connecting England and Italy."

The victories of Solferino and San Martino made the bitterness of the disgraceful Treaty of Villafranca the more hard to bear. Even had we not Mr. Story's evidence, it would be a natural conclusion that this disastrous ending to the high hopes of the Italian patriots accelerated Mrs. Browning's death. The withdrawal of hope is often worse in its physical effects than any direct bodily ill.

It was a miserable summer for both husband and wife, for more private sorrows also pressed upon them. Not even the sweet autumnal winds blowing upon Siena wafted away the shadow that had settled upon the invalid : nor was there medicine for her in the air of Rome, where the winter was spent. A temporary relief, however, was afforded by the more genial climate, and in the spring of 1860 she was able, with Browning's help, to see her Italian patriotic poems through the press. It goes without saying that these " Poems before Congress " had a grudging reception from the critics, because they dared to hint that all was not roseate-hued in England. The true patriots are those who love despite blemishes, not those who cherish the blemishes along with the virtues. To hint at a flaw is "not to be an Englishman."

The autumn brought a new sadness in the death of Miss Arabella Barrett—a dearly loved sister, the "Arabel" of so many affectionate letters. Once more a winter in Rome proved temporally restorative. But at last the day came when she wrote her last poem—" North and South," a gracious welcome to Hans Christian

Andersen on the occasion of his first visit to the Eternal City.

Early in June of 1861 the Brownings were once more at Casa Guidi. But soon after their return the invalid caught a chill. For a few days she hovered like a tired bird—though her friends saw only the seemingly unquenchable light in the starry eyes, and did not anticipate the silence that was soon to be.

By the evening of the 28th day of the month she was in sore peril of failing breath. All night her husband sat by her, holding her hand. Two hours before dawn she realised that her last breath would ere long fall upon his tear-wet face. Then, as a friend has told us, she passed into a state of ecstasy: yet not so rapt therein but that she could whisper many words of hope, even of joy. With the first light of the new day, she leaned against her lover. Awhile she lay thus in silence, and then, softly sighing "*It is beautiful!*" passed like the windy fragrance of a flower.

CHAPTER IX.

IT is needless to dwell upon what followed. The world has all that need be known. To Browning himself it was the abrupt, the too deeply pathetic, yet not wholly unhappy ending of a lovelier poem than any he or another should ever write, the poem of their married life.

There is a rare serenity in the thought of death when it is known to be the gate of life. This conviction Browning had, and so his grief was rather that of one whose joy has westered earlier. The sweetest music of his life had withdrawn : but there was still music for one to whom life in itself was a happiness. He had his son, and was not void of other solace : but even had it been otherwise he was of the strenuous natures who never succumb, nor wish to die—whatever accident of mortality overcome the will and the power.

It was in the autumn following his wife's death that he wrote the noble poem to which allusion has already been made : " Prospice." Who does not thrill to its close, when all of gloom or terror

> " Shall change, shall become first a peace out of pain,
> Then a light, then thy breast,
> O thou soul of my soul ! I shall clasp thee again,
> And with God be the rest."

There are few direct allusions to his wife in Browning's poems. Of those prior to her death the most beautiful is "One Word More," which has been already alluded to : of the two or three subsequent to that event none surpasses the magic close of the first part of "The Ring and the Book."

Thereafter the details of his life are public property. He all along lived in the light, partly from his possession of that serenity which made Goethe glad to be alive and to be able to make others share in that gladness. No poet has been more revered and more loved. His personality will long be a stirring tradition. In the presence of his simple manliness and wealth of all generous qualities one is inclined to pass by as valueless, as the mere flying spray of the welcome shower, the many honours and gratifications that befell him. Even if these things mattered, concerning one by whose genius we are fascinated, while undazzled by the mere accidents pertinent thereto, their recital would be wearisome—of how he was asked to be Lord Rector of this University, or made a doctor of laws at that : of how letters and tributes of all kinds came to him from every district in our Empire, from every country in the world : and so forth. All these things are implied in the circumstance that his life was throughout "a noble music with a golden ending."

In 1866 his father died in Paris, strenuous in life until the very end. After this event Miss Sarianna Browning went to reside with her brother, and from that time onward was his inseparable companion, and ever one of the dearest and most helpful of friends. In latter years brother and sister were constantly seen

together, and so regular attendants were they at such
functions as the "Private Views" at the Royal Academy
and Grosvenor Gallery, that these never seemed complete
without them. A Private View, a first appearance of
Joachim or Sarasate, a first concert of Richter or
Henschel or Hallé, at each of these, almost to a certainty,
the poet was sure to appear. The chief personal happiness of his later life was in his son. Mr. R. Barrett
Browning is so well known as a painter and sculptor
that it would be superfluous for me to add anything
further here, except to state that his successes were his
father's keenest pleasures.

Two years after his father's death, that is in 1868, the
"Poetical Works of Robert Browning, M.A., Honorary
Fellow of Baliol College, Oxford," were issued in six
volumes. Here the equator of Browning's genius may
be drawn. On the further side lie the "Men and
Women" of the period anterior to "The Ring and the
Book": midway is the transitional zone itself: on the
hither side are the "Men and Women" of a more
temperate if not colder clime.

The first part of "The Ring and the Book" was not
published till November. In September the poet was
staying with his sister and son at Le Croisic, a picturesque
village at the mouth of the Loire, at the end of the great
salt plains which stretch down from Guérande to the
Bay of Biscay. No doubt, in lying on the sand-dunes
in the golden September glow, in looking upon the there
somewhat turbid current of the Loire, the poet brooded
on those days when he saw its inland waters with her
who was with him no longer save in dreams and
memories. Here he wrote that stirring poem, "Hervé

Riel," founded upon the valorous action of a French sailor who frustrated the naval might of England, and claimed nothing as a reward save permission to have a holiday on land to spend a few hours with his wife, "la belle Aurore." "Hervé Riel" (which has been translated into French, and is often recited, particularly in the maritime towns, and is always evocative of enthusiastic applause) is one of Browning's finest action-lyrics, and is assured of the same immortality as "How they brought the Good News from Ghent to Aix," or the "Pied Piper " himself.

In 1872 there was practical proof of the poet's growing popularity. Baron Tauchnitz issued two volumes of excellently selected poems, comprising some of the best of "Men and Women," "Dramatis Personæ," and "Dramatic Romances," besides the longer "Soul's Tragedy," "Luria," "In a Balcony," and "Christmas Eve and Easter Day"—the most Christian poem of the century, according to one eminent cleric, the heterodox self-sophistication of a free-thinker, according to another: really, the reflex of a great crisis, that of the first movement of the tide of religious thought to a practically limitless freedom. This edition also contained "Bishop Blougram," then much discussed, apart from its poetic and intellectual worth, on account of its supposed verisimilitude in portraiture of Cardinal Wiseman. This composition, one of Browning's most characteristic, is so clever that it is scarcely a poem. Poetry and Cleverness do not well agree, the muse being already united in perfect marriage to Imagination. In his Essay on Truth, Bacon says that one of the Fathers called poetry *Vinum Dæmonum*, because it filleth the imagination. Certainly if it be not *vinum dæmonum* it is not Poetry.

In this year also appeared the first series of "Selections" by the poet's latest publishers: "Dedicated to Alfred Tennyson. In Poetry—illustrious and consummate: In Friendship—noble and sincere." It was in his preface to this selection that he wrote the often-quoted words: "Nor do I apprehend any more charges of being wilfully obscure, unconscientiously careless, or perversely harsh." At or about the date of these "Selections" the poet wrote to a friend, on this very point of obscurity, "I can have little doubt that my writing has been in the main too hard for many I should have been pleased to communicate with ; but I never designedly tried to puzzle people, as some of my critics have supposed. On the other hand, I never pretended to offer such literature as should be a substitute for a cigar or a game at dominoes to an idle man. So perhaps, on the whole, I get my deserts, and something over—not a crowd, but a few I value more."

In 1877 Browning, ever restless for pastures new, went with his sister to spend the autumn at La Saisiaz (Savoyard for "the sun"), a villa among the mountains near Geneva; this time with the additional company of Miss Anne Egerton Smith, an intimate and valued friend. But there was an unhappy close to the holiday. Miss Smith died on the night of the fourteenth of September, from heart complaint. "La Saisiaz" is the direct outcome of this incident, and is one of the most beautiful of Browning's later poems. Its trochaics move with a tide-like sound.

At the close, there is a line which might stand as epitaph for the poet—

"He, at least, believed in Soul, was very sure of God."

In the following year "La Saisiaz" was published along with "The Two Poets of Croisic," which was begun and partly written at the little French village ten years previously. There is nothing of the eight-score stanzas of the "Two Poets" to equal its delightful epilogue, or the exquisite prefatory lyric, beginning

> " Such a starved bank of moss
> Till that May-morn
> Blue ran the flash across:
> Violets were born."

Extremely interesting—and for myself I cannot find "The Two Poets of Croisic" to be anything more than "interesting"—it is as a poem distinctly inferior to "La Saisiaz." Although detached lines are often far from truly indicative of the real poetic status of a long poem, where proportion and harmony are of more importance than casual exfoliations of beauty, yet to a certain extent they do serve as musical keys that give the fundamental tone. One certainly would have to search in vain to find in the Croisic poem such lines as

> " Five short days, scarce enough to
> Bronze the clustered wilding apple, redden ripe the mountain ash."

Or these of Mont Blanc, seen at sunset, towering over icy pinnacles and teeth-like peaks,

> " Blanc, supreme above his earth-brood, needles red and white and
>   green,
> Horns of silver, fangs of crystal set on edge in his demesne."

Or, again, this of the sun swinging himself above the dark shoulder of Jura—

" Gay he hails her, and magnific, thrilled her black length burns to
gold."

Or, finally, this sounding verse—

" Past the city's congregated peace of homes and pomp of spires."

The other poems later than "The Ring and the
Book" are, broadly speaking, of two kinds. On the
one side may be ranged the groups which really cohere
with "Men and Women." These are "The Inn Album,"
the miscellaneous poems of the "Pacchiarotto" volume,
the "Dramatic Idyls," some of "Jocoseria," and some of
"Asolando." "Ferishtah's Fancies" and "Parleyings"
are not, collectively, dramatic poems, but poems of
illuminative insight guided by a dramatic imagination.[1]
They, and the classical poems and translations (render-
ings, rather, by one whose own individuality dominates
them to the exclusion of that *nearness* of the original
author, which it should be the primary aim of the
translator to evoke), the beautiful "Balaustion's Adventure," "Aristophanes' Apology," and "The Agamemnon
of Æschylus," and the third group, which comprises
"Prince Hohenstiel-Schwangau," "Red Cotton Nightcap

---

[1] In a letter to a friend, Browning wrote :—"I hope and believe
that one or two careful readings of the Poem [Ferishtah's Fancies]
will make its sense clear enough. Above all, pray allow for the
Poet's inventiveness in any case, and do not suppose there is more
than a thin disguise of a few Persian names and allusions. There
was no such person as Ferishtah—the stories are all inventions.
. . . The Hebrew quotations are put in for a purpose, as a
direct acknowledgment that certain doctrines may be found in the
Old Book, which the Concocters of Novel Schemes of Morality
put forth as discoveries of their own."

Country," and "Fifine at the Fair"—these three groups are of the second kind.

Remarkable as are the three last-named productions, it is extremely doubtful if the first and second will be read for pleasure by readers born after the close of this century. As it is impossible, in my narrow limits, to go into any detail about poems which personally I do not regard as essential to the truest understanding of Browning, the truest because on the highest level, that of poetry—as distinct from dogma, or intellectual suasion of any kind that might, for all its æsthetic charm, be in prose—it would be presumptuous to assert anything derogatory of them without attempting adequate substantiation. I can, therefore, merely state my own opinion. To reiterate, it is that, for different reasons, these three long poems are foredoomed to oblivion— not, of course, to be lost to the student of our literature and of our age, a more wonderful one even than that of the Renaissance, but to lapse from the general regard. That each will for a long time find appreciative readers is certain. They have a fascination for alert minds, and they have not infrequent ramifications which are worth pursuing for the glimpses afforded into an always evanishing Promised Land. "Prince Hohenstiel-Schwangau" (the name, by the way, is not purely fanciful, being formed from Hohen Schwangau, one of the castles of the late King of Bavaria) is Browning's complement to his wife's "Ode to Napoleon III." "Red Cotton Nightcap Country" is a true story, the narrative of the circumstances pertinent to the tragic death of one Antonio Mellerio, a Paris jeweller, which occurred in 1870 at St. Aubin in Normandy, where,

indeed, the poet first heard of it in all its details. It is
a story which, if the method of poetry and the method
of prose could for a moment be accepted as equivalent,
might be said to be of the school of a light and
humorously grotesque Zola. It has the fundamental
weakness of "The Ring and the Book"—the weakness
of an inadequate ethical basis. It is, indeed, to that
great work what a second-rate novelette is to a masterpiece of fiction.

"Fifine at the Fair," on the other hand, is so powerful
and often so beautiful a poem that one would be rash
indeed were he, with the blithe critical assurance which
is so generally snuffed out like a useless candle by a later
generation, to prognosticate its inevitable seclusion from
the high place it at present occupies in the estimate of
the poet's most uncompromising admirers. But surely
equally rash is the assertion that it will be the "poem of
the future." However, our concern is not with problem-
atical estimates, but with the poem as it appears to *us*.
It is one of the most characteristic of Browning's productions. It would be impossible for the most indolent
reader or critic to attribute it, even if anonymous, to
another parentage. Coleridge alludes somewhere to
certain verses of Wordsworth's, with the declaration that
if he had met them howling in the desert he would have
recognised their authorship. "Fifine" would not even
have to howl.

Browning was visiting Pornic one autumn, when he
saw the gipsy who was the original of "Fifine." In the
words of Mrs. Orr, "his fancy was evidently set roaming
by the gipsy's audacity, her strength—the contrast which
she presented to the more spiritual types of womanhood;

and this contrast eventually found expression in a pathetic theory of life, in which these opposite types and their corresponding modes of attraction became the necessary complement of each other. As he laid down the theory, Mr. Browning would be speaking in his own person. But he would turn into some one else in the act of working it out—for it insensibly carried with it a plea for yielding to those opposite attractions, not only successively, but at the same time; and a modified Don Juan would grow up under his pen."

One drawback to an unconditional enjoyment of Balzac is that every now and again the student of the *Comédie Humaine* resents the too obvious display of the forces that propel the effect—a lesser phase of the weariness which ensues upon much reading of the mere "human documents" of the Goncourt school of novelists. In the same way, we too often see Browning working up the electrical qualities, so that, when the fulmination comes, we understand "just how it was produced," and, as illogically as children before a too elaborate conjurer, conclude that there is not so much in this particular poetic feat as in others which, like Herrick's maids, continually do deceive. To me this is affirmable of "Fifine at the Fair." The poet seems to know so very well what he is doing. If he did not take the reader so much into his confidence, if he would rely more upon the liberal grace of his earlier verse and less upon the trained subtlety of his athletic intellect, the charm would be the greater. The poem would have a surer duration as one of the author's greater achievements, if there were more frequent and more prolonged insistence on the note struck in the lines (§ lxxiii.) about the hill-stream,

infant of mist and dew, falling over the ledge of the
fissured cliff to find its fate in smoke below, as it disappears into the deep, "embittered evermore, to make
the sea one drop more big thereby:" or in the cloudy
splendour of the description of nightfall (§ cvi.) : or in
the windy spring freshness of

> " Hence, when the earth began afresh its life in May,
>   And fruit-trees bloomed, and waves would wanton, and the bay
>   Ruffle its wealth of weed, and stranger-birds arrive,
>   And beasts take each a mate." . . .

But its chief fault seems to me to be its lack of
that transmutive glow of rhythmic emotion without
which no poem can endure. This rhythmic energy is,
inherently, a distinct thing from intellectual emotion.
Metric music may be alien to the adequate expression of
the latter, whereas rhythmic emotion can have no other
appropriate issue. Of course, in a sense, all creative art
is rhythmic in kind: but here I am speaking only of
that creative energy which evolves the germinal idea
through the medium of language. The energy of the
intellect under creative stimulus may produce lordly
issues in prose : but poetry of a high intellectual order
can be the outcome only of an intellect fused to white
heat, of intellectual emotion on fire—as, in the fine
saying of George Meredith, passion is noble strength
on fire. Innumerable examples could be taken from
any part of the poem, but as it would not be just to
select the most obviously defective passages, here are
two which are certainly fairly representative of the
general level—

> " And I became aware, scarcely the word escaped my lips, that
> swift ensued in silence and by stealth, and yet with certitude, a

formidable change of the amphitheatre which held the Carnival; *although the human stir continued just the same amid that shift of scene."* (No. CV.)

"And where i' the world is all this wonder, you detail so trippingly, espied? My mirror would reflect a tall, thin, pale, deep-eyed personage, pretty once, it may be, doubtless still loving— a certain grace yet lingers if you will—but all this wonder, where?" (No. XL.)

Here, and in a hundred other such passages, we have the rhythm, if not of the best prose, at least not that of poetry. Will "Fifine" and poems of its kind stand re-reading, re-perusal over and over? That is one of the most definite tests. In the pressure of life can we afford much time to anything but the very best—nay, to the vast mass even of that which closely impinges there-upon?

For myself, in the instance of "Fifine," I admit that if re-perusal be controlled by pleasure I am content (always excepting a few scattered noble passages) with the Prologue and Epilogue. A little volume of those Summaries of Browning's—how stimulating a companion it would be in those hours when the mind would fain breathe a more liberal air!

As for "Jocoseria,"[1] it seems to me the poorest of Browning's works, and I cannot help thinking that

---

[1] In a letter to a friend, along with an early copy of this book, Browning stated that "the title is taken from the work of Melander (*Schwartzmann*), reviewed, by a curious coincidence, in the *Blackwood* of this month. I referred to it in a note to 'Paracelsus.' The two Hebrew quotations (put in to give a grave look to what is mere fun and invention) being translated amount to (1) 'A Collection of Many Lies': and (2), an old saying, 'From Moses to Moses arose none like Moses' . . . . . ."

ultimately the only gold grain discoverable therein will be "Ixion," the beautiful penultimate poem beginning—

> " Never the time and the place
> And the loved one altogether ; "

and the thrush-like overture, closing—

> "What of the leafage, what of the flower ?
> Roses embowering with nought they embower !
> Come then ! complete incompletion, O comer,
> Pant through the blueness, perfect the summer !
> Breathe but one breath
> Rose-beauty above,
> And all that was death
> Grows life, grows love,
> Grows love ! "

In 1881 the "Browning Society" was established. It is easy to ridicule any institution of the kind—much easier than to be considerate of other people's earnest convictions and aims, or to be helpful to their object. There is always a ridiculous side to excessive enthusiasm, particularly obvious to persons incapable of enthusiasm of any kind. With some mistakes, and not a few more or less grotesque absurdities, the members of the various English and American Browning Societies are yet to be congratulated on the good work they have, collectively, accomplished. Their publications are most interesting and suggestive : ultimately they will be invaluable. The members have also done a good work in causing some of Browning's plays to be produced again on the stage, and in Miss Alma Murray and others have found sympathetic and able exponents of some of the poet's most attractive *dramatis personæ*. There can

be no question as to the powerful impetus given by
the Society to Browning's steadily-increasing popularity.
Nothing shows his judicious good sense more than the
letter he wrote, privately, to Mr. Edmund Yates, at the
time of the Society's foundation.

"The Browning Society, I need not say, as well as Browning
himself, are fair game for criticism. I had no more to do with the
founding it than the babe unborn; and, as Wilkes was no Wilkeite,
I am quite other than a Browningite. But I cannot wish harm to
a society of, with a few exceptions, names unknown to me, who are
busied about my books so disinterestedly. The exaggerations
probably come of the fifty-years'-long charge of unintelligibility
against my books; such reactions are possible, though I never
looked for the beginning of one so soon. That there is a grotesque
side to the thing is certain; but I have been surprised and touched
by what cannot but have been well intentioned, I think. Anyhow,
as I never felt inconvenienced by hard words, you will not expect
me to wax bumptious because of undue compliment: so enough
of 'Browning,'—except that he is yours very truly, 'while this
machine is to him.'"

The latter years of the poet were full of varied interest
for himself, but present little of particular significance for
specification in a monograph so concise as this must
perforce be. Every year he went abroad, to France or
to Italy, and once or twice on a yachting trip in the
Mediterranean.[1] At home—for many years, at 19

[1] It was on his first experience of this kind, more than a quarter of
a century earlier, that he wrote the nobly patriotic lines of " Home
Thoughts from the Sea," and that flawless strain of bird-music,
"Home Thoughts from Abroad:" then, also, that he composed
"How they brought the Good News." Concerning the last, he
wrote, in 1881 (*vide The Academy*, April 2nd), "There is no sort
of historical foundation about [this poem]. I wrote it under the

Warwick Crescent, in what some one has called the dreary Mesopotamia of Paddington, and for the last three or four years of his life at 29 De Vere Gardens, Kensington Gore—his avocations were so manifold that it is difficult to understand where he had leisure for his vocation. Everybody wished him to come to dine; and he did his utmost to gratify Everybody. He saw everything; read all the notable books; kept himself acquainted with the leading contents of the journals and magazines; conducted a large correspondence; read new French, German, and Italian books of mark; read and translated Euripides and Æschylus; knew all the gossip of the literary clubs, salons, and the studios; was a frequenter of afternoon-tea parties; and then, over and above it, he was Browning: the most profoundly subtle mind that has exercised itself in poetry since Shakspere. His personal grace and charm of manner never failed. Whether he was dedicating " Balaustion's Adventure " in terms of gracious courtesy, or handing a flower from some jar of roses, or lilies, or his favourite daffodils, with a bright smile or merry glance, to the lady of his regard, or when sending a copy of a new book of poetry with an accompanying letter expressed with rare felicity, or when generously prophesying for a young poet the only true success if he will but listen and act upon "the inner voice,"—he was in all these, and in all things, the ideal gentleman. There is so charming and characteristic a

bulwark of a vessel off the African coast, after I had been at it long enough to appreciate even the fancy of a gallop on the back of a certain good horse, ' York,' then in my stable at home. It was written in pencil on the fly-leaf of Bartoli's *Simboli*, I remember."

touch in the following note to a girl-friend, that I must find room for it :—

29 De Vere Gardens, W.,
6th-July 1889.

MY BELOVED ALMA,—I had the honour yesterday of dining with the Shah, whereupon the following dialogue:—

"Vous êtes poëte?"

"On s'est permis de me le dire quelquefois."

"Et vous avez fait des livres?"

"Trop de livres."

"Voulez-vous m'en donner un, afin que je puisse me ressouvenir de vous?"

"Avec plaisir."

I have been accordingly this morning to town, where the thing is procurable, and as I chose a volume of which I judged the binding might take the imperial eye, I said to myself, "Here do I present my poetry to a personage for whom I do not care three straws; why should I not venture to do as much for a young lady I love dearly, who, for the author's sake, will not impossibly care rather for the inside than the outside of the volume?" So I was bold enough to take one and offer it for your kind acceptance, begging you to remember in days to come that the author, whether a good poet or no, was always, my Alma, your affectionate friend,

ROBERT BROWNING.

His look was a continual and serene gleam. Lamartine, who remarks this of Bossuet in his youth, adds a phrase which, as observant acquaintances of the poet will agree, might be written of Browning—"His lips quivered often without utterance, as if with the wind of an internal speech."

Except for the touching and beautiful letter which he wrote from Asolo about two months before his death, to Mr. Wilfrid Meynell, about a young writer to whom the latter wished to draw the poet's kindly attention—a letter which has a peculiar pathos in the words, " I shall soon depart for Venice, on my way homeward "—except for this letter there is none so well worth repetition here as his last word to the Poet-Laureate.   The friendship between these two great poets has in itself the fragrance of genius.   The letter was written just before Browning left London.

29 De Vere Gardens, W.,
August 5th, 1889.

MY DEAR TENNYSON,—To-morrow is your birthday—indeed, a memorable one.   Let me say I associate myself with the universal pride of our country in your glory, and in its hope that for many and many a year we may have your very self among us—secure that your poetry will be a wonder and delight to all those appointed to come after.   And for my own part, let me further say, I have loved you dearly.   May God bless you and yours.

At no moment from first to last of my acquaintance with your works, or friendship with yourself, have I had any other feeling, expressed or kept silent, than this which an opportunity allows me to utter—that I am and ever shall be, my dear Tennyson, admiringly and affectionately yours,

ROBERT BROWNING.

Shortly after this he was at Asolo once more, the little hill-town in the Veneto, which he had visited in his youth, and where he heard again the echo of Pippa's song—

" God's in His heaven,
All's right with the world ! "

Mr. W. W. Story writes to me that he spent three days with the poet at this time, and that the latter seemed, except for a slight asthma, to be as vigorous in mind and body as ever.   Thence, later in the autumn, he went to Venice, to join his son and daughter-in-law at the home where he was "to have a corner for his old age," the beautiful Palazzo Rezzonico, on the Grand Canal.   He was never happier, more sanguine, more joyous, than here. He worked for three or four hours each morning, walked daily for about two hours, crossed occasionally to the Lido with his sister, and in the evenings visited friends or went to the opera. But for some time past, his heart—always phenomenally slow in its action, and of late ominously intermittent—had been noticeably weaker. As he suffered no pain and little inconvenience, he paid no particular attention to the matter. Browning had as little fear of death as doubt in God. In a controlling Providence he did indeed profoundly believe. He felt, with Joubert, that "it is not difficult to believe in God, if one does not worry oneself to define Him."[1]

"How should externals satisfy my soul?" was his cry in "Sordello," and it was the fundamental strain of all his poetry, as the fundamental motive is expressible in

> "—a loving worm within its sod
> Were diviner than a loveless god
> Amid his worlds "—

love being with him the golden key wherewith to unlock the world of the universe, of the soul, of all

[1] "Browning's 'orthodoxy' brought him into many a combat with his rationalistic friends, some of whom could hardly believe that he took his doctrine seriously. Such was the fact, however; indeed, I have heard that he once stopped near an open-air assembly which an atheist was haranguing, and, in the freedom of his *incognito*, gave strenuous battle to the opinions uttered. To one who had spoken of an expected 'Judgment Day' as a superstition, I heard him say: 'I don't see that. Why should there not be a settling day in the universe, as when a master settles with his workmen at the end of the week?' There was something in his tone and manner which suggested his dramatic conception of religious ideas and ideals."—MONCURE D. CONWAY.

nature. He is as convinced of the two absolute facts
of God and Soul as Cardinal Newman in writing of
"Two and two only, supreme and luminously self-
evident beings, myself and my Creator." Most fervently
he believes that

> "Haply for us the ideal dawn shall break . . .
> And set our pulse in tune with moods divine "—

though, co-equally, in the necessity of "making man sole
sponsor of himself." Ever and again, of course, he was
betrayed by the bewildering and defiant puzzle of life :
seeing in the face of the child the seed of sorrow, "in
the green tree an ambushed flame, in Phosphor a
vaunt-guard of Night." Yet never of him could be
written that thrilling saying which Sainte-Beuve uttered
of Pascal, "That lost traveller who yearns for home,
who, strayed without a guide in a dark forest, takes many
times the wrong road, goes, returns upon his steps, is
discouraged, sits down at a crossing of the roads, utters
cries to which no one responds, resumes his march with
frenzy and pain, throws himself upon the ground and
wants to die, and reaches home at last only after all
sorts of anxieties and after sweating blood." No darkness, no tempest, no gloom, long confused his vision of
'the ideal dawn.' As the carrier-dove is often baffled,
yet ere long surely finds her way through smoke and
fog and din to her far country home, so he too, however distraught, soon or late soared to untroubled ether.
He had that profound inquietude, which the great French
critic says 'attests a moral nature of a high rank, and a
mental nature stamped with the seal of the archangel.'
But, unlike Pascal—who in Sainte-Beuve's words exposes

in the human mind itself two abysses, "on one side an elevation toward God, toward the morally beautiful, a return movement toward an illustrious origin, and on the other side an abasement in the direction of evil"— Browning sees, believes in, holds to nothing short of the return movement, for one and all, toward an illustrious origin.

The crowning happiness of a happy life was his death in the city he loved so well, in the arms of his dear ones, in the light of a world-wide fame. The silence to which the most eloquent of us must all one day lapse came upon him like the sudden seductive twilight of the Tropics, and just when he had bequeathed to us one of his finest utterances.

It seems but a day or two ago that the present writer heard from the lips of the dead poet a mockery of death's vanity—a brave assertion of the glory of life. "Death, death! It is this harping on death I despise so much," he remarked with emphasis of gesture as well as of speech—the inclined head and body, the right hand lightly placed upon the listener's knee, the abrupt change in the inflection of the voice, all so characteristic of him—"this idle and often cowardly as well as ignorant harping! Why should we not change like everything else? In fiction, in poetry, in so much of both, French as well as English, and, I am told, in American art and literature, the shadow of death—call it what you will, despair, negation, indifference—is upon us. But what fools who talk thus! Why, *amico mio*, you know as well as I that death is life, just as our daily, our momentarily dying body is none the less alive and ever recruiting new forces of existence. Without death,

which is our crapelike churchyardy word for change, for
growth, there could be no prolongation of that which we
call life. Pshaw! it is foolish to argue upon such a
thing even. For myself, I deny death as an end of
everything. Never say of me that I am dead!"

On the evening of Thursday, the 12th of December
(1889), he was in bed, with exceeding weakness. In the
centre of the lofty ceiling of the room in which he lay, and
where it had been his wont to work, there is a painting
by his son. It depicts an eagle struggling with a serpent,
and is illustrative of a superb passage in Shelley's
" Revolt of Islam." What memories, what deep
thoughts, it must have suggested; how significant, to
us, the circumstance ! But weak as the poet was, he yet
did not see the shadow which had begun to chill the
hearts of the watchers. Shortly before the great bell of
San Marco struck ten, he turned and asked if any news
had come concerning "Asolando," published that day.
His son read him a telegram from the publishers, telling
how great the demand was and how favourable were the
advance-articles in the leading papers. The dying poet
smiled and muttered, " How gratifying !" When the last
toll of St. Mark's had left a deeper stillness than before,
those by the bedside saw a yet profounder silence on the
face of him whom they loved.

It is needless to dwell upon the grief everywhere felt
and expressed for the irreparable loss. The magnificent
closing lines of Shelley's " Alastor " must have occurred
to many a mourner; for gone, indeed, was "a surpassing
Spirit." The superb pomp of the Venetian funeral, the

solemn grandeur of the interment in Westminster Abbey,
do not seem worth recording: so insignificant are all
these accidents of death made by the supreme fact
itself. Yet it is fitting to know that Venice has never
in modern times afforded a more impressive sight, than
those craped processional gondolas following the high
flower-strewn funeral-barge through the thronged water-
ways and out across the lagoon to the desolate Isle of
the Dead: that London has rarely seen aught more
solemn than the fog-dusked Cathedral spaces, echoing at
first with the slow tramp of the pall-bearers, and then with
the sweet aerial music swaying upward the loved familiar
words of the 'Lyric Voice' hushed so long before.
Yet the poet was as much honoured by those humble
friends, Lambeth artizans and a few poor working-
women, who threw sprays of laurel before the hearse—
by that desolate, starving, woe-weary gentleman, shiver-
ing in his threadbare clothes, who seemed transfixed
with a heart-wrung though silent emotion, ere he hurriedly drew from his sleeve a large white chrysanthemum,
and throwing it beneath the coffin as it was lifted
inward, disappeared in the crowd, which closed again
like the sea upon this lost wandering wave.

Who would not honour this mighty dead? All who
could be present were there, somewhere in the ancient
Abbey. One of the greatest, loved and admired by the
dead poet, had already put the mourning of many into
the lofty dignity of his verse :—

> " Now dumb is he who waked the world to speak,
> And voiceless hangs the world beside his bier,
> Our words are sobs, our cry of praise a tear :
> We are the smitten mortal, we the weak.

We see a spirit on Earth's loftiest peak
Shine, and wing hence the way he makes more clear :
See a great Tree of Life that never sere
Dropped leaf for aught that age or storms might wreak :
Such ending is not Death : such living shows
What wide illumination brightness sheds
From one big heart—to conquer man's old foes :
The coward, and the tyrant, and the force
Of all those weedy monsters raising heads
When Song is murk from springs of turbid source."[1]

One word more of " light and fleeting shadow." In the greatness of his nature he must be ranked with Milton, Defoe, and Scott. His very shortcomings, such as they were, were never baneful growths, but mere weeds, with a certain pleasant though pungent savour moreover, growing upon a rich, an exuberant soil. Pluck one of the least lovely—rather call it the unworthy arrow shot at the body of a dead comrade, so innocent of ill intent : yet it too has a beauty of its own, for the shaft was aflame from the fulness of a heart whose love had withstood the chill passage of the years.

———

On the night of Browning's death a new star suddenly appeared in Orion. The coincidence is suggestive if we like to indulge in the fancy that in that constellation—

" No more subjected to the change or chance
Of the unsteady planets——"

gleam those other " abodes where the Immortals are." Certainly, a wandering fire has passed away from us.

[1] George Meredith.

Whither has it gone? To that new star in Orion: or whirled to remote silences in the trail of lost meteors? Whence, and for how long, will its rays reach our storm and gloom-beleaguered earth?

Such questions cannot meanwhile be solved. Our eyes are still confused with the light, with that ardent flame, as we knew it here. But this we know, it was indeed "a central fire descending upon many altars." These, though touched with but a spark of the immortal principle, bear enduring testimony. And what testimony! How heartfelt: happily also how widespread, how electrically stimulative!

But the time must come when the poet's personality will have the remoteness of tradition: when our perplexed judgments will be as a tale of sound and fury, signifying nothing. It is impossible for any student of literature, for any interested reader, not to indulge in some forecast as to what rank in the poetic hierarchy Robert Browning will ultimately occupy. The commonplace as to the impossibility of prognosticating the ultimate slow decadence, or slower rise, or, it may be, sustained suspension, of a poet's fame, is often insincere, and but an excuse of indolence. To dogmatise were the height of presumption as well as of folly: but to forego speculation, based upon complete present knowledge, for an idle contentment with narrow horizons, were perhaps foolisher still. But assuredly each must perforce be content with his own prevision. None can answer yet for the generality, whose decisive franchise will elect a fit arbiter in due time.

So, for myself, let me summarise what I have already written in several sections of this book, and particularly

in the closing pages of Chapter VI.   There, it will
be remembered—after having found that Browning's
highest achievement is in his second period—emphasis
was laid on the primary importance of his life-work
in its having compelled us to the assumption of a fresh
critical standpoint involving the construction of a new
definition.   In the light of this new definition I think
Browning will ultimately be judged.   As the sculptor
in "Pippa Passes" was the predestinated novel thinker
in marble, so Browning himself appears· as the predestinated novel thinker in verse ; the novel thinker,
however, in degree, not in kind.   But I do not for a
moment believe that his greatness is in his status as a
thinker : even less, that the poet and the thinker are
indissociable.   Many years ago Sainte-Beuve destroyed
this shallow artifice of pseudo-criticism : "Venir nous
dire que tout poëte de talent est, par essence, un grand
penseur, et que tout vrai *penseur* est nécessairement
artiste et poëte, c'est une prétention insoutenable et que
dément à chaque instant la réalité."

When Browning's enormous influence upon the spiritual
and mental life of our day—an influence ever shaping
itself to wise and beautiful issues—shall have lost much
of its immediate import, there will still surely be discerned in his work a formative energy whose resultant
is pure poetic gain.   It is as the poet he will live :
not merely as the "novel thinker in verse."   Logically,
his attitude as 'thinker' is unimpressive.   It is the
attitude, as I think some one has pointed out, of
acquiescence with codified morality.   In one of his
Causeries, the keen French critic quoted above has a
remark upon the great Bossuet, which may with singular

aptness be repeated of Browning :—" His is the Hebrew
genius extended, fecundated by Christianity, and open
to all the acquisitions of the understanding, but retaining
some degree of sovereign interdiction, and closing its
vast horizon precisely where its light ceases." Browning
cannot, or will not, face the problem of the future
except from the basis of assured continuity of individual
existence. He is so much in love with life, for life's
sake, that he cannot even credit the possibility of incon-
tinuity; his assurance of eternity in another world is at
least in part due to his despair at not being eternal in
this. He is so sure, that the intellectually scrupulous
detect the odours of hypotheses amid the sweet savour
of indestructible assurance. Schopenhauer says, in one
of those recently-found Annotations of his which are so
characteristic and so acute, " that which is called ' mathe-
matical certainty' is the cane of a blind man without
a dog, or equilibrium in darkness." Browning would
sometimes have us accept the evidence of his 'cane' as
all-sufficient. He does not entrench himself among con-
ventions : for he already finds himself within the fortified
lines of convention, and remains there. Thus is true
what Mr. Mortimer says in a recent admirable critique
—" His position in regard to the thought of the age
is paradoxical, if not inconsistent. He is in advance
of it in every respect but one, the most important of
all, the matter of fundamental principles ; in these he is
behind it. His processes of thought are often scientific
in their precision of analysis; the sudden conclusion
which he imposes upon them is transcendental and
inept." Browning's conclusions, which harmonise so
well with our haphazard previsionings, are sometimes

so disastrously facile that they exercise an insurrectionary
influence. They occasionally suggest that wisdom of
Gotham which is ever ready to postulate the certainty
of a fulfilment because of the existence of a desire.
It is this that vitiates so much of his poetic reasoning.
Truth may ring regnant in the lines of Abt Vogler—

> " And what is our failure here but a triumph's evidence
> For the fulness of the days? "—

but, unfortunately, the conclusion is, in itself, illogical.

We are all familiar with, and in this book I have
dwelt more than once upon, Browning's habitual attitude
towards Death. It is not a novel one. The frontage is
not so much that of the daring pioneer, as the sedate
assurance of ' the oldest inhabitant.' It is of good hap,
of welcome significance : none the less there is an aspect
of our mortality of which the poet's evasion is uncompromising and absolute. I cannot do better than quote
Mr. Mortimer's noteworthy words hereupon, in connection, moreover, with Browning's artistic relation to
Sex, that other great Protagonist in the relentless duel
of Humanity with Circumstance. " The final inductive
hazard he declines for himself; his readers may take it if
they will. It is part of the insistent and perverse
ingenuity which we display in masking with illusion the
more disturbing elements of life. Veil after veil is torn
down, but seldom before another has been slipped
behind it, until we acquiesce without a murmur in the
concealment that we ourselves have made. Two facts
thus carefully shrouded from full vision by elaborate
illusion conspicuously round in our lives—the life-giving

and life-destroying elements, Sex and Death. We are compelled to occasional physiologic and economic discussion of the one, but we shrink from recognising the full extent to which it bases the whole social fabric, carefully concealing its insurrections, and ignoring or misreading their lessons. The other, in certain aspects, we are compelled to face, but to do it we tipple on illusions, from our cradle upwards, in dread of the coming grave, purchasing a drug for our poltroonery at the expense of our sanity. We uphold our wayward steps with the promises and the commandments for crutches, but on either side of us trudge the shadow Death and the bacchanal Sex, and we mumble prayers against the one, while we scourge ourselves for leering at the other. On one only of these can Browning be said to have spoken with novel force—the relations of sex, which he has treated with a subtlety and freedom, and often with a beauty, unapproached since Goethe. On the problem of Death, except in masquerade of robes and wings, his eupeptic temperament never allowed him to dwell. He sentimentalised where Shakspere thought." Browning's whole attitude to the Hereafter is different from that of Tennyson only in that the latter 'faintly,' while he strenuously, "trusts the larger hope." To him all credit, that, standing upon the frontiers of the Past, he can implicitly trust the Future.

> " High-hearted surely he;
> But bolder they who first off-cast
> Their moorings from the habitable Past."

The teacher may be forgotten, the prophet may be hearkened to no more, but a great poet's utterance is never temporal, having that in it which conserves it against the antagonism of time, and the ebb and flow of literary ideals. What range, what extent of genius! As Mr. Frederick Wedmore has well said, ' Browning is not a book—he is a literature.'

But that he will "stand out gigantic" in *mass* of imperishable work, in that far-off day, I for one cannot credit. His poetic shortcomings seem too essential to permit of this. That fatal excess of cold over emotive thought, of thought that, however profound, incisive, or scrupulously clear, is not yet impassioned, is a fundamental defect of his. It is the very impetuosity of this mental energy to which is due the miscalled obscurity of much of Browning's work—miscalled, because, however remote in his allusions, however pedantic even, he is never obscure in his thought. His is that "palace infinite which darkens with excess of light." But mere excess in itself is nothing more than symptomatic. Browning has suffered more from intellectual exploitation than any writer. It is a ruinous process—for the poet. "He so well repays intelligent study." That is it, unfortunately. There are many, like the old Scotch lady who attempted to read Carlyle's *French Revolution*, who think they have become "daft" when they encounter a passage such as, for example,

> "Rivals, who . . .
>
> 　Tuned, from Bocafoli's stark-naked psalms,
> 　To Plara's sonnets spoilt by toying with,
> ' As knops that stud some almug to the pith
> ' Prickèd for gum, wry thence, and crinklèd worse
> ' Than pursèd eyelids of a river-horse
> ' Sunning himself o' the slime when whirrs the breeze—
> 　*Gad-fly*, that is."

The old lady persevered with Carlyle, and, after a few days, found "she was nae sae daft, but that she had tackled a varra dee-fee-cult author." What would even that indomitable student have said to the above quotation, and to the poem whence it comes? To many it is not the poetry, but the difficulties, that are the attraction. They rejoice, after long and frequent dippings, to find their plummet, almost lost in remote depths, touch bottom. Enough 'meaning' has been educed from 'Childe Roland,' to cite but one instance, to start a School of Philosophy with: though it so happens that the poem is an imaginative fantasy, written in one day. Worse still, it was not inspired by the mystery of existence, but by 'a red horse with a glaring eye standing behind a dun one on a piece of tapestry that used to hang in the poet's drawing-room.'[1] Of all his faults, however, the worst is that jugglery, that inferior legerdemain, with the elements of the beautiful in verse: most obvious in "Sordello," in portions of "The Ring and the Book," and in so many of the later poems. These inexcusable violations are like the larvæ within certain vegetable growths: soon or late they will destroy their environment before they perish themselves. Though possessive above all others of that science of the percipient in the allied arts of painting and music, wherein he found the unconventional Shelley so missuaded by convention, he seemed ever more alert to the substance than to the manner of poetry. In a

---

[1] One account says 'Childe Roland' was written in three days; another, that it was composed in one. Browning's rapidity in composition was extraordinary. "The Return of the Druses" was written in five days, an act a day; so, also, was the "Blot on the 'Scutcheon."

letter of Mrs. Browning's she alludes to a friend's "melodious feeling" for poetry. Possibly the phrase was acci-
dental, but it is significant. To inhale the vital air of
poetry we must love it, not merely find it "interesting,"
"suggestive," "soothing," "stimulative": in a word, we
must have a "melodious feeling" for poetry before we can
deeply enjoy it. Browning, who has so often educed from
his lyre melodies and harmonies of transcendent, though
novel, beauty, was too frequently, during composition,
without this melodious feeling of which his wife speaks.
The distinction between literary types such as Browning
or Balzac on the one hand, and Keats or Gustave Flaubert
on the other, is that with the former there exists a
reverence for the vocation and a relative indifference to the
means, in themselves—and, with the latter, a scrupulous
respect for the mere means as well as for that to which
they conduce. The poet who does not love words
for themselves, as an artist loves any chance colour
upon his palette, or as the musician any vagrant
tone evoked by a sudden touch in idleness or reverie,
has not entered into the full inheritance of the sons of
Apollo. The writer cannot aim at beauty, that which
makes literature and art, without this heed—without,
rather, this creative anxiety: for it is certainly not
enough, as some one has said, that language should be
used merely for the transportation of intelligence, as a
wheelbarrow carries brick. Of course, Browning is not
persistently neglectful of this fundamental necessity for
the literary artist. He is often as masterly in this as in
other respects. But he is not always, not often enough,
alive to the paramount need. He writes with "the verse
being as the mood it paints:" but, unfortunately, the

mood is often poetically unformative. He had no
passion for the quest for seductive forms. Too much of
his poetry has been born prematurely. Too much of it,
indeed, has not died and been born again—for all
immortal verse is a poetic resurrection. Perfect poetry
is the deathless part of mortal beauty. The great artists
never perpetuate gross actualities, though they are the
supreme realists. It is Schiller, I think, who says in
effect, that to live again in the serene beauty of art, it is
needful that things should first die in reality. Thus
Browning's dramatic method, even, is sometimes disastrous in its untruth, as in Caliban's analytical reasoning
—an initial absurdity, as Mr. Berdoe has pointed out,
adding epigrammatically, 'Caliban is a savage, with
the introspective powers of a Hamlet, and the theology
of an evangelical Churchman.' Not only Caliban, but
several other of Browning's personages (Aprile, Egla-
mour, etc.) are what Goethe calls *schwankende Gestalten*,
mere "wavering images."

Montaigne, in one of his essays, says that to stop
gracefully is sure proof of high race in a horse : certainly to stop in time is imperative upon the poet. Of
Browning may be said what Poe wrote of another, that
his genius was too impetuous for the minuter techni-
calities of that elaborate *art* so needful in the building
up of monuments for immortality. But has not a greater
than Poe declared that "what distinguishes the artist
from the amateur is *architectoniké* in the highest sense ;
that power of execution which creates, forms, and con-
stitutes : not the profoundness of single thoughts, not
the richness of imagery, not the abundance of illustra-
tion." Assuredly, no "new definition" can be an

effective one which conflicts with Goethe's incontro-vertible dictum.

But this much having been admitted, I am only too willing to protest against the uncritical outcry against Browning's musical incapacity.

A deficiency is not incapacity, otherwise Coleridge, at his highest the most perfect of our poets, would be lowly estimated.

> " Bid shine what would, dismiss into the shade
> What should not be—and there triumphs the paramount
> Surprise o' the master." . . .

Browning's music is oftener harmonic than melodic: and musicians know how the general ear, charmed with immediately appellant melodies, resents, wearies of, or is deaf to the harmonies of a more remote, a more complex, and above all a more novel creative method. He is, among poets, what Wagner is among musicians; as Shakspere may be likened to Beethoven, or Shelley to Chopin. The common assertion as to his incapacity for metric music is on the level of those affirmations as to his not being widely accepted of the people, when the people have the chance ; or as to the indifference of the public to poetry generally—and this in an age when poetry has never been so widely understood, loved, and valued, and wherein it is yearly growing more acceptable and more potent !

A great writer is to be adjudged by his triumphs, not by his failures : as, to take up Montaigne's simile again, a famous race-horse is remembered for its successes and not for the races which it lost. The tendency with certain critics is to reverse the process. Instead of saying with

the archbishop in Horne's "Gregory VII.," "He owes it
all to his Memnonian voice! He has no genius:" or of
declaring, as Prospero says of Caliban in "The Tempest,"
"He is as disproportioned in his manners as in his
shape:" how much better to affirm of him what Ben
Jonson wrote of Shakspere, "Hee redeemed his vices
with his vertues: there was ever more in him to bee
praysed than to bee pardoned." In the balance of
triumphs and failures, however, is to be sought the
relative measure of genius—whose equipoise should be
the first matter of ascertainment in comparative criticism.

For those who would discriminate between what Mr.
Traill succinctly terms his *generic* greatness as thinker
and man of letters, and his *specific* power as poet, it is
necessary to disabuse the mind of Browning's "message." The question is not one of weighty message, but
of artistic presentation. To praise a poem because of its
optimism is like commending a peach because it loves
the sunshine, rather than because of its distinguishing
bloom and savour. The primary concern of the artist
must be with his vehicle of expression. In the instance
of a poet, this vehicle is language emotioned to the
white-heat of rhythmic music by impassioned thought
or sensation. Schopenhauer declares it is all a question
of style now with poetry; that everything has been sung,
that everything has been duly cursed, that there is
nothing left for poetry but to be the glowing forge of
words. He forgets that in quintessential art there is
nothing of the past, nothing old: even the future has
part therein only in that the present is always encroach-
ing upon, becoming, the future. The famous pessimistic
philosopher has, in common with other critics, made, in

14

effect, the same remark—that Style exhales the odour of
the soul : yet he himself has indicated that the strength
of Shakspere lay in the fact that 'he had no taste,' that
'he was not a man of letters.'   Whenever genius has
displayed epic force it has established a new order.   In
the general disintegration and reconstruction of literary
ideals thus involved, it is easier to be confused by the
novel flashing of strange lights than to discern the
central vivifying altar-flame.   It may prove that what
seem to us the regrettable accidents of Browning's
genius are no malfortunate flaws, but as germane thereto
as his Herculean ruggednesses are to Shakspere, as the
laboured inversions of his blank verse are to Milton, as
his austere concision is to Dante.   Meanwhile, to the
more exigent among us at any rate, the flaws seem flaws,
and in nowise essential.

But when we find weighty message and noble utterance
in union, as we do in the magnificent remainder after
even the severest ablation of the poor and mediocre
portion of Browning's life-work, how beneficent seem the
generous gods !   Of this remainder most aptly may be
quoted these lines from "The Ring and the Book,"

> "Gold as it was, is, shall be evermore ;
> Prime nature with an added artistry."

How gladly, in this dubious hour—when, as an eminent
writer has phrased it, a colossal Hand, which some call
the hand of Destiny and others that of Humanity, is
putting out the lights of Heaven one by one, like candles
after a feast—how gladly we listen to this poet with
his serene faith in God, and immortal life, and the
soul's unending development !   "Hope hard in the

subtle thing that's Spirit," he cries in the Prologue to "Pacchiarotto": and this, in manifold phrasing, is his *leit-motif,* his fundamental idea, in unbroken line from the "Pauline" of his twenty-first to the "Asolando" of his seventy-sixth year. This superb phalanx of faith— what shall prevail against it?

How winsome it is, moreover: this, and the humanity of his song. Profoundly he realised that there is no more significant study than the human heart. "The development of a soul: little else is worth study," he wrote in his preface to "Sordello": so in his old age, in his last "Reverie"—

> " As the record from youth to age
> Of my own, the single soul—
> So the world's wide book: one page
> Deciphered explains the whole
> Of our common heritage."

He had faith also that "the record from youth to age" of his own soul would outlast any present indifference or neglect—that whatever tide might bear him away from our regard for a time would ere long flow again. The reaction must come: it is, indeed, already at hand. But one almost fancies one can hear the gathering of the remote waters once more. We may, with Strafford,

> " feel sure
> That Time, who in the twilight comes to mend
> All the fantastic day's caprice, consign
> To the low ground once more the ignoble Term,
> And raise the Genius on his orb again,—
> That Time will do me right." . . .

Indeed, Browning has the grand manner, for all it is

more that of the Scandinavian Jarl than of the Italian count or Spanish grandee.

And ever, below all the stress and failure, below all the triumph of his toil, is the beauty of his dream. It was "a surpassing Spirit" that went from out our midst.

> " One who never turned his back but marched breast forward,
>   Never doubted clouds would break,
>   Never dreamed, though right were worsted, wrong would triumph,
>   Held we fall to rise, are baffled to fight better,
>   Sleep to wake."

"Speed, fight on, fare ever There as here!" are the last words of this brave soul. In truth, "the air seems bright with his past presence yet."

> " Sun-treader—life and light be thine for ever ;
>   Thou art gone from us—years go by—and spring
>   Gladdens, and the young earth is beautiful,
>   Yet thy songs come not—other bards arise,
>   But none like thee—they stand—thy majesties,
>   Like mighty works which tell some Spirit there
>   Hath sat regardless of neglect and scorn,
>   Till, its long task completed, it hath risen
>   And left us, never to return."

INDEX.

A. | B.

ERRATA AND ADDENDA.

Page 101, l. 7, "shattered" *should be* "shuttered."
Page 101, l. 24, "no other" *should be* "any other."
Page 105, l. 20, "it" *should be* "Sordello."
Page 113, l. 23, "reached" *should be* "reaches."
Page 177, l. 4, "alluded to" *should be* "quoted in part.

TO INDEX, *add*

more that of the Scandinavian Jarl than of the Italian count or Spanish grandee.

And ever, below all the stress and failure, below all the triumph of his toil, is the beauty of his dream. It was "a surpassing Spirit" that went from out our midst.

" One who never turned his back but marched breast forward,
    Never doubted clouds would break,
Never dreamed, though right were worsted, wrong would triumph,
Held we fall to rise, are baffled to fight better,
    Sleep to wake."

" Speed
words o
with his

    "

INDEX.

BIBLIOGRAPHY.

BY

JOHN P. ANDERSON

(British Museum).

I. WORKS.

Poems. 2 vols. A new edition. London, 1849, 16mo.
Vol. i., *Paracelsus; Pippa Passes, a Drama; King Victor and King Charles, a Tragedy; Colombe's Birthday, a Play.* Vol. ii., *A Blot in the 'Scutcheon, a Tragedy; The Return of the Druses, a Tragedy; Luria, a Tragedy; A Soul's Tragedy; Dramatic Romances and Lyrics.*

The Poetical Works of Robert Browning. Third edition. 3 vols. London, 1863, 8vo.
Vol. i., *Lyrics; Romances; Men and Women.* Vol. ii., *Tragedies and other Plays.* Vol. iii., *Paracelsus; Christmas Eve and Easter-Day; Sordello.*

The Poetical Works of Robert Browning. 6 vols. London, 1868, 8vo.
Vol. i., *Pauline; Paracelsus; Strafford.* Vol. ii., *Sordello; Pippa Passes.* Vol. iii., *King Victor and King Charles; Dramatic Lyrics; The Return of the Druses.* Vol. iv., *A Blot in the 'Scutcheon; Colombe's Birthday; Dramatic Romances.* Vol. v., *A Soul's Tragedy; Luria; Christmas Eve and Easter-Day; Men and Women.* Vol. vi., *In a Balcony; Dramatis Personæ.*

Complete works of Robert Browning. A reprint from the latest English edition. Chicago, 1872-74, 8vo.
Nos. 1-19 of the "Official Guide of the Chicago and Alton R. R. and Monthly Reprint and Advertiser."

The Poetical Works of Robert Browning. 2 vols. Leipzig, 1872, 8vo.
  Vols. 1197, 1198 of the "Tauchnitz Collection of British Authors."

The Poetical Works of Robert Browning. 16 vols. London, 1888-9, 8vo.
  Vol. i. contains *Pauline* and *Sordello.* Vol. ii., *Paracelsus* and *Strafford.* Vol. iii., *Pippa Passes; King Victor and King Charles; The Return of the Druses; A Soul's Tragedy.* Vol. iv., *A Blot in the 'Scutcheon; Colombe's Birthday; Men and Women.* Vol. v., *Dramatic Romances; Christmas Eve and Easter-Day.* Vol. vi., *Dramatic Lyrics; Luria.* Vol. vii., *In a Balcony; Dramatis Personæ.* Vols. viii.-x., *The Ring and the Book,* 3 vols. Vol. xi., *Balaustion's Adventure; Prince Hohenstiel-Schwangau; Fifine at the Fair.* Vol. xii., *Red Cotton Night-Cap Country; The Inn Album.* Vol. xiii., *Aristophanes' Apology; The Agamemnon of Æschylus.* Vol. xiv., *Pacchiarotto and how he worked in Distemper, with other Poems.* Vol. xv., *Dramatic Idyls; Jocoseria.* Vol. xvi., *Ferishtah's Fancies; Parleyings with Certain People.*

II. SINGLE WORKS.

The Agamemnon of Æschylus, transcribed by Robert Browning. London, 1877, 8vo.

Aristophanes' Apology, including a transcript from Euripides, being the Last Adventure of Balaustion. London, 1875, 8vo.

Asolando: Fancies and Facts. London, 1890 [1889], 8vo.
  Now in seventh edition.

Balaustion's Adventure; including a transcript from Euripides [*i.e.*, a translation of the "Alcestis"]. London, 1871, 8vo.
  Now in third edition.

Bells and Pomegranates. 8 Nos. London, 1841-1846, 8vo.

No. i., *Pippa Passes,* 1841. No. ii., *King Victor and King Charles,* 1842. No. iii., *Dramatic Lyrics,* 1842. No. iv., *The Return of the Druses,* 1843. No. v., *A Blot in the 'Scutcheon,* 1843. No. vi., *Colombe's Birthday,* 1844. No. vii., *Dramatic Romances and Lyrics,* 1845. No. viii., *Luria;* and *A Soul's Tragedy,* 1846.

Christmas Eve and Easter-Day. A poem. London, 1850, 16mo.

Cleon. *Moxon:* London, 1855, 8vo.
  Reprinted in *Men and Women.*

Dramatic Idyls. 2 series. London, 1879-80, 8vo.
  The First Series now in 2nd edition.

Dramatis Personæ. London, 1864, 8vo.
  Three poems in this book were reprinted from advance copies in the Atlantic Monthly in vol. 13, 1864, viz., *Gold Hair,* pp. 596-599; *Prospice,* p. 694; *Under the Cliff,* pp. 737, 738.

——Second edition. London, 1864, 8vo.

Ferishtah's Fancies. London, 1884, 8vo.
  Now in third edition.

Fifine at the Fair. London, 1872, 8vo.

Gold Hair: a Legend of Pornic. [London], 1864, 8vo.
  Reprinted in *Dramatis Personæ.* Gold Hair appeared in the Atlantic Monthly, May 1864, and *Dramatis Personæ* was published on May 28, 1864.

The Inn Album. London, 1875, 8vo.

Jocoseria. London, 1883, 8vo.
  Now in third edition.

La Saisiaz. The Two Poets of Croisic. London, 1878, 8vo.

Men and Women. 2 vols. London, 1855, 8vo.

Pacchiarotto and how he worked in distemper: with other poems. London, 1876, 8vo.

Paracelsus. London, 1835, 8vo.

Parleyings with Certain People of

Importance in their Day. Introduced by a Dialogue between Apollo and the Fates, etc. London, 1887, 8vo.

Pauline, a Fragment of a Confession. London, 1833, 8vo.
There are only five known copies extant, two of which are in the British Museum.

——A reprint of the original edition of 1833. Edited by T. J. Wise. London, 1886, 12mo.
Four copies were printed on vellum.

The Pied Piper of Hamelin, with 35 illustrations by Kate Greenaway. London [1889], 4to.
Appeared originally in *Dramatic Lyrics* (Bells and Pomegranates, No. III.), 1842.

Prince Hohenstiel - Schwangau: Saviour of Society. London, 1871, 8vo.

Red Cotton Night-Cap Country; or Turf and Towers. London, 1873, 8vo.

The Ring and the Book. 4 vols. London, 1868-69, 8vo.
Now in second edition.

Sordello. London, 1840, 8vo.

The Statue and the Bust. *Moxon*: London, 1855, 8vo.
Reprinted in *Men and Women*.

Strafford: an historical tragedy. London, 1837, 8vo.

——[Acting edition for the use of the North London Collegiate School for Girls.] [London, 1882.] 8vo.

——Another edition. With notes and preface by E. H. Hickey, and an introduction by S. R. Gardiner. London, 1884, 8vo.

Two Poems. By Elizabeth Barrett Browning and Robert Browning. London, 1854, 8vo.
These two poems, "A Plea for the Ragged Schools of London," by Elizabeth B. Browning, and "The Twins," by Robert Browning, were printed by Miss Arabella Barrett, for a bazaar in aid of a "Refuge for Young Destitute Girls." "The Twins" was reprinted in "Men and Women," in 1850.

III. CONTRIBUTIONS TO MAGAZINES, ETC.

Sonnet.—"Eyes, calm beside thee, (Lady couldst thou know !") Dated August 17, 1834 ; signed "Z." (*Monthly Repository*, vol. 8 N.S., 1834, p. 712.)

The King.—"A King lived long ago." Signed "Z." (*Monthly Repository*, vol. 9 N.S., 1835, pp. 707, 708.)
Reprinted with six fresh lines and revised throughout, in Pippa Passes (1841).

Porphyria.—"The rain set early in to-night." Signed "Z." (*Monthly Repository*, vol. 10 N.S., 1836, pp. 43, 44.)

Johannes Agricola. — "There's Heaven above ; and night by night." Signed "Z." (*Monthly Repository*, vol. 10 N.S., 1836, pp. 45, 46.)
Porphyria and *Johannes Agricola* were reprinted in "Bells and Pomegranates," No. iii., with the title *Madhouse Cells*.

Lines.—"Still ailing, wind? Wilt be appeased or no?" Signed "Z." (*Monthly Repository*, vol. 10 N.S., 1836, pp. 270, 271.)
Reprinted revised, in *Dramatis Personæ*, 1864, as the first six stanzas of VI. of "James Lee."

The Laboratory (Ancient Régime). (*Hood's Magazine*, vol. 1, 1844, pp. 513, 514.)
Reprinted in *Dramatic Romances and Lyrics* (1845), as the first of two poems called "France and England."

Claret and Tokay. (*Hood's Magazine*, vol. 1, 1844, p. 525.)
Reprinted in *Dramatic Romances and Lyrics* (1845).

Garden Fancies. I. The Flower's Name; II. Sibrandus Schafnaburgensis. (*Hood's Magazine*, vol. 2, 1844, pp. 45-48.)
Reprinted in *Dramatic Romances and Lyrics* (1845).

The Boy and the Angel. (*Hood's Magazine*, vol. 2, 1844, pp. 140-142.)
Reprinted revised, and with five fresh coup'ets, in *Dramatic Romances and Lyrics* (1845).

The Tomb at St. Praxed's (Rome 15—). (*Hood's Magazine*, vol. 3, 1845, pp. 237-239.)
Reprinted in *Dramatic Romances and Lyrics* (1845).

The Flight of the Duchess. (*Hood's Magazine*, vol. 3, 1845, pp. 313-318.)
Reprinted in *Dramatic Romances and Lyrics* (1845).

Letters of Percy Bysshe Shelley. [A fabrication.] With an introductory essay, by Robert Browning. London, 1852, 8vo.

——On the poet, objective and subjective; on the latter's aim; on Shelley as man and poet. [Being a reprint of the Introductory Essay to "Letters of Percy Bysshe Shelley."] London, 1881, 8vo.
Published for the Browning Society.

——A reprint of the Introductory Essay prefixed to the volume of Letters of Shelley. Edited by W. Tyas Harden. London, 1888, 8vo.

Ben Karshook's Wisdom. (*The Keepsake*, 1856, p. 16.)

May and Death. (*The Keepsake*, 1857, p. 164.)
Reprinted in *Dramatis Personæ* (1845).

Orpheus and Eurydice. F. Leighton. 8 lines. (*Royal Academy Exhibition Catalogue* 1864, p. 13.)
Reprinted in *Poetical Works*, 1868, where it is included in *Dramatis Personæ*.

Gold Hair. *See* note to *Dramatis Personæ*.

Prospice. *See* note to *Dramatis Personæ*.

Under the Cliff. *See* note to *Dramatis Personæ*.

A selection from the poetry of Elizabeth Barrett Browning. [First series edited by Robert Browning.] 2 series. London, 1866-80, 8vo.

Hervé Riel. (*Cornhill Magazine*, vol. 23, 1871, pp. 257-260.)
Reprinted in *Pacchiarotto and other Poems*, 1876.

"Oh Love, Love:" the Lyric of Euripides in his Hippolytus. (*Euripides. By J. P. Mahaffy*, p. 116.) London, 1879, 12mo.

"The Blind Man to the Maiden said." (*The Hour will Come*, by *Wilhelmine von Hillern. From the German by Clara Bell*, vol. ii., p. 174.) London [1879], 8vo.
Printed anonymously; quoted with statement of authorship in the *Whitehall Review*, March 1, 1883. Reprinted in *Browning Society's Papers*, Pt. iv., p. 410.

Ten new lines to "Touch him ne'er so lightly." (*Dramatic Idyls*, 2nd ser., 1880, p. 149.)
Lines written in an autograph album, Oct. 14, 1880. (*Century Magazine*, vol. 25, 1882, pp. 159, 160.)
Printed without Mr. Browning's consent. Reprinted in the *Browning Society's Papers*, Pt. iii., p. 43.

Sonnet on Goldoni (dated "Venice, Nov. 27, 1883"). Written for the Album of the Committee of the Goldoni Monument at Venice, and inserted on the first page. (*Pall Mall Gazette*, Dec. 8, 1883.)

Reprinted in the Browning Society's Papers, Pt. v., p. 98.*

Sonnet on Rawdon Brown (dated Nov. 28, 1883). (*Century Magazine*, vol. 27, 1884, p. 640.)

Reprinted in the Browning Society's Papers, Pt. v., p. 132.*

Paraphrase from Horace. Four lines, written impromptu for Mr. Felix Moscheles. (*Pall Mall Gazette*, Dec. 13, 1883, p. 6.)

Reprinted in the Browning Society's Papers, Pt. v., p. 99.*

Helen's Tower: Sonnet, dated "April 26, 1870." Written for the Earl of Dufferin, who built a tower in memory of his mother, Helen, Countess of Gifford, on his estate at Clandeboye. (*Pall Mall Gazette*, Dec. 28, 1883, p. 2.)

Reprinted in *Sonnets of this Century*, edited by William Sharp, 1886, and in the Browning Society's Papers, Pt. v., p. 97.*

The Founder of the Feast: Sonnet. (Dated "April 5, 1884.") Inscribed by Mr. Browning in the Album presented to Mr. Arthur Chappell, director of the St. James's Hall Concerts, etc. (*The World*, April 16, 1884.)

Reprinted in the Browning Society's Papers, Pt. vii., p. 18.*

"The Names." Sonnet on Shakespeare. Contributed to the "Shaksperian Show-Book" of the Shaksperian Show, held at the Albert Hall, on May 29-31, 1884.

Reprinted in the *Pall Mall Gazette*), May 29, and in the Browning Society's Papers, Pt. v., p. 105.*

The Divine Order and other Sermons and Addresses, by the late Thomas Jones. Edited by Brynmor Jones. With a short introduction by Robert Browning. London, 1884, 8vo.

Why I am a Liberal: Sonnet. (*Why I am a Liberal*, edited by Andrew Reid. London, 1885, p. 11.)

Reprinted in *Sonnets of this Century*, edited by William Sharp, 1886, and in the Browning Society's Papers, Pt. viii., p. 92.*

Prefatory Note to the *Poetical Works of Elizabeth Barrett Browning*, 1889, dated "Dec. 10, 1887."

To Edward Fitzgerald. "I chanced upon a new book yesterday." 12 lines, dated "July 8, 1889" (*Athenæum*, July 13, 1889, p. 64).

IV. PRINTED LETTERS.

Letter to Laman Blanchard [? April, 1841], dated "Craven Cottage, Saturday." (*Poetical Works of Laman Blanchard*, pp. 6-8.) London, 1876, 8vo.

Letters to Henry Fothergill Chorley on his novels Pomfret (1845) and Roccabella (1860). (*Autobiography, Memoir, and Letters of Henry Fothergill Chorley*, vol. ii., pp. 25, 26, 169-174.)

Letter to R. H. Horne, dated Pisa, Dec. 4 [1846]. Another dated London, Sept. 24 [1851], signed Robert and Elizabeth Barrett Browning. (*Letters of Elizabeth Barrett Browning to R. H. Horne*, 1877, vol. ii., pp. 182-3, 194-5.) London, 1877, 8vo.

Letter to William Etty, R.A., dated "Bagni di Lucca, Sept. 21, 1849." (*Life of William Etty, R.A. By Alexander*

Gilchrist, vol. ii., pp. 280-81.) London, 1855, 8vo.

Letter to Leigh Hunt (dated " Bagni di Lucca, 6th Oct., 1857 "). (*Correspondence of Leigh Hunt, edited by his eldest son*, vol. ii., pp. 264-267.) London, 1862, 8vo.

Letter to the Editor of *The Daily News*, dated " 19 Warwick Crescent, W., Feb. 9," stating that his contribution to the French Relief Fund was his publishers' payment for a lyrical poem (Hervé Riel). (*Daily News*, Feb. 10, 1871.)

Letter to the Editor of *The Daily News*, dated " Nov. 20." On line 131, " Gave us the doctrine of the enclitic De " of the poem, *A Grammarian's Funeral.* (*Daily News*, Nov. 21, 1874.)

Letter to the Rev. Alexander B. Grosart, on the Poem of *The Lost Leader* and *Wordsworth*, dated " 19 Warwick Crescent, Feb. 24, 1875." (*The Prose Works of William Wordsworth. Edited by the Rev. A. B. Grosart*, vol. i., p. xxxvii.) London, 1876, 8vo.

The Lord Rectorship of St. Andrew's. Letter to the Editor of *The Times*, dated " 19 Warwick Crescent, Nov. 19." (*Times*, Nov. 20, 1877.)

Letter to F. J. Furnivall. (*Academy*, Dec. 20, 1878.)

Letter to Mr. J. O. Halliwell-Phillipps, and printed by the latter in 1881.

Letter to Mr. Charles Kent, dated " 29 De Vere Gardens, W., 28 August, 1889." Accompanied by a presentation copy of the 3rd vol. of the new collective edition of " Poems." (*Athenæum*, Dec. 21, 1889, p. 860).

In Berdoe's " Browning's Message to his Time," etc., London, 1890, there are a number of letters from Browning.

In the new edition of Kingsland's " Robert Browning," London, 1890, there are several letters from Browning.

V. SELECTIONS.

Selections from the Poetical Works of Robert Browning. [Edited by J. Forster and B. W. Procter.] London, 1863 [1862], 16mo.

Moxon's Miniature Poets. A Selection from the Works of Robert Browning. London, 1865, 8vo.

Selections from the Poetical Works of Robert Browning. 2 series. London, 1872-80, 8vo.

Favourite Poems. Illustrated. Boston, 1877, 16mo.

A Selection from the Works of Robert Browning. With a memoir of the author, and explanatory notes. Edited by F. H. Ahn. Berlin, 1882, 8vo. Vol. viii. of Ahn's "Collection of British and American Standard Authors."

Stories from Robert Browning. By F. M. Holland. With an introduction by Mrs. Sutherland Orr. London, 1882, 8vo.

Lyrical and Dramatic Poems selected from the works of Robert Browning. With an extract from Stedman's " Victorian Poets." Edited by E. T. Mason. New York, 1883, 8vo.

Selections from the Poetry of Robert Browning. With an introduction by R. G. White. New York [1883], 8vo.

Pomegranates from an English Garden: a selection from the

poems of Robert Browning. With introduction and notes by J. M. Gibson. New York, 1885, 8vo.

Select Poems of Robert Browning. Edited, with notes, by William J. Rolfe and Heloise E. Hersey. New York, 1886, 8vo.

Lyrics, Idyls, and Romances from the poetic and dramatic works of Robert Browning. Boston, 1887, 8vo.

Good and true Thoughts from Robert Browning. Selected by Amy Cross. New York, 1888, 4to.
Printed in blue ink, and on one side of the leaf.

The Browning Reciter : Poems for Recitation, by Robert Browning and other writers. Edited by A. H. Miles. London, 1889, 8vo.
Part of the "Platform Series."

VI. APPENDIX.

BIOGRAPHY, CRITICISM, ETC.

Alexander, William John.—An Introduction to the poetry of Robert Browning. Boston, 1889, 8vo.

Austin, Alfred.—The Poetry of the Period. London, 1870, 8vo.
Robert Browning, pp. 38-76. Appeared originally in *Temple Bar*, vol. 26, 1869, pp. 316-333.

Bagehot, Walter.—Literary Studies. 2 vols. London, 1879, 8vo.
Wordsworth, Tennyson. and Browning; or, Pure, Ornate, and Grotesque Art in English Poetry, vol. ii., pp. 338-390. Appeared originally in the *National Review*, vol. 19, 1864, pp. 27-67.

Barnett, Professor.—Browning's Jews and Shakespeare's Jew. Read at the 54th meeting of

the Browning Society, Nov. 25th, 1887. London, 1888, 8vo.
The Browning Society's Papers, Pt. x., pp. 207-220.

Beale, Dorothea.—The Religious Teaching of Browning. (Read at the 10th meeting of the Browning Society, Oct. 27th, 1882.) London, 1882, 8vo.
The Browning Society's Papers, Pt. iii., pp. 323-338.

Berdoe, Edward.—Browning as a Scientific Poet. (Read at the meeting of the Browning Society, April 24th, 1885.) London, 1885, 8vo.
The Browning Society's Papers, Pt. vii., pp. 33-54.

——Browning's Estimate of Life. (Read at the meeting of the Society, Oct. 28, 1887.) London, 1888, 8vo.
The Browning Society's Papers, Pt. x., pp. 200-206.

——Browning's Message to his Time: His Religion, Philosophy, and Science. [With fac-simile letters of Browning and portrait.] London, 1890, 8vo.

Birrell, Augustine.—Obiter Dicta. London, 1884, 8vo.
On the alleged obscurity of Mr. Browning's poetry, pp. 55-95.

Browning, Robert.—Robert Browning's Poetry. Outline Studies published for the Chicago Browning Society. Chicago, 1886, 8vo.

Browning Society.—The Browning Society's Papers. In progress. London, 1881, etc., 8vo.

Buchanan, Robert. — Master-Spirits. London, 1873, 8vo.
Browning's Masterpiece, pp. 89-109. A revised reprint of the Athenæum reviews of the "Ring and the Book" in December and March 1870.

Bulkeley, Rev. J. H. — James Lee's Wife. (Read at the 16th meeting of the Browning

Society, May 25, 1883.) London, 1883, 8vo.
The Browning Society's Papers, Pt. iv., pp. 455-468.

——The Reasonable Rhythm of some of Browning's poems. Read at the 42nd meeting of the Browning Society, May 28, 1886. London, 1886, 8vo.
The Browning Society's Papers, Pt. viii., pp. 119-131.

Burt, Mary E. — Browning's Women, etc. Chicago, 1887, 8vo.

Bury, John B.—Browning's Philosophy. (Read at the 6th meeting of the Browning Society, April 28, 1882.) London, 1882, 8vo.
The Browning Society's Papers, Pt. iii., pp. 259-277.

——On "Aristophanes' Apology." Read at the 38th meeting of the Browning Society, Jan. 29, 1886. London, 1886, 8vo.
The Browning Society's Papers, Pt. viii., pp. 79-86.

C. C. S., *i.e.*, C. S. Calverley.— Fly Leaves. Cambridge, 1872, 8vo.
"The Cock and the Bull," a Parody on *The Ring and the Book*, pp. 113-120.

Cooke, Bancroft. — An Introduction to Robert Browning. A criticism of the purpose and method of his earlier works. London [1883], 8vo.

Cooke, George Willis.—Poets and Problems. London [1886], 8vo.
Browning, pp. 269-388.

Cooper, Thompson.—Men of Mark, etc., London, 1881, 4to.
Robert Browning, with photograph. Fifth Series, No. 17.

Corson, Hiram.—The Idea of Personality, as embodied in Robert Browning's Poetry. (Read at the 8th meeting of the Browning

Society, June 23, 1882.) London, 1882, 8vo.
The Browning Society's Papers, Pt. iii., pp. 293-321.

——An Introduction to the Study of Robert Browning's Poetry. Boston, 1886, 8vo.

Courtney, W. L. — Studies New and Old. London, 1888, 8vo.
Robert Browning, Writer of Plays, pp. 100-123.

Devey, J.—A Comparative Estimate of Modern English Poets. London, 1873, 8vo.
Browning, pp. 376-421.

Dowden, Edward.—Mr. Tennyson and Mr. Browning. (*The Afternoon Lectures on Literature and Art delivered in . . . Dublin,* 1867 *and* 1868, pp. 141-179.) Dublin, 1869, 8vo.
Reprinted in E. Dowden's "Studies in Literature," 1878, pp. 191-239.

——Studies in Literature, 1789-1877. London, 1878, 8vo.
Mr. Browning's place in recent literature, pp. 80-84; Mr. Tennyson and Mr. Browning, pp. 191-239.

——Transcripts and Studies. London, 1888, 8vo.
Mr. Browning's "Sordello," pp. 474-525.

Eyles, F. A. H.—Popular Poets of the Period, etc. London, 1888, etc., 8vo.
Robert Browning, by Alexander H. Japp, No. 7, pp. 193-199.

Fleming, Albert. — Andrea del Sarto. Read at the 39th meeting of the Browning Society, Feb. 26, 1886. London, 1886, 8vo.
The Browning Society's Papers, Pt. viii., pp. 95-102.

Forman, H. Buxton.—Our Living Poets. London, 1871, 8vo.
Robert Browning, pp. 103-152.

Fotheringham, James. — Studies in the Poetry of Robert Browning. London, 1887, 8vd.
——Second edition, revised and enlarged. London, 1888, 8vo.

Friswell, J. Hain.—Modern Men of Letters honestly criticised. London, 1870, 8vo.
Robert Browning, pp. 119-131.

Fuller, S. Margaret.—Papers on Literature and Art. 2 parts. London, 1846, 8vo.
Browning's Poems, pt. ii., pp. 31-45.

Furnivall, Frederick J.—A Bibliography of Robert Browning, from 1833-81. London, 1881-82, 8vo.
The Browning Society's Papers, 1881-4, Pts. i. and ii.

——How the Browning Society came into being. With some words on the characteristics and contrasts of Browning's early and late work. London, 1884, 8vo.

——A grammatical analysis of "O Lyric Love." Read at the 48th meeting of the Browning Society, Feb. 25, 1886. London, 1888, 8vo.
The Browning Society's Papers, Pt. ix., pp. 165-168.

Galton, Arthur.—Urbana Scripta. Studies of five living poets, etc. London, 1885, 8vo.
Mr. Browning, pp. 59-76.

Gannon, Nicholas J.—An Essay on the characteristic errors of our most distinguished living poets. Dublin, 1853, 8vo.
Robert Browning, pp. 25-32.

Glazebrook, Mrs. M. G. — "A Death in the Desert." Read at the 48th meeting of the Browning Society, Feb. 25, 1887. London, 1888, 8vo.
The Browning Society's Papers, vol. ix., pp. 153-164.

Halliwell-Phillipps, James O.— Copy of Correspondence [between J. O. Halliwell-Phillipps and Robert Browning, concerning expressions respecting Halliwell-Phillipps, used by F. J.

Furnivall in the preface to a fac-simile of the second edition of Hamlet, published in 1880]. [Brighton ? 1881] fol.

Hamilton, Walter.—Parodies of the Works of English and American Authors. London, 1889, 8vo.
Robert Browning, vol. vi., pp. 46-55.

Haweis, Rev. H. R.—Poets in the Pulpit. London, 1880, 8vo.
Robert Browning. New Year's Eve, pp. 117-143.

Herford, C. H.—Prince Hohenstiel-Schwangau. London, 1886, 8vo.
The Browning Society's Papers, Pt. viii., pp. 133-145.

Hodgkins, Louise Manning.— Nineteenth Century Authors. Robert Browning. Boston [1889], 8vo.

Holland, F. May.—Sordello. A Story from Robert Browning. New York, 1881, 8vo.
Very scarce.

Horne, R. H.—A New Spirit of the Age. 2 vols. London, 1844, 8vo.
Robert Browning (with a portrait engraved by J. C. Armytage) and J. W. Marston, vol. ii., pp. 153-186.

Hutton, Richard Holt.—Essays, Theological and Literary. 2 vols. London, 1871, 8vo.
Mr. Browning, vol. ii., pp. 190-247.

Johnson, Rev. Prof. Edwin. — On "Bishop Blougram's Apology." (Read at the 7th meeting of the Browning Society, May 26, 1882.) London, 1882, 8vo.
The Browning Society's Papers, Pt. iii., pp. 279-292.

——Conscience and Art in Browning. London, 1882, 8vo.
The Browning Society's Papers, Pt. iii., pp. 345-379.

——On "Mr. Sludge the Medium." Read at the 31st meeting of the

Browning Society, March 27, 1885. London, 1885, 8vo.
The Browning Society's Papers, Pt. vii., pp. 13-32.

Kingsland, William G. — Robert Browning: chief poet of the age. An essay addressed primarily to beginners in the study of Browning's poems. London, 1887, 8vo.
——New edition, with biographical and other additions. London, 1890, 8vo.

Landor, Walter Savage. — The Works of Walter Savage Landor. 2 vols. London, 1846, 8vo.
Poem "To Robert Browning," vol. ii., p. 673.

M'Cormick, William S. — Three Lectures on English Literature. Paisley, 1889, 8vo.
The poetry of Robert Browning, pp. 125-184.

Macdonald, George.—Orts. London, 1882, 8vo.
Browning's "Christmas Eve," pp. 195-217.
——The Imagination and other Essays. Boston [1883], 8vo.
Browning's "Christmas Eve," pp. 195-217.

McNicoll, Thomas.—Essays on English Literature. London, 1861, 8vo.
New Poems of Browning and Landor (1856), pp. 298-314.

McCrie, George.—The Religion of our Literature. Essays upon Thomas Carlyle, Robert Browning, Alfred Tennyson, etc. London, 1875, 8vo.
Robert Browning, pp. 69-109.

Macready, William Charles. — Macready's Reminiscences and Selections from his diaries and letters. 2 vols. London, 1875, 8vo.
Numerous references to Browning.

Mayor, Joseph B.—Chapters on English Metre. London, 1886, 8vo.
Tennyson and Browning, Chap. xii., pp. 184-196.

Morison, J. Cotter. — "Caliban upon Setebos," with some notes on Browning's Subtlety and Humour. (Read at the 24th Meeting of the Browning Society, April 25, 1884.) London, 1884, 8vo.
The Browning Society's Papers, Pt. v., pp. 489-493.

Morrison, Jeanie.—Sordello. An outline analysis of Mr. Browning's Poem. London, 1889, 8vo.

Nettleship, John T.—Essays on Robert Browning's Poetry. London, 1868, 8vo.
——New edition. New York, 1890, 8vo.
——On Browning's "Fifine at the Fair." To be read at the 4th Meeting of the Browning Society, Feb. 24, 1882. London, 1882, 8vo.
The Browning Society's Papers, Pt. ii., p. 199-230.
——Classification of Browning's Works. London, 1882, 8vo.
The Browning Society's Papers, Pt. ii., pp. 231-234.
——Browning's Intuition, specially in regard of music and the Plastic Arts. (Read at the 13th Meeting of the Browning Society, Feb. 23, 1883.) London, 1883, 8vo.
The Browning Society's Papers, Pt. iv., pp. 381-396.
——On the development of Browning's Genius in his capacity as poet or maker. Read at the 35th Meeting of the Browning Society, Oct. 30, 1885. London, 1886, 8vo.
The Browning Society's Papers, Pt. viii., pp. 55-77.

Noel, Hon. Roden.—Essays on Poetry and Poets. London, 1886, 8vo.
Robert Browning, pp. 256-282; Robert Browning's Poetry, pp. 283-303.

Notes and Queries.—Notes and Queries. 7 Series. London, 1849-1889, 4to.
Numerous references to Browning.

O'Byrne, George.—Robert Browning. In Memoriam. An Epicedium. Nottingham [1890], 8vo.

O'Conor, William Anderson.—Essays in Literature and Ethics. Manchester, 1889, 8vo.
Browning's "Childe Roland," pp. 1-24.

Ormerod, Helen J.—Some Notes on Browning's Poems referring to Music. Read at the 51st Meeting of the Browning Society, May 27, 1887. London, 1888, 8vo.
The Browning Society's Papers, Pt. ix., pp. 180-193.

——Abt Vogler, the Man. Read at the 55th Meeting of the Browning Society, Jan. 27th, 1888. London, 1888, 8vo.
The Browning Society's Papers, Pt. x., pp. 221-236.

Orr, Mrs. Sutherland.—A Handbook to the Works of Robert Browning, London, 1885, 8vo.
——Second edition, revised. London, 1886, 8vo.
——Classification of Browning's Poems. London, 1882, 8vo.
The Browning Society's Papers, Pt. ii., pp. 235-238.

Outram, Leonard S.—Love's Value. Colombe's Birthday. Act IV. (The Avowal of Valence.) Read at the 38th Meeting of the Browning Society, Jan. 29, 1886. London, 1886, 8vo.
The Browning Society's Papers, Pt. viii., pp. 87-94.

Pearson, Howard S.—On Browning as a Landscape Painter. Read at the 41st Meeting of the Browning Society, April 30, 1886. London, 1886, 8vo.
The Browning Society's Papers, Pt. viii., pp. 103-118.

Pollock, Frederick.—Leading cases done into English. By an Apprentice of Lincoln's Inn [Frederick Pollock]. Second edition. London, 1876, 8vo.
IV. "Scott v. Shepherd (1 Sm. L. C. 477.), Any Pleader to any Student," pp. 15-19. A Parody on Browning.

Portrait.—The Portrait. Vol. I. London, 1877, 4to.
Robert Browning, by G. Barnett Smith, 4 pages. The portrait is from a photograph by Elliott & Fry.

Portrait Gallery.—National Portrait Gallery. London [1877], 4to.
Robert Browning (with portrait), 4th Series, pp. 73-80.

Powell, Thomas.—The Living Authors of England. New York, 1849, 8vo.
Robert Browning, pp. 71-85.

——Pictures of the Living Authors of Britain. London, 1851, 8vo.
Robert Browning, pp. 61-75.

Radford, Ernest.—Illustrations to Browning's Poems; with a notice of the artists and the pictures, by E. Radford. 2 pts. London, 1882-3, fol.
Published for the Browning Society.

Raleigh, W. A.—On some prominent points in Browning's Teaching. (Read at the 22nd Meeting of the Browning Society, Feb. 22, 1884.) London, 1884, 8vo.
The Browning Society's Papers, Pt. v., pp. 477-488.

Reeve, Lovell.—Portraits of Men of Eminence in Literature,

Science, and Art, with biographical memoirs, etc. 6 vols. London, 1863-67, 8vo.
Robert Browning, vol. i., pp. 109-112.

Revell, William F.—Browning's Poems on God and Immortality as bearing on life here. (Read at the 14th Meeting of the Browning Society, March 30, 1883.) London, 1883, 8vo.
The Browning Society's Papers, Pt. iv., pp. 435-454.

——Browning's Views of Life. Address on Oct. 28, 1887. London, 1888, 8vo.
The Browning Society's Papers, Pt. x., pp. 197-199.

Sharp, William.—Browning and the Arts. London, 1882, 8vo.
The Browning Society's Papers, Pt. iii., pp. 34*-40*.

Sharpe, Rev. John.—On "Pietro of Abano" and the leading ideas of "Dramatic Idyls." Second series, 1880. (Read at the 2nd Meeting of the Browning Society, Nov. 25, 1881.) London, 1882, 8vo.
The Browning Society's Papers, Pt. ii., pp. 191-197.

——Jocoseria. (Read at the 20th Meeting of the Browning Society, Nov. 23, 1883.) London, 1884, 8vo.
The Browning Society's Papers, Pt. v., pp. 93*-97*.

Shirley, *pseud.* [*i.e.*, John Skelton]. —A Campaigner at Home. London, 1865, 8vo.
Robert Browning, pp. 247-283. Appeared originally in Fraser's Magazine, vol. 67, 1863, pp. 240-256.

Stedman, Edmund Clarence.—Victorian Poets. Boston, 1876, 8vo.
Robert Browning, pp. 293-341.

——Another edition. Boston, 1887, 8vo.

Stoddart, Anna M. — "Saul." Read at the 59th Meeting of the Browning Society, May 25, 1888. London, 1888, 8vo.
The Browning Society's Papers, Pt. x., pp. 264-274.

Swinburne, Algernon C. — The Works of George Chapman: Poems and Minor Translations. London, 1875, 8vo.
On Browning, pp. xiv.-xix. of the "Essay on George Chapman's poetical and dramatic works."

——Specimens of Modern Poets. The Heptalogia, or the Seven against Sense, etc. London, 1880, 8vo.
John Jones, pp. 9-30. A parody on James Lee.

Symons, Arthur. — Is Browning Dramatic? (Read at the 29th Meeting of the Browning Society, Jan. 30, 1885.) London, 1885, 8vo.
The Browning Society's Papers, Pt. vii., pp. 1-12.

——An Introduction to the Study of Browning. London, 1886, 8vo.

——Some Notes on Mr. Browning's last volume. (On Parleyings with Certain People.) Read at the 50th Meeting of the Browning Society, April 29, 1887. London, 1888, 8vo.
The Browning Society's Papers, Pt. ix., pp. 169-179.

Thomson, James.—Notes on the Genius of Robert Browning. (Read at the 3rd Meeting of the Browning Society, Jan. 27, 1882.) London, 1882, 8vo.
The Browning Society's Papers, Pt. ii., pp. 239-250.

Todhunter, Dr. John.—"The Ring and the Book." (Read at the 19th Meeting of the Browning Society, Oct. 26, 1883.) London, 1884, 8vo.
The Browning Society's Papers, Pt. v., pp. 85*-92*.

——"Strafford" at the Strand Theatre, Dec. 21, 1886. Read

at the 47th Meeting of the Browning Society, Jan. 28, 1887. London, 1883, 8vo.
The Browning Society's Papers, Pt. ix., pp. 147-152.

Turnbull, Mrs. — Abt Vogler. (Read at the 17th Meeting of the Browning Society, June 22, 1883.) London, 1883, 8vo.
The Browning Society's Papers, Pt. iv., pp. 469-476.

——In a Balcony. (Read at the Annual Meeting of the Browning Society, July 4, 1884.) London, 1884, 8vo.
The Browning Society's Papers, Pt. v., pp. 499-502.

Wall, Annie.—Sordello's Story retold in prose. Boston, 1886, 8vo.

West, E. D.—One aspect of Browning's Villains. (Read at the 15th Meeting of the Browning Society, April 27, 1883.) London, 1883, 8vo.
The Browning Society's Papers, Pt. iv., pp. 411-434.

Westcott, B. F.—On some points in Browning's View of Life. A paper read before the Cambridge Browning Society, November, 1882. Cambridge, 1883, 8vo.
Printed also in the Browning Society's Papers, Pt. iv., pp. 307-410.

Whitehead, Miss C. M.—Browning as a Teacher of the Nineteenth Century. Read at the 58th Meeting of the Browning Society, April 27, 1888. London, 1888, 8vo.
The Browning Society's Papers, Pt. x., pp. 237-263.

MAGAZINE ARTICLES, ETC.

Browning, Robert.—Sharpe's London Magazine, vol. 8, 1849, pp. 60-62, 122-127.—Revue des Deux Mondes, by J. Milsand, 15 Aug. 1851, pp. 661-689. —London Quarterly Review, vol. 6, 1856, pp. 493-501,

Browning, Robert.
vol. 22, p. 30, etc.—Revue Contemporaine, by J. Milsand, vol. 27, 1856, pp. 511-546.— Fraser's Magazine, by J. Skelton, vol. 67, 1863, pp. 240-256; reprinted in "A Campaigner at Home," 1865.— Victoria Magazine, by M. D. Conway, vol. 2, 1864, pp. 298-316.— Contemporary Review, vol. 4, 1867, pp. 1-15, 133-148; same article, Eclectic Magazine, vol. 5 N.S., pp. 314-323, 501-513.—Revue des Deux Mondes, by Louis Etienne, tom. 85, 1870, pp. 704-735.—Appleton's Journal (with portrait), by R. H. Stoddard, vol. 6, 1871, pp. 533-536.—Once a Week, vol. 9 N.S., 1872, pp. 164-167.— Scribner's Monthly, by E. C. Stedman, vol. 9, 1874, pp. 167-183.—Galaxy, by J. H. Browne, vol. 19, 1875, pp. 764-774.— St. James's Magazine, by T. Bayne, vol. 32, 1877, pp. 153-164.—Dublin University Magazine (with portrait), vol. 3 N.S., 1878, pp. 322-335, 416-443.—Gentleman's Magazine, by A. N. McNicoll, vol. 244, 1879, pp. 54-67.—Congregationalist, vol. 8, 1879, pp. 915-922. —International Review, by G. Barnett Smith, vol. 6, 1879, pp. 176-194.—Literary World (Boston), by F. J. Furnivall, H. E. Scudder, etc., vol. 13, 1882, pp. 76-81.—Critic, by J. H. Morse, vol. 3, 1883, pp. 263, 264. —Contemporary Review, by Hon. Roden Noel, vol. 44, 1883, pp. 701-718; same article, Littell's Living Age, vol. 159, pp. 771-781.—British Quarterly Review, vol. 80, 1884, pp. 1-28. —Family Friend, by J. Fuller

Browning, Robert.

vol. 13, 1871, pp. 178, 179.—
Fortnightly Review, by Sidney
Colvin, vol. 10 N.S., 1871, pp.
478-490.—Edinburgh Review,
vol. 135, 1872, pp. 221-249.—
London Quarterly Review, vol.
37, 1871, pp. 346-368.—Athenæum, Aug. 12, 1871, pp. 199,
200.—Penn Monthly, by R. E.
Thompson, vol. 6, 1875, pp.
928-940.—St. Paul's Magazine,
by E. J. Hasell, vol. 12, 1873,
pp. 680-699; vol. 13, pp. 49-66.—
Pioneer, Oct. 1887, pp. 159-162.
——*Bells and Pomegranates.*
Christian Remembrancer, vol.
11 N.S., 1846, pp. 316-330.—
People's Journal, by H. F.
Chorley, vol. 2, 1847, pp. 38-
40, 104-106.
——*Browning Society.* Saturday
Review, vol. 53, 1882, pp. 12,
13 ; vol. 58, 1884, pp. 721, 722.
——*Childe Roland.* Papers of
the Manchester Literary Club,
by the Rev. W. A. O'Conor,
vol. 3, 1877, pp. 12-25.—Critic
(New York), by J. E. Cooke,
vol. 8, 1886, pp. 201, 202, and
by A. Bates, pp. 231, 232.
————*Childe Roland, Childe
Harold, and the Sangrail.*
Papers of the Manchester
Literary Club, by John Mor-
timer, vol. 3, 1877, pp. 26-31.
——*Christmas Eve and Easter-Day.*
Prospective Review, vol. 6,
1850, pp. 267-279. — Littell's
Living Age (from the Examiner),
vol. 25, pp. 403-409. — The
Germ, No. 4, by W. M. Ros-
setti, pp. 187-192.—Day of Rest,
by George MacDonald, vol. 1,
1873, pp. 34-36, 55, 56.
——*Clubs in the United States.*
Literary World (Boston), by H.
Corson, vol. 14, 1883, p. 127.

Browning, Robert.

——*Day with the Brownings at
Pratolino.* Scribner's Monthly,
by E. C. Kinney, vol. 1, 1870,
pp. 185-188.
——*Dead in Venice.* (Verses.)
Athenæum, Dec. 21, 1889, p.
860.
—— *The "Detachment" of.* Athenæum, Jan. 4, 1890, pp. 18, 19.
——*Dramatic Idyls.* Fortnightly
Review, by Grant Allen, vol.
26 N.S., 1879, pp. 149-154.—
Contemporary Review, by Mrs.
Sutherland Orr, vol. 35, 1879,
pp. 289-302.—Saturday Review,
June 21, 1879, pp. 774, 775.—
Fraser's Magazine, vol. 20 N.S.,
1879, pp. 103-124.—St. James's
Magazine, by T. Bayne, vol. 8,
fourth series, 1880, pp. 108-
118.—Athenæum, May 10, 1879,
pp. 593-595. — Academy, by
Frank Wedmore, May 10, 1879,
pp. 403, 404.—Athenæum, July
10, 1880, pp. 39-41.—Literary
World, July 23, 1880, pp. 49-51.
——*Dramatis Personæ.* St. James's
Magazine, by R. Bell, vol. 10,
1864, pp. 477-491. — New
Monthly Magazine, by T. F.
Wedmore, vol. 133, 1865, pp.
186-194. — Dublin University
Magazine, vol. 64, 1864, pp.
578-579.—Eclectic Review, by
E. Paxton Hood, vol. 7 N.S.,
1864, pp. 62-72.
——*Early Writings of.* Century,
by E. W. Gosse, vol. 23, 1881,
pp. 189-200.
——*Ferishtah's Fancies.* Athe-
næum, Dec. 6, 1884, pp. 725-
727.—Saturday Review, vol. 58,
1884, pp. 727, 728.—Spectator,
Dec. 6, 1884, pp. 1614-1616.—
Academy, by H. C. Beeching,
Dec. 13, 1884, pp. 385, 386.—

Browning, Robert.
Critic (New York), Dec. 13, 1884, p. 279.—Oxford Magazine, vol. 3, 1885, pp. 161, 162.
——*Fifine at the Fair.* Old and New, by C. C. Everett, vol. 6, 1872, pp. 609-615.—Canadian Monthly, by Goldwin Smith, vol. 2, 1872, pp. 285-287.—Temple Bar, vol. 37, 1873, pp. 315-328.—Literary World, July 12, 1872, pp. 17, 18, and July 19, pp. 42, 43.—Fortnightly Review, by Sidney Colvin, vol. 12 N.S., 1872, pp. 118-120.—Saturday Review, vol. 34, 1872, pp. 220, 221.
——*First Poem of.* St. James's Magazine, vol. 7 N.S., 1871, pp. 485-496.
——*Funeral of.* Scots Magazine, by Elizabeth R. Chapman, Feb. 1890, pp. 216-223.
——*Handbook to the Works of, Orr's.* Academy, by J. T. Nettleship, vol. 27, 1885, pp. 429-431. — Athenæum, Sept. 26, 1885, pp. 396, 397.
——*in* 1869. Cornhill Magazine, vol. 19, 1869, pp. 249-256.
——*In a Balcony.* Theatre, by B. L. Mosely, May 1, 1885, pp. 225-230.
——*In Memoriam.* New Review, by Edmund W. Gosse, Jan. 1890, pp. 91-96.
——*Inn Album.* Macmillan's Magazine, by A. C. Bradley, vol. 33, 1876, pp. 347-354.—Nation, by Henry James, junr., vol. 22, 1876, pp. 49, 50.—International Review, by Bayard Taylor, vol. 3, 1876, pp. 402-404. — Athenæum, Nov. 27, 1875, pp. 701, 702.—Academy, by J. A. Symonds, Nov. 27, 1875, pp. 543, 544.—Spectator, December 11, 1875, pp. 1555-

Browning, Robert.
1557. — Examiner, Dec. 11, 1875, pp. 1389-1390.
——*in Westminster Abbey.* Speaker, by Henry James, Jan. 4, 1890, pp. 10-12.
——*Jocoseria.* National Review, by W. J. Courthope, vol. 1, 1883, pp. 548-561.—Atlantic Monthly, vol. 51, 1883, pp. 840-845. — Cambridge Review, vol. 4, 1883, pp. 352, 353.—Gentleman's Magazine, by R. H. Shepherd, vol. 254, 1883, pp. 624-630.—Academy, by J. A. Symonds, vol. 23, 1883, pp. 213, 214.—Athenæum, March 24, 1883, pp. 367, 368.—Saturday Review, vol. 55, 1883, pp. 376, 377. — Spectator, March 17, 1883, pp. 351-353.
——*Kingsland's.* Literary Opinion, May 1, 1887.
——*La Saisiaz. The Two Poets of Croisic.* Academy, by G. A. Simcox, vol. 13, 1878, pp. 478-480. — Athenæum, May 25, 1878, pp. 661-664.—Saturday Review, June 15, 1878, pp. 759, 760.
——*Love Poems of.* Journal of Education, by Arthur Sidgwick, May 1, 1882, pp. 139-143.
——*Lyrical and Dramatic Poems.* Literary World (Boston), Feb. 24, 1883, p. 58.
——*Men and Women.* Bentley's Miscellany, vol. 39, 1856, pp. 64-70.—British Quarterly Review, vol. 23, 1856, pp. 151-180. — Rambler, vol. 5 N.S., 1856, pp. 55-71. — Christian Remembrancer, vol. 31 N.S., 1856, pp. 281-294; vol. 34 N.S., 1857, pp. 361-390.—Dublin University Magazine, vol. 47, 1856, pp. 673-675.—Fraser's Magazine, by G.

Browning, Robert.
Brimley, vol. 53, 1856, pp. 105-116.—Irish Quarterly Review, vol. 6, 1856, pp. 21-28.—Westminster Review, vol. 9 N.S., 1856, pp. 290-296.
——*Note on.* Art Review, by W. Mortimer, Jan. 1890, pp. 28-32.
——*One Way of Love.* Literary World (Boston), by C. R. Corson, July 26, 1884, pp. 250, 251.
——*Pacchiarotto.* Academy, by Edward Dowden, July 29, 1876, pp. 99, 100.—Athenæum, July 22, 1876, pp. 101, 102.
——*Paracelsus.* New Monthly Magazine, by John Forster, vol. 46, 1836, pp. 289-308.—Examiner, by John Forster, Sept. 6, 1835, pp. 563-565.—Theologian, vol. 2, 1845, pp. 276-282.—Monthly Repository, by W. J. Fox, vol. 9 N.S., 1835, pp. 716-727.—Fraser's Magazine, by J. Heraud, vol. 13, 1836, pp. 363-374.—Leigh Hunt's Journal, vol. 2, 1835, pp. 405-408.—Revue des Deux Mondes, by Philarète Chasles, tom. xxii., 1840, pp. 127-133.
——*Parleyings with Certain People.* Literary Opinion, March 1, 1887.
——*Pauline.* Monthly Repository, by W. J. Fox, vol. 7 N.S., 1833, pp. 252-262.—Athenæum, April 6, 1833, p. 216.
——*Place of, in Literature.* Contemporary Review, by Mrs. Sutherland-Orr, vol. 23, 1874, pp. 934-965; same article, Littell's Living Age, vol. 122, pp. 67-85.
——*Plays and Poems.* North American Review, by J. R. Lowell, vol. 66, 1848, pp. 357-400.

Browning, Robert.
——*Poems.* British Quarterly Review, vol. 6, 1847, pp. 490-509.—Eclectic Review, vol. 26 N.S., 1849, pp. 203-214.—Eclectic Magazine, vol. 18, 1849, pp. 453-469.—Christian Examiner, by C. C. Everett, vol. 48, 1850, pp. 361-372. — Massachusetts Quarterly Review, vol. 3, 1850, pp. 347-385.—Fraser's Magazine, vol. 43, 1851, pp. 170-182.—Putnam's Monthly Magazine, vol. 7, 1856, pp. 372-381.—North British Review, vol. 34, 1861, pp. 350-374.—Chambers's Journal, vol. 19, 1863, pp. 91-95; vol. 20, pp. 39-41.—National Review, vol. 17, 1863, pp. 417-446.—Eclectic Review, by E. P. Hood, vol. 4 N.S., 1863, pp. 436-454; vol. 7 N.S., 1864, pp. 62-72.—Edinburgh Review, vol. 120, 1864, pp. 537-565.—Christian Examiner, by C. C. Everett, vol. 77, 1864, pp. 51-64.—Quarterly Review, vol. 118, 1865, pp. 77-105.—Nuova Antologia di Scienze, Lettere ed Arti, by Enrico Nencioni, July 1867, pp. 468-481.—North British Review, by J. Hutchinson Stirling, vol. 49, 1868, pp. 353-408.—Temple Bar, by Alfred Austin, vol. 26, 1869, pp. 316-333; vol. 27, pp. 170-186; vol. 28, pp. 33-48.—British Quarterly Review, vol. 49, 1869, pp. 435-459.—Saint Paul's Magazine, by E. J. H[assell], vol. 7, 1871, pp. 257-276; same article, Eclectic Magazine, vol. 13 N.S., pp. 267-279, and in Littell's Living Age, vol. 108, pp. 155-166.—Church Quarterly Review, by the Hon. and Rev. Arthur Lyttleton, vol. 7, 1878, pp. 65-92.—Cambridge Review,

Browning, Robert.

vol. 3, 1881, pp. 126, 127.—
Scottish Review, vol. 2, 1883,
pp. 349-358.—London Quarterly
Review, vol. 65, 1886, pp. 238-
250.
—— Prince Hohenstiel - Schwangau. New Englander, by J.
S. Sewall, vol. 33, 1874, pp.
493-505.—Examiner, Dec. 23,
1871, pp. 1267, 1268.—Academy, by G. A. Simcox, Jan.
15, 1872, pp. 24-26.—Literary
World, Jan. 5, 1872, pp. 8, 9.
——Red Cotton Night-Cap Country.
Nation, by J. R. Dennett, vol.
17, 1873, pp. 116-118.—Contemporary Review, by Mrs.
Sutherland-Orr, vol. 22, 1873,
pp. 87-106. — Penn Monthly
Magazine, vol. 4, 1873, pp.
657-661.—Athenæum, May 10,
1873, pp. 593, 594.
——Ring and the Book. Athenæum, Dec. 26, 1868, pp. 875,
876; March 20, 1869, pp. 399,
400.—Edinburgh Review, vol.
130, 1869, pp. 164-186.—Dublin Review, vol. 13 N.S., 1869,
pp. 48-62.—Chambers's Journal,
July 24, 1869, pp. 473-476.—
Fortnightly Review, by John
Morley, vol. 5 N.S., 1869, pp.
331-343. — Macmillan's Magazine, by J. A. Symonds, vol. 19,
1869, pp. 258-262, and by J. R.
Mozley, pp. 544-552.—North
American Review, by E. J.
Cutler, vol. 109, 1869, pp. 279-
283.—Nation, by J. R. Dennett, vol. 8, 1869, pp. 135, 136.
—Tinsley's Magazine, vol. 3,
1869, pp. 665-674.—Christian
Examiner, by J. W. Chadwick,
vol. 86, 1869, pp. 295-315.
—Gentleman's Magazine, by
James Thomson, vol. 251, 1881,
pp. 682-695.—St. James's Maga-

Browning, Robert.

zine, vol. 2 N.S., 1869, pp.
460-464.—Saint Paul's, vol. 7,
1871, pp. 377-397; same
article, Eclectic Magazine, vol.
13 N.S., pp. 400-412, and in
Littell's Living Age, vol. 108,
pp. 771-783. — North British
Review, vol. 51, 1870, pp. 97-
126.—Quarterly Review, vol.
126, 1869, pp. 328-359.
—— Some of the Teachings
of " The Ring and the Book."
Poet-Lore, by F. B. Horn-
brooke, July 1889, pp. 314-320.
——Science of. Poet-Lore, by
Edward Berdoe, Aug. 15, 1889,
pp. 353-362.
—— Selections from. London
Quarterly Review, by Frank T.
Marzials, vol. 20, 1863, pp. 527-
532.—Literary World, May 19,
1883, p. 157.
——Sequence of Sonnets on death
of. Fortnightly Review, by
Algernon C. Swinburne, Jan.
1890, pp. 1-4.
——Some Thoughts on. Mac-
millan's Magazine, by M. A.
Lewis, vol. 46, 1882, pp. 205-
219; same article, Littell's
Living Age, vol. 154, pp. 238-
246.
——Sonnets to. Macmillan's Magazine, by Aubrey de Vere, Feb.
1890, p. 258. — Blackwood's
Edinburgh Magazine, by Sir
Theodore Martin, Jan. 1890,
p. 112.—Household Words, vol.
4, 1852, p. 213.
——Sonnets of. Manchester Quarterly, by Benjamin Sagar, vol.
6, 1887, pp. 148-159.
——Sordello. Fraser's Magazine,
by E. Dowden, vol. 76, pp.
518-530. — Macmillan's Magazine, by R. W. Church, vol.
55, 1887, pp. 241-253.

Browning, Robert.
—— ——*Sordello at the East End.* Journal of Education, July 1, 1885, pp. 281-283.
——*Stories from, Holland's.* Academy, by J. A. Blaikie, vol. 22, 1882, pp. 287, 288.
——*Strafford: a Tragedy.* Edinburgh Review, vol. 65, 1837, pp. 132-151.
——*Study of.* Overland Monthly, by Caroline Le Conte, vol. 3, 2nd series, 1884, pp. 645-651.—Literary World (Boston), vol. 17, 1886, p. 44.
——*Two Sonnets to.* New Monthly Magazine, vol. 48, 1836, p. 48.
——*Types of Womanhood.* Woman's World, by Annie E.

Browning, Robert.
Ireland, Nov. 1889, pp. 47-50.
——*Verses on.* Art Review (with portrait), by William Sharp, Feb. 1890, pp. 33-36.—Murray's Magazine, by Rev. H. D. Rawnsley, Feb. 1890, pp. 145-150.—Belford's Magazine (poem of 20 six-line stanzas), by William Sharp, March 1890.
——*Wordsworth and Tennyson.* National Review, by Walter Bagehot, vol. 19, 1864, pp. 27-67; reprinted in "Literary Studies," 1879; same article, Eclectic Magazine, vol. 1 N.S., pp. 273-284, 415-427, and in Littell's Living Age, vol. 84, pp. 3-24.

VII. CHRONOLOGICAL LIST OF WORKS.